GOLDEN BALLAST

GOLDEN BALLAST

H. DEVERE STACPOOLE

WILDSIDE PRESS

Originally published in 1924.
Published by Wildside Press LLC.
Visit us online at wildsidepress.com.

CHAPTER 1

THE FLYING MAN

On the morning of the first of April, 1921, Mr. Isaac Forsythe, of the firm of Forsythe, Forsythe & Clove, was seated at his desk in Old Serjeant's Inn opening his morning correspondence. He was a grey man with side whiskers and glasses that seemed always on the point of tumbling off his nose, a perfect specimen of the old-time family lawyer and the last of a firm that had held and practised in Old Serjeant's Inn for one hundred and ten years.

Clove, whose name still stuck to the business, had died somewhere about the time of Queen Victoria's accession to the throne, and on the tin deed boxes on the office shelves were names and titles that to a student of the petty history of the nineteenth century would have recalled scandals and deeds and actions forgotten or half forgotten in a world trampled by the Great War.

Envelope after envelope as it was opened was held up to the light, to see that no inclosure had been missed, torn in two and cast into the waste-paper basket, letter after letter when read was placed under an agate paper weight to be dealt with later on. The blue day—it was a blue day, if you remember—looked in through the dusty windows, but without finding any response in the mind or soul of the grey man at the desk, who was in the act of opening the last of his correspondence when a knock at the door was followed by the announcement:

"Mr. Richard Sebright to see you, sir."

"Show him in," said the lawyer.

A fresh-faced, bright-looking boy in grey tweed came in, one of the sort that fell in thousands and thousands in the war that has put an end to all wars, a creature pleasant to look at as April; clean, with black, brilliantined hair, but wearing an anxious look.

He held a bowler in one hand and a stick in the other, but he did not seem to know exactly what to do with them.

"Take a seat," said the lawyer. "You are Mr. Richard Sebright?"

"Yes, my name is Sebright," said the other, taking a chair and placing his hat and stick on the floor while he produced a letter from his pocket. "I got this letter from you and I thought it better to turn up at once, in case it was anything important, you know. I got it first post this morning, sent on from Cox's."

"Born at Hildersditch, I believe, Mr. Sebright?"

"Yes, we lived there. I mean I was born there—all right."

"And educated—"

"At Malvern—schoolhouse."

"Just so," said the lawyer, opening a drawer and taking out some papers. "You had an aunt?"

"I had an aunt, but I've never seen her. She was dotty—I mean she never got on with the mater; she was her sister and lived at Folkestone—"

"And her name?"

"Masters—that was my mother's name before she married."

"Your mother and father are—er—no longer living, I believe?"

"No, they are dead."

"Just so. Now can you give me any papers of identity?"

"I beg your pardon?"

"Anything to show that in a legal sense you *are* Mr. Sebright?"

Dicky Sebright pondered a moment over this proposition, then brightening:

"Cox's know me and there's my army papers."

"And a birth certificate?"

"Oh, yes, I can get that."

"That's all right," said Mr. Forsythe. "That I am sure will be quite all right, and now to our business, Mr. Sebright. Your aunt, I regret to tell you, died last Monday week and has left you heir to what small property she possessed, which, deducting death duties and legal expenses, will amount to some seven hundred and fifty pounds—as nearly as possible."

"Seven hundred and fifty!" cried Dicky, light leaping to his eyes and a fresher color to his cheeks. "I say, you aren't making an April fool of me, are you?—I mean, what made her do it? She hated us all—seven hundred and fifty—*pounds*?"

"Pounds," replied Mr. Forsythe, who seemed scarcely to hear all Dicky's talk and who was turning over the legal documents with the tips of his fingers while he scanned them through his tilted glasses. "Pounds. And the money will be at your disposal in a few days when the necessary formalities have been complied with. Meanwhile," with an up glance that took in Dicky's worn tweed suit, "if you are at all in need of money I can help you with an advance—without interest," he finished, and put away the papers, laughing as if at some subtle legal joke.

"Thanks," said the other. He could say nothing more for the moment, though it was not grief that stayed his tongue, but good fortune. He had never seen his aunt, so how could he grieve for her? And he didn't pretend to. He picked up his hat and his stick, but he did not rise from his seat, and the lawyer, having locked up his papers, dropped his legal manner and turned in his chair for a chat. All at once the legal machine had become a man.

"And how long have you left the air force?" he asked.

Dicky told him.

"What are you doing now?"

"Nothing. You see when I was demobed, I—well, I bust all the money they gave me—it didn't last long. Then I got a job, but I couldn't stick it."

"Oh, you couldn't stick it?"

"No; it was in an office. The money was all right, but it was being stuck all day at a desk that got me. I couldn't breathe in the place—but I was there eight months."

The lawyer said nothing for a moment, contemplating the flying man, this eagle who had been tossed from the nest of a public school into the sky and dropped from the sky into a place where sparrows had a better chance of picking up a decent living than eagles.

"I understand. I ought, of course, to say to you that in busting' your money you acted foolishly, that in not retaining your post in that office you acted more than foolishly, and so forth and so on, but I understand. Well now, I just want to say to you about this legacy; here is a small sum that may yet be a big sum if you apply it rightly. And if you will take an old man's advice, I would say to you, follow where your instinct leads you. London is no use for you. Get into the open."

"That's what I want," cried the other.

"Go to the colonies."

"No," said Dicky suddenly and firmly. "I'm not going to the colonies. At least not now—not yet a bit."

"Not yet a bit. And what, may I ask, do you propose to do now?"

"I'm going to have a good time."

"Oh, you are going to have a good time—a good time." Old Forsythe disturbed some papers on his desk almost in an irritable manner and as though he were looking for some documentary reply to the outrageous statement.

"But, my dear sir, a good time is all very well *in* its time, which is not at the outset of a young man's career, if you will permit me to say so. Look at me. For forty-seven years I have worked in this office. I did not set out to have a good time; work was my one object, work, that is to say, duty to myself and to the business I found to my hand." He paused as though he had slightly lost the thread of his argument, and Dicky, whose eyes had been downcast at the pattern of the Turkish carpet, looked up.

"I think, somehow, things are different now, sir," said he. "I'm not talking of going on the racket or anything like that when I'm talking of a good time, but I've seen a lot of things in the last few years and the chaps that were always bothering about the future were the ones usually that never came home in the morning. You see, a chap like me that ought to have been dead half a dozen times, when he gets a bit of luck, wants to grab it and enjoy it unless something snatches it away. I want to get down to the sea for a few months. It's the only thing I care for much. I want to get a boat and get out. After that it will be different."

The grim and grey legal man turned, and taking a check book from a drawer began to write. Then he handed an open check for fifty pounds to the other.

"Cash that and put the money in Cox's," he commanded. "Perhaps you are right. I didn't know. Send me your address and I will notify you when the rest of the business wants finishing. Go and enjoy yourself, and don't get drowned"—with a kindly touch of the hand on Dicky's shoulder as he went out.

Then, alone again, he returned to the old grind, the eternal round of business that he called life.

CHAPTER 2

THE MYSTERY OF THE "BALTRUM"

Outside in the April sunshine Dicky Sebright made for the National Provincial Bank, cashed his check and turned his steps toward Cox's. With plenty of will of his own and more than enough obstinacy, he was, still, carrying out old Forsythe's orders with the straightforward simplicity of a child, and if the lawyer had told him to turn three times round on leaving the bank, shut his eyes and say "Abracadabra," he might have done it.

Dicky was no pup, sure of himself and disdainful of his elders; he had known himself to be as an airman not so much a man helping to win the war as a midge buzzing in the dreams of Foch, and though he had seen more of life and death than the dusty lawyer he had not seen more of the world. He reckoned Forsythe a "downy bird" and a likable one and a useful man to appeal to if ever in difficulties, also a pilot whose sailing directions were worth following.

He banked the whole of his fifty pounds, having enough money to carry on with, went to the residential club where he was staying, paid his bill, obtained his portmanteau and deposited it at Liverpool Street Station. Then he made for the docks.

Have you ever thought when standing, say, in Piccadilly Circus, that you are in a seaport town; that a bus ride for a few pence will take you to where the great deep-sea ships are lying, miles and miles of them, fluttering to the breeze all the flags of the world, ships from Japan, ships from India, Australia and China, tea ships from the Canton River and grain ships from the Golden Gate?

Dicky had often come down here to the docks urged by a craving for that romance which in West End literary circles is said to be dying; but he was not seeking romance to-day, only a suit of oilskins which he obtained at Hart & Wiseman's off the West India Dock Road.

He caught the twelve-fifty-six train from Liverpool Street to Hildersditch, the home of his childhood, and at three o'clock of a perfect early spring day was seated in front of the Anchor Inn smoking a pipe, talking to the landlord and looking again at a picture which he had known from his earliest youth.

It was low tide and the uncovered mud banks, showing a glimpse of the blue-gray North Sea beyond, filled the air with a scent better by far than the smell of roses. Gulls' voices came on the wind across the pool where a few small yachts lay, still dressed in their winter outfit, and where a "house boat to let" had not yet found her tenant. On the foreshore an old scow drawn up beyond tide mark was the only hint of the varnished rowboats that June would lay out for the summer visitors—and yet amidst all that not-too-likely prospect, unseen, hidden, Fortune warm and rosy, wealth beyond a plain man's dreams of riches, and love enduring and constant, lay, all three waiting for the adventurer lucky enough to seize them.

That adventurer wasn't Bone, the landlord of the Anchor, an old salt who had taken to inn keeping and pig raising for a living, a true-blue pessimist who still carried the weight of the fo'c's'le hatch on his back.

"I'm not sayin'," said Bone, "that you won't be able to get a boat down Mersea way or Britlinsea; I'm only sayin' there ain't no boat here that'll suit you. A ten tonner, you want. Well, there ain't no ten tonner to buy or hire, not here. There ain't no life in this place nor no money, and," concluded this amazing innkeeper, "it's my 'pinion you'd be better fixed down Mersea way."

"What's that big ketch out there?" asked Dicky, indicating a ketch-rigged boat from which a dinghy was pushing off.

"Oh, she—well, she ain't so much a ketch as a bloomin' mystery. That's what she is. Old Captain Dennis, he was an Irishman, died at Christmas. He took her over from Captain Salt—he's the board-of-trade man. That ketch she come in last October with two chaps on her, Frenchies they said they was, and they dropped their hook and they must have had a quarrel or somethin', for they was found dead in the cabin, both of them, shot through, and there she lay with no papers to show where she'd come from—nothin' but the stiffs and they couldn't speak.

"Captain Dennis, he was an Irishman, died last Christmas. He came up here last September in a fifteen-ton yawl, him and his darter and a man to help work the boat. Then he sold the yawl off to Bright of Mersea Island for three hundred and fifty pounds and came ashore to live for the winter, and couldn't stick it with the rheumatism. He said if he couldn't get on the water again he'd die, so Captain Salt he gave him leave to take up his quarters on the *Baltrum*, that's the name of the ketch, and there he stuck the winter, dyin' at Christmas, as I was tellin' you."

"And who's on her now?"

"Miss Dennis and the chap, Larry they call him, an old navy quartermaster they tell me he was, that served under Captain Dennis. And there they stick, him and she, livin' on charity, you may say, and too proud to speak to the likes of us—likes of us! Why, they reckons themselves above the visitors. Captain Salt is the only man good enough for them, because he was in the navy."

"How do you mean, living on charity?" asked Dicky.

Mr. Bone expectorated, took a pipe from his pocket and accepted a fill of tobacco.

"Well, they ain't payin' no rent for the *Baltrum* and what's that but livin' on charity? They don't deal with no shops here, but gets their goods from the stores up in Lun'on on the cheap, and Strudwick the inkim-tax collector put off last March to see if he couldn't tax them, and the girl said she'd no inkim and Larry said he'd lay for him with a stretcher if he put a foot on board. That's them, proud as Punch an' poor as Lazurus and livin' on canned meat an' charity and maybe worse."

"How do you mean worse?"

"Well, I'd like to know where that strayed pig of mine went to," burst out Mr. Bone, "and what his innards were doin' lyin' on the sand spit with the birds peckin' at them, and what them big parcels was that Larry fetched from the post office, if they wasn't sugar and saltpeter for saltin' him down. I'm not sayin' they was, but I'm just askin', what was they? And there's more than that. Ducks has gone from this place, I'm not sayin' no one's took them, I'm just sayin' ducks has gone. I'm not the man to let myself in for no axions for slander, but I often lies awake at nights thinkin' what's to happen to the oyster beds when the season comes if that chap Larry is still loose and about."

"Well, I'm hanged," said Dicky, half laughing, yet half sharing the indignation of the other. "Why don't you clear them out?"

"Clear them out?" said Bone. "That's easy said. You don't know them Irish. They've got leave to stay there till the hooker's sold—and who's to buy her? She's no yacht. If she ever was one she's been so knocked to pieces it'd take the better part of two hundred pounds to make her look respectable, and Salt he's fixed three hundred as the goviment price for her. Salt, he's the coast-guard capt'in, as I was tellin' you. She's salvage, and you know what the goviment is."

Mr. Sebright, having relit his pipe, sat for a moment smoking and looking across the water at the *Baltrum*.

She interested him. Despite her unkempt look she had lines that appealed even to his untrained eye. He could handle a boat and the passion for the sea was on him. The bother was he had never had the opportunity to acquire firsthand knowledge of cruising. He had always been the guest of some more fortunate small-yacht owner. His idea on coming to Hildersditch had been to hire a ten tonner and a knowledgeable man and work out his own education and salvation. The *Baltrum* was distinctly fascinating, but she was too big for him. Yet was she?

He had Knight's "Small Boat Sailing," published the year before, in his pocket. He had bought it at the bookshop opposite Liverpool Street Station and he had been studying it in the train, and the passage about ketch-rigged boats recurred to him. The *Alerte* was a yawl so handy that Knight and a single companion worked her off Trinidad and even cruised as far as Bahia and back, a distance of fourteen hundred miles, and Knight reckoned the ketch as handy to work as a yawl, perhaps handier.

"Where does Captain Salt live?" he asked, suddenly turning to the other.

"The captain? Why, he lives away back in the village," replied Bone. "First house on the right along out on the Mersea Road. You ain't thinkin' of takin' the *Baltrum*, are you?"

"I don't know," replied the other. "If I were, do you think I could get a man to help me work her?"

"Oh, you'd get a man easy enough," said Bone, "if there was anythin' of him left after Larry had done with him, and the girl. I'm tellin' you. It's not the buyin' of the boat that's the trouble; it's the lot on board her, and the chap that buys her will have to smoke them out like horneys, or hell get stung— b'gosh."

"I'll see," said Dicky.

CHAPTER 3

CAPTAIN SALT

Captain Salt was seated that evening after supper reading Jane Austen's "Sense and Sensibility" when the servant brought in Mr. Sebright's card.

The captain, a quick little grey-bearded man, was tired with his day's work; he had been dealing all the afternoon with something more terrible than a tiger, a German mine washed ashore on the west-center sand spit, but he ordered the visitor to be shown in.

Taking to him after a few minutes' conversation, he put Jane Austen definitely aside and produced whisky.

"Now where did Bone get that yarn from?" said he. "The government hasn't put a price on the *Baltrum*; she'll be sold all right, but most likely it will be by auction. If they'd let me handle her I'd have got rid of her by this, but not they. You see," said Salt, getting up and taking a lot of forms and blue papers from a drawer in his bureau, "government departments, whether it's admiralty or civil service, don't act like reasonable beings. Here's the *Baltrum's* papers, sheaves and sheaves of them, asking all sorts of silly questions that no one bothers about when answered, and making all sorts of silly replies to straightforward letters." He pushed the papers back in the drawer and lit a pipe. "I've had more trouble over that two-cent ketch than if she'd been a stranded battleship, all because the chaps on board of her were Germans."

"Germans? Bone said they were French."

"He's a fool. Everything pointed to their being Germans.

"There wasn't much about it in the papers, but this is the way it happened. She came in here one afternoon last October when I was away down at Mersea. I had my men with me, so there was no one to board her, but next morning Longshot, he's my man, went off to her. She was lying there with her riding light still burning and no one on deck. He went down below and found two dead men in the cabin; one chap had shot the other evidently in some quarrel and then shot himself. He had the pistol still clutched in his hand; it was a German automatic, army pattern. They were black-bearded chaps; they weren't French, I'd swear that—either Russians or Germans, and the pistol was German.

"So I reported them German. There were no papers, no contraband, nothing. Not a scrap of writing on either of them and only three days' food in the lockers. We set the wires going, but Germany knew nothing of them. The name of the boat told nothing, for Baltrum—that's the big German island over there by Juist—had no knowledge of such a boat. Norway, Sweden, Denmark, Holland and France knew nothing. You see, it became an international police matter, for the chaps were possibly criminals wanted abroad; of course I had to have them photographed and the boat and all, but there was no result. No port in any of those countries knew of such a boat or of having collected harbour dues on her."

"That's strange," said Dicky.

"Of course, she may have come from some fishing village in the Baltic or somewhere like that," said the captain. "All the same she could not have used any of the seaboard continental towns within a long time else she'd have been remembered. The customs have pretty sharp eyes and long memories. So there you have it, a thirty-ton ketch putting in from nowhere, as you may say; two fellows on board of her, one of whom shoots the other and then commits suicide; no papers, no money, not a brass farthing of money on them. What's to be made out of it?"

"Might they have come from Russia?"

"I've thought of that," said Salt. "Of course we couldn't ask any questions there, but Petrograd or any Black Sea port is a long way from here for two chaps to work her. I've lain awake nights trying to think the business out, trying to imagine what they fought over. Whatever it was, they must have been on the rocks without any money and in a strange port. Then old Captain Dennis blew along and I let him live on her on condition he kept a riding light going. A ship goes to pieces worse than a house if it's left empty and the boys were mucking her about, fishing off her and stealing gear."

"Bone told me Miss Dennis was on her now," said the other. "She and a man—"

"Larry—yes. When the old chap died they stuck there. I hadn't the heart to turn them off and Larry keeps the riding light going and looks after the ship—but they'll have to go if she's sold."

"Well, as I told you, I am looking out for a boat," said Dicky. "She's bigger than I want, but if she's likely to go cheap I wouldn't mind that."

"What do you want buying a boat for at all?" asked the other. "You'd do much better by hiring one. A boat's all trouble. First there's the buying of her, then there's the putting her away for the winter and getting her out in the spring, then she's always wanting something—she's worse than a wife to keep. Something is always giving out or wanting replacing; if it's not new gaff jaws it's new ground tackle, or a spar's sprung—or maybe it's a leak. Oh, Lord, no!—owning is a fool's game. Besides you'd want two men to help you work a boat like that, and there's six pounds a week gone clear."

"There's not one to be hired," said Dicky. "Not here, anyhow."

"No, but you might get one at Mersea or Brightlingsea—"

"And that's what I don't want. I was born here and know the waters, and besides, I don't like those big small-yacht towns nor the crowd you get there. It's like living in a regatta."

"Well," said Salt, "if you will, you will. Go over and see the *Baltrum* if you want to. You will find Miss Dennis quite a nice girl and if you are a prospective purchaser she can take you out to try the boat—it's covered by government insurance. Then I'll let you know when it's to be auctioned, when they send me news of it."

CHAPTER 4

MISS DENNIS

At nine o'clock next morning, borrowing Bone's old dinghy, Mr. Sebright pushed off for the *Baltrum*. The Pool was brimming with the flood, mud banks and sand spits were hidden and the wind from the north-of-east promised a fine day, but it was cold.

Out here on the water the supreme deadness of a small yachting center before the opening of the season struck the heart and mind more sharply and freshly than from on shore. Sebright passed the house boat, dead and deserted, with the little choppy waves smacking her planking, and a natty little yawl labeled the *Sunflower* showed him her stern and dropped behind, while now on the breeze from the east-center shoal came the *tonk-tonk-tonk* of the Black Jack bell buoy and the creak of gulls from the Long Spit that is never covered even by the springs.

Then the *Baltrum* in all her beauty showed close as he glanced over his shoulder.

She had leaped on him all of a sudden, the blisters of her paint, the desolation of her decks, the head of a disused tar brush sticking up close to the bowsprit, and clothes of some sort drying on her after rail.

From the galley stovepipe a thin wreath of smoke struggled against the breeze. That was the only sign of life on board of her; that and the clothes drying on the rail.

He rowed along the starboard side, rounded the anchor chain and then let the dinghy drift a bit while he sat contemplating old Captain Dennis' refuge against rheumatism.

She didn't look it. In some curious way the nip in the air and the creaking of the gulls and the *tonk-tonk* of the bell buoy all seemed part of her—and the cold blue of the wind-swept Pool and a sudden sense of desolation caused by the passing of a cloud across the face of the sun. The Pool had gone grey and the distant spire of Hildersditch, still sun touched, seemed to call him back to the land.

"Go to Mersea or Britlin'sea," said the spire. "This place is God-forsaken and so's she. She's beastly. Besides, what's the good of owning? Much better hire; a boat's worse than a wife to keep." It was talking sometimes like Bone and sometimes like Captain Salt, and the dinghy was drifting.

Another moment and he could have taken to the sculls again and made for shore, when up from the fo'c's'le hatch of the *Baltrum* came a man.

A big old man who rose slowly as seals rise on ice floes, straightened himself, looked into the north-of-east from where the wind was coming, and then noted the stranger and the dinghy.

Dicky, recognizing that this must be the redoubtable Larry, took up the sculls again, stopped the drift of the dinghy and with a stroke or two brought her nearer the *Baltrum*.

Bell buoy, gulls, and the nip in the wind were forgotten for the moment at the sight of the heavy and unfriendly figure standing now with hands resting on the starboard rail and eyes fixed on the dinghy.

"Hallo," cried Dicky.

"What are you wantin'?" replied Larry.

"This the *Baltrum*?"

"What are you wantin' with the *Baltrum*? Mind me paint an' keep your distance—what are you wantin' with the *Baltrum*?"

The vague antagonism that had been forming in the mind of Mr. Sebright suddenly took shape.

"I'm thinking of buying her," said he, urged not by design but the devil. "Have you any objections?"

"Thinkin' of *buyin'* her," said Larry. "Buyin' this ould cockroach trap— and what you want to buy her for?"

Dicky checked in his reply. Another figure had come on deck, from the saloon hatch this time. It swept the washing off the after rail, threw it down the hatch and then came to the side.

Oh, what a pretty girl! The last skirt of the cloud swept away from the face of the sun as she looked over, the light falling on her weather-worn old pilot jacket with one brass button missing, her nut-brown hair and the hand that grasped the rail.

"She's not for sale," said Miss Dennis, who had evidently overheard the whole conversation. "She's not fit to be sold and she belongs to the government."

"She's droppin' to bits," cut in Larry, "and not more than held up be the anchor chain. Sure it's takin' our lives in our hands we are stayin' on board of her at all."

Dicky laughed and then, suddenly, Miss Dennis—trying to frown— laughed; even Larry unbent. As if by magic the whole situation changed.

"We don't want to sell her," said Miss Dennis, "and that's the truth."

"I know," said Dicky, "and I'm not particularly keen on buying her. But the bother is *someone* will, because Captain Salt told me she was going to be auctioned."

"When did he tell you that?" asked the girl anxiously.

"Last night."

Miss Dennis brooded for a moment on this news.

"He said something to me a long time ago about auctioning her," said she, "but I thought he'd forgot it—said something about auctioning her in London at some place in the city where they sell old stores and things."

"An' how'n the divil would they take her to London," cut in Larry, "unless they put her on wheels?"

Dicky explained that this would not be necessary, and gloom fell on the company—for a moment. Then the spirit of hospitality intervened and seized Miss Dennis.

"Well, come on board, now you're here and look at her," said she. "Larry will see to the boat." She dropped the little ladder and he came on board, standing for a moment to look around him before going below.

The deck of the *Baltrum* ran flush fore and aft and had none of the distressful appearance of the hull seen from the dinghy. Once on her, the *Baltrum's* homely and sterling qualities made themselves felt even by the half-trained mind of Mr. Sebright.

Ships have personalities, just like men, and you never can gauge the personality of any craft till you get on her deck. The *Baltrum* said to you, "I mayn't be lovely, but I'm honest. I'm not ashamed of my beam, neither, nor of my age, nor of the fact that maybe I'm some Dutchman's idea of a yacht. Dutchmen have a lot of sense. You try me in a heavy sea and then try that little wedge-faced *Sunflower* back there, and you'll learn that paint isn't character—that wench!—Lord, wouldn't I like to see her off Terschelling in the winter—just once!"

Down below she spoke even louder, assisted by the voice of Miss Dennis, who seemed quite to have forgotten her rôle of deprecator.

Aft of the main saloon was a little cabin used by the girl; there was plenty of head room and none of the fixings had been removed; telltale compass, lamps, furniture and bunk bedding all remained, also the crockery ware in a tiny pantry and the pots and pans in the microscopic galley.

"She's comfortable, isn't she?" said the girl, as they returned to the main cabin, where she produced cigarettes. "She's thirty tons and you could go round the world in her—not that there's any chance of us doing that. My only wish is to be let alone and not be turned out. I'm not thinking of myself, but Larry. He's been in the family twelve years, ever since father left the navy, and what's to become of him if we leave here I don't know, for I've only a hundred and ten pounds a year and that wouldn't keep us both ashore. You see, father's pension died with him," went on Miss Dennis, "and the money we got from the *Sheila*—that's our old boat—all went in debts and things, and I'm sure I don't know what we'd have done only for Captain Salt. He let us come here—maybe you know about—"

"Yes, he told me," replied the other, shocked by the disastrous financial conditions so innocently revealed to him, and not knowing exactly what to say.

"He told you about the two dead men they found here?" asked she.

"Yes, he told me."

Miss Dennis sighed and looked across the cabin at a patch of blue sky revealed by a porthole; her gaze seemed fixed a thousand miles away.

"Many a person wouldn't have touched the boat after that," said she, "but father didn't mind. He didn't think it was unlucky, it was the other way about; he said she was a lucky boat, he said if we stuck to her we'd be sure to have great luck and when he was dying," she finished, with a quiver in her voice, "he seemed to see things he couldn't tell of, but it was all as if he saw something bright and grand, and his last words were, 'Sink her at her moorings before you let them turn you off.'"

A slight heave from the outer sea and the last of the flood was answered by the tinkle of a lamp swinging on its gimbals and a faint creak from the timbers as the *Baltrum* moved and settled again. Through the open skylight came the far-away voice of the bell buoy.

"That's why I don't want to leave her," she went on; "that and not knowing what to do with Larry if I went to live on shore. Besides, I'm fond of her. She's good. I don't know if you understand what I mean; it's like houses. There are some houses I wouldn't live in for earths—they're bad, I don't know why, but I just know it. It's the same with boats. The *Sheila* was bad, we never had any luck with her."

"I know what you mean," said he. "I've been in houses that have given me the shivers. I haven't had the same experience with boats, don't know enough of them, but I like this old hooker. She's homy, somehow, and you shan't leave her, not if I can help it."

Miss Dennis, whose hands were folded in her lap, turned her face to him like a child in perplexity.

"It's not you I'm bothering about, but the auction," said she. "I knew at once after I'd spoken to you only a minute that you'd never buy her over our heads, but if she's put up for auction *someone* will buy her and that's just as bad."

"A jolly sight worse," said he, "for if I bought her I wouldn't turn you out. You see it wouldn't matter to me, not having my own crew. Larry would be as good as any other man."

"Better," said she.

"And we could manage to sail her between us—couldn't we?"

"Of course we could," said she, brightening. "I'm as good as a man and we wouldn't charge anything—you might give Larry something for his work, but I wouldn't charge you anything, and as I was saying, I'm as good as a man."

"You're used to the sea?"

"Twelve years," said she. "Ever since I was eight, that's twelve years ago. Father was in the navy, I've told you, haven't I? And after he left it my mother died and he bought the *Port Patrick*. She was a twenty tonner. He used to sail her with only me and we berthed mostly in Kingstown harbor. Then Larry turned up and we took him along to give him a job and he's stuck to us ever since."

"Have you any friends ashore?"

"I've some relatives in Ireland," said she, "but father never got on with them. He said the best thing to do with relatives is to keep clear of them; and they weren't yacht people. Once you take to our way of living," concluded Miss Dennis, "you cut yourself off from shore folk of your own class. I don't know how it is, but it's so."

She was speaking the truth.

The small yachtsman, if he is a whole hogger, belongs to a circle more exclusive than any high-art circle. His aims and ambitions are different from those of shore folk, his life is different, his ways are different. The Dennises had spent their summers from the first of the herring to the last of the mackerel in and about Kingstown harbor, fishing off the Mugglins where the great cod feed on their way from Cahore and Mizzen Head to Lambay; fishing in Dublin Bay where the Dover sole run two inches thick and the prawns are twice the length of your thumb; then in the autumn when the last of the mackerel had departed, and before the Atlantic winter reached across the Wicklow Mountains, these happy-go-lucky people would pick up their hook, pay their bills—maybe—and steer for the south, making for Funchal or Teneriffe. Santa Cruz harbor, Teneriffe, was their favorite winter haunt. It is a pleasant little harbor, palm girt, and an ideal winter cruising base, for from here you can run to Palma, that little, colored island forty miles to the west, or drop over to Las Palmas where the great Union Castle liners come in, or potter about Hiero and Gommera, or even hunt for the treasure supposed to be hidden on the Selvagees, those barren islands lying in the turquoise sea between Las Palmas and Madeira.

Can you imagine a cheaper or more pleasant existence?

Yet it had its drawbacks—not that Sheila or her father bothered about them. These drawbacks were mostly social, as we understand the word. Old female relatives living in Kingstown and Black Rock were never done talking of the madness of Captain Dennis in subjecting his daughter to such a life, only fit for a boy, and not even for a boy who wanted to get on in the world. They prophesied that she would never make a decent match, and their prophesies seemed to have a sufficient basis. But the old captain, though destitute of much worldly wisdom, had a certain naïve philosophy of his own which told him that a healthy body is better even than the favourable opinion of maiden aunts, that decent matches often end in disaster and that God would look after Sheila. He was a well-educated man and did not neglect her education; history, geography and the love of Charles Dickens being included in the curriculum that taught her how to knot and splice.

When the war came on the captain, infuriated with the admiralty for not reinstating him in his old position, rheumatism and all, sulked till the sea danger became desperate and then he smuggled himself on board of a mine sweeper; but three months of this work crocked him for good.

She told all this, and the young man in return gave a sketch of his war experiences. Then he rose to go.

"Now look here," he said, "if you really mean it, I'd like better than anything to take a hand in this business. We could get her ready for sea by May. I'm not bothering about the auction; if it comes off maybe I'd be able to buy her, for I have a little money, but anyhow it would be fun fitting her out and I wouldn't mind painting her at my own expense. What do you say?"

"I'm sure I'd like it well enough," replied she, "and I'll talk it over with Larry, but if they sell her after you've painted her what—"

"Oh, I'll risk that," said he laughing, "if Salt doesn't object. He can't very well, for it's improving the property and my being a prospective purchaser gives me a standing with him; but there's one thing I'd like to mention, and that's terms. I hate talking about money, but it's this way—if I bought or hired a boat it would cost me a good deal, and I don't want to save money through your kindness in taking me on. When the cruising season starts I'd expect to pay for the *Baltrum* just as much as I would for any other boat."

"But she's not ours," said Sheila.

"Oh, yes, she is, as long as Salt gives you permission to use her."

"Well," said Sheila, after a moment's thought, "it's a new idea to me. It's like taking paying guests, isn't it? I've got to think it over and talk to Larry—it's so hard to know what to think. Yes, I suppose it would be right to pay something if you want to—but, I'll see."

"Miss Shaila," came a voice from the skylight, suspiciously near, Dicky thought.

The girl glanced up.

"What is it, Larry?"

"I want to spake to you about the galley stove, Miss Shaila."

"Well, I'll be up in a minute," she replied.

"Come off again to-morrow," said she, turning to Sebright, "and then I'll be able to tell you more." He followed her up the saloon stairs to the deck where Larry was waiting for them, got into the boat and rowed off.

His heart felt curiously light as he made for the shore, the sun was shining, the bell buoy had lost its dreariness of voice, and the future that an hour before had seemed pretty blank showed warm in color and traced with all sorts of unfinished sketches.

He had not found companionship, but he had come in contact with it in the persons of Miss Dennis and Larry. Companionship, the something that helps you to live the everyday life of every day, that shares the little burdens and banishes loneliness and gives existence warmth.

* * * *

"Miss Shaila," said Larry, as they watched the dinghy row ashore, "it wasn't the stove was botherin' me mind, but that young chap."

"How was he bothering you?" asked the girl.

"Faith, I dunno, but I was listenin' to what you said, him and you, and him offerin' to pay for the boat and you refusin' it."

"I wasn't. I only thought he was offering to pay too much."

Larry, who had fetched a bucket of water over the side, was preparing to peel some potatoes; he talked as he worked, squatting beside the bucket.

"Faith an' it's aisy to say pay too much, but there ain't so many goin' about on that same job these days—an' why shouldn't he pay too much? Sure, what's the good of chaps like him unless it's to make them pay for their footin'."

"Oh, Larry," said the girl, "what are you talking about? We aren't hotel keepers."

"Him and his fine ways!" went on the other, absolutely deaf to everything but what the spirit of rapine and greed was dinging in his ear. "Belongs to the flyin' corpse and carries himself as if the deck couldn't hould him. It's aisy to see what's wrong with him; he's rotten with money—and you pushin' his hand back when he houlds the gold out!"

Sheila let him talk; the thing that surprised her was the absence of the furious opposition she had expected from him. He knew everything. He had heard the conversation in the cabin and Dick's proposition, which meant nothing less than that this stranger should join their ménage, and yet he had nothing to say, he who hated strangers as he hated the devil—nothing to her in the way of speech except the suggestion that Dicky should be fleeced.

"Larry," said she, "stop talking foolishness and tell me, what do you think of him? You know quite well you wouldn't touch a penny of his money unless you liked him. Do you like him enough to have him on board with us, money or not?"

Larry paused for a moment over the potatoes he was peeling, and drawing the back of his hand across his chin, turned his eyes toward Hildersditch church spire.

"Now you're axin' me," said he, speaking in a far-away voice and as if addressing his remarks to the spire.

Miss Dennis stood for a second watching him as one watches a seer. She knew that he was reviewing Mr. Sebright both as a man and a shipmate and maybe even as a possible husband for herself. She knew Larry and his ways.

"*Now* you're axin' me," said he, dropping the church spire and taking up the potato, which he finished off and flung in the bucket.

Miss Dennis turned aft, perplexed and just a trifle anxious as to results; for Larry, without uttering the words, had said, "I haven't made up me mind. Maybe I do and maybe I don't, but I'll be tellin' you more tomorrow." You had to know Larry a long time before you knew his talk.

CHAPTER 5

LARRY SAYS "YES"

At three o'clock that day Larry came on shore for parcels at the post office. Leaving the dinghy on the beach and coming up by the path that led to the village he saw a natty old Ford in front of the Anchor Inn and the figure of a tall man passing through the doorway.

It was Selway, the small-yacht dealer, of Bewick; carpenter, painter, tinker, tailor—as far as suits of sails went—breaker and broker both. Larry knew everyone on the beach from Brightlingsea to Bewick Flats, the number of their children, of their wives, and how many times they had been bankrupt. He had the gift for acquiring this sort of knowledge.

He knew Selway. Selway had nearly crabbed the sale of the *Sheila* and Larry had sworn revenge. That was six months and more ago, but six months were nothing to Larry when he was on the warpath.

He knew Dicky Sebright was staying at the Anchor, and he had seen Selway go in. He stopped and scratched his head.

Selway had come all the way from Bewick, four miles off; he hadn't wasted petrol coming all the way to Hildersditch to inquire as to Bone's health. Well Larry knew that news of a greenhorn would go about the coast as news of a carcass goes about the desert collecting the vultures to the feast, and he guessed that Dicky was now the carcass.

He pottered about the car for a few minutes, looking at it from all sorts of angles as though it were a natural curiosity. Then he entered the inn and went into the bar on the left of the passage, where, seated behind the counter, Miss Bone, with her hair in curl papers, was reading last Sunday's *Sunday Herald*, eating an apple and killing flies all at the same time. She paused in the midst of these industries to take Larry's order for a bottle of stone ginger beer, then having slapped the glass down on the counter and tossed the threepence in the till, she resumed her pleasures and occupations as though the other had suddenly become extinct.

Larry was not bothering about her. The door of the sitting room faced the door of the bar across the passage. It was a bit open and he could hear voices from the sitting room, the voice of Sebright and the voice of Selway.

They seemed arguing about something. Then Dicky's voice came quite clearly: "But I don't want to buy a yacht. I've made other arrangements, nearly, and I don't want to waste your time."

Then Selway: "There ain't no call for you to buy her, sir, but there ain't no harm in your lookin' at her, it's all in the day's bisness, and I'll run you over in the car and back under half an hour."

Then a back door opening caused a shift of wind that half drowned the voices, incidentally bringing a smell of fried onions from the kitchen, and Larry, swallowing the remains of his drink at one gulp, left the bar and came outside.

Now Larry was undecided about Dicky. In that mind of his that knew all the soundings from Carnsore Point to Dundrum Bay he had sized the young man up and without approving, had not disapproved of him; he was "clane and a bright young chap with money in his pocket, and a gintleman"—and when Larry dubbed a man a gentleman it was a title worth having—all the same he was a stranger and to be carefully dealt with. But if Sebright had been Beelzebub, horns, hoof, and tail complete, Larry would have taken him on board the *Baltrum*—and dealt with him afterward—rather than let Selway profit by him.

Waiting for the vulture and the victim to appear, he walked round the Ford anew, sure of what was coming, sure in his heart that if Selway got his intended once aboard the lugger, Dicky would be sold, or at least some old dud boat would be sold to Dicky, which would amount to the same thing.

Then they came out, Selway leading and talking, the young man half unwilling, yet led.

"Hullo," said he, when he saw Larry, "here's a man trying to sell me a boat." Then he checked himself. He could say nothing yet about the proposed arrangement with Miss Dennis—besides, Larry had winked at him.

"Proposin' to sell you a boat, is he?" said Larry, turning his regard upon the yacht shark. "And what's the boat you're proposin' to shove off on the gintleman, may I ax?"

"The *May Queen*," replied the man from Bewick. "You've seen her, Mr. Meehan"—Meehan was Larry's other name. "She was berthed close to the *Sheila* last autumn, twenty-ton cutter and as good as new. No, I ain't tryin' to shove her off on no one. The buyers will be thick as mackerel when the season opens, but there she lays to be looked at, stripped to the keel. Maybe, Mr. Meehan, you'd come along with us and give *your* opinion of her."

Selway winked at Larry as he spoke.

"If the gentleman doesn't mind," finished Selway.

"Oh, I don't mind," said the victim.

"Then crank her up," said Larry. As the Ford started to hum he gave Dicky a nudge with his elbow, got in beside Selway and they started.

It was low tide at Bewick Flats, where the green fields come down and kiss the mud banks that are blacker even than the Mersea mud banks, and where the high tides kiss the fields; a place of great silences and weird sounds, the home of sea lavender and poppies, where birds from the great bird city of Sylt come visiting in summer and the wild duck fighting in the winter dawns.

By the anchorage and in front of an old barn converted into a workshop stood the *May Queen*, shored up and naked to the keel.

"Begob, she's a beauty," said Larry, as they got out of the car and dropped on to the hard mud. "And when was she built, may I ax?"

"Oh, she ain't more than fifteen years old," said the other, leading the way up the ladder to the deck. "Just long enough to be well tried out and show her faults, which she hasn't any that I've found out, barring the standing rigging, which wants an overhaul."

"Sticks all right?" asked Mr. Meehan, taking a knife from his pocket, opening it and prodding the mast.

"You try 'em," replied Selway. "Go all over her and give the gentleman your opinion. You know what a boat is and I wants nothin' better than your honest, candid opinion."

Then he took his visitor down to inspect the cabin and Larry, like a spider, began to go "all over her." He dropped on the mud and inspected the stem and stern posts, ran his hand over the copper sheathing, squinted at the keel, examined the chain plates and their attachments and lastly the bowsprit. Then he dropped into the little fo'c's'le, emerging from it as the other two came on deck.

"Well," said Selway, "have you been over her?"

"I have," said Larry, "and I've got her character in me pocket, and faith it's a beauty. How much might you be askin' for her?"

"Four hundred."

"Four hundred pounds?" said Larry.

"Four hundred pounds. It'll be five when the season opens."

"Well, I wouldn't advise the gintleman to give five for her," said Mr. Meehan, "but I'll have a talk with him on the way back. We'll walk it if it's all the same to you. It's only a matter of four miles. Are you willin', sir?"

"Yes, I'd like the walk," said Dicky.

"It's no trouble to drive you," said Selway, following down the ladder. "The car's there and waiting."

"The gintleman would sooner walk," said Larry, "and here's somethin' for your trouble in showin' us over her."

He took a pound note from his pocket and placed it in the hand of Selway, who wilted as if it had been the black spot itself, pocketed it without a word and turned away toward the car.

Dicky, astonished and not knowing what to say, followed, while Larry led him up to the road by which they had come.

Mr. Meehan seemed suffering from great internal excitement; as he rolled along beside his companion he muttered and grumbled and then burst into speech, addressed apparently to the fields and gull-strewn flats.

"Oh, the blazin' scoundrel!" said Mr. Meehan. "Oh, the blazin' scoundrel—four hundred pounds for that dam' sieve and he'd have took it. Oh, the blazin' scoundrel!"

"Look here," said Dicky, "what on earth did you give him that pound for?"

"Give him a pound? Why, it was the pound he slipped me in the car comin' down without you seein' him and without a word. I took it, m'anin' to shove it down his throat after I'd seen what tricks he was up to, but faith, I've done better."

"Gave you a pound!"

"Slipped me it to crack her up to you, and if I'd been as black as him it's a commission I'd have got out of the dale. Lord save us from such as him. Four hundred pounds—do you know what's wrong with her? Well, first and foremost she's nail sick. It'd cost you a pocket full of money to renail her. Second, she's rotten under her sheathin', it's all lines runnin' fore and aft and if you took it off she's cheese underneath. If you put out with her the keel might hold for a twelve-month or drop off in a minit—the bolts are half gone, c'roded. Masts sprung and rotten, she's forty years old if an hour and bad built at that. That's her character, and now you've got it—and his. He's as bad as her."

Selway had done more than expose his black nature and the rottenness of his goods to the eyes of Dicky Sebright. He had forged a bond between Larry and the young man.

Larry, besides being himself, was something that perhaps you have never met, an Irish fisherman. Captured by Captain Dennis as one might capture a walrus, he had consented to help in working the *Port Patrick* and the *Sheila*, but he was no yachtsman; he had a supreme contempt for the tribe, born maybe of arrogance, maybe of experience, maybe of both; a contempt extending to all surface sailors, for to Larry the depths of the sea were the real things that mattered. Born at Clifden on the west coast of Ireland, of a race of fishermen who had cast their nets when Brian Boru was king, he had learned to handle a boat before he was born, and he had learned to read the floor of the sea and the colors of the water before he was ten. He could smell weather and there was little about the ways of fish that he did not know.

He had done a bit of boat building, and the tricks of the trade had taught him something of the tricks of men; his instinct helped him in this direction.

As they took their way across the great flat lands in the direction of Hildersditch church steeple they talked, became companions and exchanged ideas.

Before parting at the Anchor they had come to an arrangement over the *Baltrum* by which Mr. Sebright as party of the first part was to give her a lick of paint, a new mast winch and some repairs to the standing rigging, buy her if possible if she were put up for sale, and, having bought her, was not to dispossess the present crew, who would help to work her for nothing on condition that they were permanent tenants at no rent during the ensuing winter. On the other hand, and if she were not elsewhere sold, the parties of the second part contracted to "larn" Mr. Sebright boat handling and sea craft and take him cruising and fishing all the summer from the first of May on for a consideration of two pounds a week, if Salt did not queer the pitch and turn them all adrift—that is to say ashore.

"There's no use talkin' to Miss Shaila of money, sir," said Larry. "She's one of the sort that's robbin' herself all the time. I'll do the money business wid you and shove it into her pocket whether she likes it or no. And as for the captain, there won't be any trouble with him; he's not the sort to make trouble."

"Well, that's settled," said Dicky. "I suppose Miss Dennis won't object."

"No, sir," said Larry, "she won't object."

They parted at the inn door, where Miss Bone was standing in silk stockings, her hair out of curl papers and her face powdered. She blossomed like this every day at five o'clock.

CHAPTER 6

THE ANCHOR OF THE DINGHY

During the next couple of weeks, Mr. Sebright, lodging at the Anchor and putting off each day to see his new friends, potter about the deck and help in cleaning up and repairs, became conscious of a developing antagonism, vaguely expressed in the manner and attitude of the Bones; the way Miss Bone laid the table for dinner, the way she slapped down the dishes, the way Mrs. Bone neglected his room, and the attitude of Bone himself. It was as though between the *Baltrum* and the Anchor a great gulf were fixed, bridged by electricity and hung over by storm clouds. As a matter of fact, the Bones were getting impudent because the season was coming on when the inn would not be wanting for visitors. Hildersditch is that way. You can tell the time of the year by the attitude and faces of the shopkeepers, longshoremen, post-office people and innkeepers. Again, there was the feud between Larry and the Bones, and the fact that Larry had captured Mr. Sebright and queered Selway's deal over the *May Queen*, out of which Bone would have got a commission.

The pig that had left its innards on the sand spit was nothing to this, nor the ducks that had vanished—for the commission would have been twenty pounds at least.

One bright morning toward the middle of April things came to a crisis and the visitor at the Anchor packed his luggage and paying his bill rowed off to the *Baltrum*, though he was not due to take up his quarters there till the beginning of May.

"I've come aboard, Larry, if you'll take me," said he. "I can't stick the Anchor any longer. Is Miss Dennis on board?"

"She's gone off in the dinghy, sir, beyond the sand spit," said Larry, who was working on deck, "but sure you're welcome. Now then, 'Sunny Jim'"—to the longshoreman on the boat—"h'ist that portmantle up." He handed the portmanteau on deck and, the owner following it, dismissed the boatman.

At last he was afloat for good and all, and as he looked at his portmanteau lying on the deck, at the deck, at the rails, and the water dividing him from the distant shore, a new sensation came to him; delightful in this world where most sensations are so worn out with use.

He had definitely cut his connections with the land, become a sea creature, and, more than that, a member of a new community.

The return of Miss Dennis some twenty minutes later did not break the spell, nor the events of the day that followed. Life had suddenly become new.

And the spell lasted. Sleeping in the fo'c's'le with Larry did not break it, nor did helping to fry bacon for breakfast next morning, washing up dishes and washing down the deck. Larry had nearly completed the paint work, doing it without hired help, and the smell of paint did not matter. The weather held fine and the *Baltrum* was nearly ready for sea, and that prospect breathed life and joy even into the peeling of potatoes. Little did he know what was coming.

One morning after breakfast, the tide being favourable, he started out in the dinghy to fish for dabs. Sheila being engaged in household duties could not come, but she waved her hand to him and wished him luck.

"Good luck to you!" cried Sheila. She stood for a moment at the rail, the wind blowing her hair, then she dropped below, and the fisherman following the directions he had received rowed across the Pool, dropping anchor in six-fathom water and putting out his lines.

The anchor of the dinghy had been lost and Larry had supplied its place with a pig of the *Baltrum's* ballast, a piece of brass to judge by the metal that showed through a scratch in the rust-red-colored paint that covered it. It was not an ideal anchor, but it served, and the luck which Miss Dennis had wished him came, for the flounders were biting and in an hour he had twenty.

Getting back, he found Larry on deck mending a trawl which was to serve them when cruising; he helped in the business, which took them till dinner time. All the late afternoon he spent hunting for clams on the mud banks, and that night when he turned in he was tired, too tired to drop asleep at once. He heard the incoming tide slapping the planking and the faint and far-away voice of the bell buoy. He lay thinking of all sorts of things till suddenly his subconscious mind, that stealthy worker in the dark, disclosed something which it had probably been turning over and over all day.

The anchor of the dinghy.

"That wasn't brass," thought he. "Too heavy—and not the right color, more like copper—it ought to have been lead from the weight. It looked more like gold, might be phosphor bronze—but phosphor bronze is light, isn't it?" He was asking this of a silver flounder he had hauled up from the sea of sleep and next moment the waters of oblivion might have been over him had not Larry brought him to by turning over in his bunk with a snort.

Then his subconscious mind, taking another hand in the game, sent up for his inspection and consideration the two stiffs, the black-bearded men who had been found shot in the cabin. Then sleep fell on him like a dropped cloak and he awoke to find it two hours past sunrise and a bright morning.

When he came on deck the first thing that struck his eye was the dinghy. They had taken her on deck the night before and there she lay with the new-risen sun lighting her and the fish scales on her thwarts. The anchor was still in her, and remembering the problem as to its metal, he leaned over, and taking a knife from his pocket scraped the paint near the rope fastening. The paint came off easily in flakes, and the metal showed its rich bright yellow that yielded a tiny shaving to the testing edge of the knife.

It was almost as soft as lead—as soft as gold. Weight, color, softness—it *must* be gold!

He did not believe that it was gold, and yet the strange thing was that his heart suddenly began to knock against his ribs like a hammer.

It couldn't be gold—and yet the knocking went on. He left the dinghy and walked aft. The *Baltrum* was swinging stern toward Hildersditch with the flooding tide, and he stood with his hands on the rail and his eyes fixed on the far-off Anchor Inn and the village beyond. He could hear Sheila singing as she dressed below, and the tonk-tonk of the bell buoy as it worked to the flood. And as he stood, the full realization of what was possibly the truth came on him, and he was saying in his own mind, "It's gold—what other metal *can* it be? It was taken from the ballast. And that paint that looks like rust—no one ever painted ballast pigs before. Those two fellows that were found shot—Germans or Russians. It's German or Russian gold, and there's more of it—how much?"

He said all this to himself, yet still he did not believe.

CHAPTER 7

HOUSTON

As he stood between Doubt and Fortune he heard Sheila's voice inquiring of Larry whether there were enough eggs for breakfast, and Larry's voice from the little galley, mixed with the sizzle of frying bacon, replying in the affirmative, with an addendum on the size and price of the eggs and the condition of the hearts and souls of the people that charged tuppence apiece for them. "Oh, the murtherin' scoundrels!"

Leaving the after rail, Dicky came to the locker where carpenters' tools and odds and ends were stowed, found a mallet and chisel and turned to the dinghy. The pig lay up-ended against a thwart; during its use as an anchor a rock evidently had rubbed noses with the pig and a flange of yellow metal not bigger than a threepenny piece showed near the rope attachment. He chiselled it off, then as he held it in the palm of his hand the absurdity of the whole idea came to him like a blow, together with the old adage: "All is not gold that glitters."

Gold, nonsense! There were a dozen metals and metallic combinations that looked like gold; this was one of them. Recollections of men who had made fools of themselves by mistaking iron pyrites and mica for the precious metal crossed his mind and he was about to toss the fragment over the side when a thought restrained him, and putting it in his waistcoat pocket he returned the chisel and mallet to the locker and came down to the saloon where breakfast was waiting, determined to say nothing about the business as yet.

He was due to go to town that day by the eleven-thirty that reaches Liverpool Street at twelve-fifteen. He had to see Forsythe about some business, get his hair cut and visit his tailors. Miss Dennis also had some work for him to do and as they sat at breakfast she produced a list of her requirements, things to be got at the stores and brought back with him, thus saving time and postage.

"You don't mind, do you?" said she.

"Mind?—not a bit," said Dicky, glancing over the list and putting it in the same pocket where he had placed the fragment of metal. "I'll be back by the five-fifteen, and Larry can meet me and help to cart the stuff down to the boat."

They came on deck, where he helped Larry and got the dinghy over, though there was an hour yet before he need start. Then he lit a pipe.

He had completely forgotten the pig and all his fantastic ideas about it, he was thinking of the parcel of stuff from the stores; he hated carrying parcels, especially parcels huge enough to contain six pounds of preserving sugar, two cans of asparagus, a jar of ginger, another of chutney and two cards of darning wool. The darning wool was a little worry in itself, it was not the sort of stuff that a young man cares to ask for—Sheila had never thought of that and it seemed to him that women were sometimes strangely obtuse about some things.

These meditations were suddenly interrupted by Larry.

"Now I wonder what them chaps are after," said Larry, who was standing by the rail shading his eyes against the morning glitter.

"Which chaps?" asked Dicky.

"Them chaps in the boat," said Larry.

A boat had put off from the shore. It had passed the *Sunflower*, the house boat, the mud dredgers and a cutter that had put in from Mersea during the night. There was nothing else for it to pass but the *Baltrum*.

It was coming *toward* the *Baltrum*.

Sheila was watching it now as well as the others.

"That's Bone at the sculls," said she. "But who is it in the stern sheets?"

"Faith, I don't know," said Larry, "but I've got a feelin' down the back of me spine it's some chap comin' afther the boat—bad 'cess to him."

He was right. The scow came alongside, Bone took in his sculls, grabbed on to the rail with the boat hook and the man in the stern sheets stood up.

He was a big man, prosperous looking, in tweeds, clean shaven, with a heavy jaw, and, quite irrespective of his obvious business, the crew of the *Baltrum* took an instant dislike to him.

The stranger, evidently primed with their family history by Bone, did not mince matters.

"My name is Houston," he said. "I've come to look over the boat. Throw us a ladder."

"Throw you a lather," said Larry. "I haven't no lathers to be throwin' about. Where's your orders to look over her?"

The big man contained himself; he was evidently a person not to be rattled, a believer in law and order, and the formalities of business. Holding on to the rail with his left hand, with his right he produced a letter and handed it up.

The crew read it over each other's shoulders. It was an official order to view the ketch *Baltrum*, to be disposed of by auction on the sixth of May at eleven a. m. at the Three Bells Inn, Hildersditch, by Murdle & Jackman, auctioneers of Mersea, Hildersditch and Wyvenhole and by the order of the board of trade.

"But Captain Salt told us nothing of this," cried Sheila, "and he *told* me he'd let me know when the boat was to be sold if it ever was sold."

"Now I'll put you wise about the matter," said Larry, nudging Sheila gently aside and leaning affectionately over the rail toward the stranger. "If it's a rat thrap you want to buy with holes in it and sprung masts and a garboard strake that's outwore its houldin' bolts, this is the chance of your lifetime. But if it's a say-boat you're wantin', or a yacht, be chance, then you pop down to Bewick Flats and Misther Selway will suit you. Ax Bone if I'm not telling you the truth."

"Will you kindly throw down the ladder?" said Houston, without moving an eyelid. "I have no time to waste, as I have to catch the eleven-thirty back to town."

Sheila put the little ladder over and Houston come on board without saying "Thank you," stood for a moment and looked around him just as though he were alone on the deck.

Then Dicky knew that he surely loathed this man, so prosperous-looking, heavy, material, utterly contained and satisfied with himself, so insulting in his aloofness. It was quite plain that he had taken them at Bone's valuation— he probably had put up at Bone's for the night—and looked on them as a lot of interlopers only a cut above tramps. He was not the man to understand Sheila and Larry or the poverty of old Captain Dennis or the humours of pig sticking as conducted by Mr. Meehan.

"Larry," said Sheila, as Houston, having contemplated the sticks and strings, made a move toward the saloon companionway, "will you show this gentleman over the boat down below?"

"Thanks," said Houston, "but I would prefer to go over the boat alone."

"Oh, no, you don't," said Larry, leading the way. "Not whiles our property is about, if it's all the same to you. Not that I'm mistrustin' you," continued he, vanishing from sight followed by the other, "but tayspoons is tayspoons. Stip careful for them brass-bound steps is slippy and sure it'd be the pity of the world if you tumbled an' hurt yourself."

Sheila followed them down.

The breakfast things had not been cleared away in the cabin and the newcomer took them in with the rest of the fixings; to Sheila his cold disapproving gaze seemed to blight everything from the cabin furniture to the memory of happy days here with her father. He examined the bunk cushions, he examined the swinging lamp, the carpet. He opened lockers. The lockers of an Irish yacht and the cupboards of an Irish house are better left uninvestigated by the cold eye of the Anglo-Saxon.

Sheila had stuffed the starboard lockers of the *Baltrum* with all sorts of odds and ends, some edible, some not. Lubricating oil, Brasso, a can of peaches, a can of tomatoes, an old revolver and a sou'wester were among the contents of the first locker explored by Houston. He closed it, went to the others and then turned from them to the lazaret, looked into the after cabin and then came forward, inspecting the rest of the boat in a manner that showed he was not on a yacht for the first time.

Then up on deck he examined the spars and rigging and lastly dropping into the boat he gave his attention to the chain plates.

Then he rowed off, raising his hat with sudden remembered civility to Sheila, but totally ignoring the others.

"Divil go with him," said Larry.

Sheila gazed after the retreating boat.

"He'll buy her," said Sheila, "if it's only to spite us. I know the sort of man he is—at least I know I hate him. What makes him so beastly?"

"I don't know," said Dicky, "but if he buys her he'll have to outbid me. What day did that paper say the sale's to be?"

"The sixth of May," replied Sheila. "That's Tuesday next, and I'll never—never—never forgive Captain Salt for not telling us—though maybe he doesn't know. It would be just like the government to send the advertisements out without telling him."

"I'll see him when I get back tonight," said Dicky, "and now I must be off if I'm to catch that train."

Five minutes later he was being rowed ashore, Sheila waving to him and calling directions as to what he was not to forget at the stores. Landed at the Hard he sent Larry back with the boat and took his way to the station.

Bone, who was working in his patch of garden, pretended not to see him, and away ahead, bag in hand, and also making for the train, was Houston.

It was only this morning that the mind of Mr. Sebright began to sense antagonism in the air of Hildersditch. As a matter of fact the "Dennis people," as Sheila and Larry had come to be called, had for a long time been laying down the bed plates of unpopularity; to say nothing of vanished pigs and ducks, Larry's sharp tongue and the fact that they did not deal at the local shops, Hildersditch was against them because they were "strangers." On this strip of coast everyone not born on the soil is a stranger. That is to say an outsider.

Hildersditch tolerates outsiders who come and spend money in the place; holds them at a distance, criticizes, makes fun of them, yet tolerates them.

The Dennises spent no money, dug their own bait for fishing, caught more fish than the natives, camped free of charge in the *Baltrum* and were reported to be pig stickers and fowl snatchers—you can fancy.

The antagonism of Hildersditch was felt by Dicky this morning as a chill emanation coming from Bone, from Littler of the local shop standing in his doorway and looking up and down the street, from the railway porter at the station, from the very soil itself.

It was unpleasant, but Dicky had come of a fighting breed. He knew that Hildersditch would throw up its hat to see Sheila and Larry and himself cleared off the *Baltrum*, and, sniffing the battle afar off, he took a mental oath to beat Hildersditch if it cost him his last penny. The *Baltrum* could always be resold, the great thing was not to be turned off her, and turned off her by Houston.

The sight of Houston on the railway platform smoking a cigar and reading the morning paper did not damp the fighting spirit of the Sebrights. To avoid Houston he got into a smoking carriage at the far end of the train, a smoking carriage containing a huge crocodile-skin travelling bag, a bundle of rugs, golf sticks, a perfume of Turkish cigarettes, the *Pink Un*, the *Times* and several other newspapers strewn about, and a stout young man in tweeds.

A fresh-faced, pleasant, rather bibulous-looking young man, who, on seeing the other, cried:

"Good Lord, Dicky! Where the devil have you sprung from?"

"Corder!" said Dicky. "Well, I'm blest!"

CHAPTER 8

JAMES

Wilfred Corder, otherwise known as James for some occult reason or another, was perhaps twenty-five years old—as years go.

But a man is not equally old all through and all over. There were spots in James—and very important spots—that were not more than fifteen years of age.

The son of Henry Corder, head of a great manufacturing company, James, on the death of his father, had found himself the sole possessor of some two million pounds, half in real estate and half in company shares. He took no interest in the manufacturing company or in real estate. The great round wonderful world was enough for James; the golf clubs and courses, the yachting centres, the fishing grounds, the clubs and the pleasant companions therein to be met.

"Absolutely irresponsible," said Hanover, the head of the manufacturing company; "no good for anything but play, and it's well for the business he hasn't taken the craze to mix himself up in it."

But Hanover was only partly right. James had strange streaks of caution in his nature, a certain business sense, and taste that preserved him from vulgarity. His yacht was a proof of this, no millionaire's yellow-funneled packet boat, but a schooner of one hundred and eighty tons, built for weather, auxiliary engined and fit to go anywhere.

"Well," said Dicky, "here's luck. I got into this carriage to avoid a beastly chap and find you."

"Who's the chap?" asked James.

Dicky explained and Corder absorbed the tale. Keen though he was over anything to do with yachts or boats, the story of the Dennises and their make-shift way of living seemed to interest him more than the story of the *Baltrum*.

"And they've been living in her for nothing all the winter," said he, "and now the government steps in and sells her over their heads and this perisher Houston is going to be a buyer. Well, you've got to beat him, Dicky. When's the auction to be?"

Dicky told.

"If I've a day to spare I'll maybe drop down and see it," said James. "Eleven o'clock, is it? I could run down by car. I'm staying at the Savoy and the yacht's at Grove's yard at Tilbury. She's just finished refitting; you remember her at Torquay, it's the same old boat and I never want a better."

At Liverpool Street Mr. Corder proposed luncheon at the Savoy, and Dicky fell to the lure; they had champagne and liqueurs, and at three o'clock Dicky found himself getting into a taxi and ordering the driver to take him to the bank.

Despite the champagne or maybe because of its reaction he felt heavy and dull and dissatisfied with the world. Corder's wealth and sumptuous rooms and manner of life contrasted themselves with the streets, the shabby old taxi and his own prospects. Then he ought not to have gone to luncheon—he had wasted hours and he would have to see the solicitor some other day.

The interview at the bank did not improve his state of mind. His balance had shrunk. He had been paying out some checks and that process has a tendency toward making balances shrink. He found that he had exactly four hundred and twenty-five pounds to his credit, and leaving the twenty-five he drew out the four hundred—eight fifty-pound notes, which he placed in the breast pocket of his coat, and getting into the taxi again told the driver to take him to the stores.

Auctioneers want money down from strangers, or a reliable local reference. There was no one in Hildersditch to whom he could refer except Captain Salt, whom he knew only slightly, that was why he drew the money; and as he sat waiting in a block of the traffic his heaviness of spirit deepened into pessimism. The money in his pocket cried to him that it would not be enough, that Houston was a rich man who would beat him hands down in this game. Also it told him some home truths, among others that it was nearly all the money he possessed in the world and that when it was spent he would be on his beam ends.

It was past five o'clock when, taking a taxi from the stores to Liverpool Street, he remembered that he ought to have paid a visit to his tailor, and that he had not had his hair cut, also that he would be too late for the five-fifteen train and must take the six-ten. With these recollections and facts his subconscious mind suddenly turned up the remembrance of the bit of metal in his waistcoat pocket and the reason why he had placed it there.

He told the driver to stop at Ambrose's in the Strand.

Ambrose is a pawnbroker and also a gun dealer. One half of the shop is given over to the sale of guns, revolvers, rifles and sporting gear, the other to the jewelry and pawnbroking business.

Dicky was known there. He had bought a second-hand rifle once at the right-hand counter and once when he was hard up he had pawned his watch at the counter on the left.

He found the sleek-haired assistant at the jewelry counter selling a bangle to a woman customer, waited his turn and handed over the bit of metal.

"A friend of mine has asked me to see if that's gold or not," said Dicky. "Would you mind testing it?"

"Certainly not," said the other.

He took the thing in the palm of his hand and vanished with it into the back premises while Dicky contemplated the rings in the show cases, the clocks pointing to different hours and the umbrellas and walking sticks—unredeemed pledges and bargains.

Moments became minutes, the taxi was ticking away outside and Mr. Sebright for the second or third time that day told himself that he was a fool.

Then at last from the shop beyond came the sleek-haired assistant. He was carrying the bit of metal between finger and thumb. He placed it in a small envelope which he picked off a shelf and handed it across the counter.

"That's gold," said the assistant.

CHAPTER 9

GOLD

"High grade—somewhere about twenty-two carat," finished the assistant.

"Gold!" said Dicky.

It seemed to him that he had known from the very first the tremendous truth that the ballast of the *Baltrum* was gold.

When the assistant had picked up the little envelope and carefully placed the bit of metal in it, a knock had come to his heart; in that moment, he knew; the full announcement scarcely stirred him more. He placed the envelope in his pocket and stood for a minute talking to the other.

What he said he scarcely knew. He wanted to get out of the shop, he wanted to get out without creating suspicion or giving any clue to the tremendous secret that had suddenly become his, and so admirably does the mind adapt itself to emergencies that the man behind the counter noticed nothing very remarkable in his tone, manner or conversation.

Then Dicky found himself pushing the swing door open. The roar of the Strand hit him in the face and for the first time the reality stood before him dressed in the garb of the "Arabian Nights."

The whole passing street—for the Strand is always passing—the newsboys, the cab drivers, clerks and typists, the rich and the ragged, all become part of this dream, come true.

"Gold, high grade, somewhere about twenty-two carat," said the pulse of the traffic.

"Gold!" yelled the newsboys.

And there was not a soul in all that crowded street that knew what he knew; not a soul in the whole world but himself who knew that at Hildersditch, in the Pool, on board the ketch *Baltrum*, pigs and pigs of high-grade gold were lying hidden under the guise of ballast. He got into the taxi, and the man having already received his directions, started.

Dicky, lighting a cigarette and leaning back in his seat, gave himself up to thought.

What would Sheila say?

The thought opened the door to others less pleasant. This great and glorious discovery was not altogether a jam cupboard. The *Baltrum* had to be bought. The gold was not his yet, nor could it be his till the auction was over and the cash paid down. Suppose Houston were to outbid him, and there would be others besides Houston, and he—Dicky—had only four hundred pounds.

Would it be possible before the auction to take the ballast off and hide it on one of the sand spits and reballast with bags of sand? Turning this over in his mind he came to the conclusion that it would be impossible. There were too many eyes at Hildersditch. The only chance of making profit over this business lay in keeping the stuff on board the ketch and sailing with her to some place where the gold could be disposed of. To do this she had to be bought and to buy her he had to beat Houston, and who knows whom competing with him in open market and under the presidency of a pitiless auctioneer.

That was the fight that lay before Dicky, and old Roman gladiators have entered the Circus Maximus better prepared and to meet less trying possibilities.

At Liverpool Street, over a cup of tea in the tea rooms, he came to the determination to dismiss the future and enjoy the present. Luck had been with him up to this, and why should it not be with him till the end?

At Hildersditch station he found Larry waiting for him to carry the parcels to the boat. The salt-water smell of the place was good after the stuffiness of London, and as they rowed across the dark water of the Pool toward the riding light of the *Baltrum* Dicky found himself wondering how men with banking accounts and free wills ever submit themselves to the thraldom of the cities.

"I'd sooner break stones for a living down here," said he to himself, "than live in London on ten thousand a year." Then aloud, "*Baltrum*, ahoy!"

"Ahoy," came a girl's voice from the darkness.

"Aisy does it," said Larry, drawing in his sculls and taking the boat hook. "Be ready wid the lather, Miss Shaila."

They came gliding alongside, the boat hook rasped on the rail, the ladder came down and Dicky sprang on board.

"You haven't forgotten the things?" asked Sheila's voice.

"No, they are in the boat," said he. "Hand the parcel up, Larry. I've forgotten nothing but to have my hair cut and go to the tailor's and see old Forsythe, but I met a man and that delayed me."

"Then come down to supper," said Sheila.

CHAPTER 10

THE NEWS

It was good to come down out of the night into that cozy interior. The swinging lamp was lit and the table laid, coffee, hot cakes, and half a home-cured ham waiting.

The ancestry of the ham did not worry Dicky or whether it had come to its present position illicitly or by purchase; he was too full of the great subject in his mind to notice whether he was drinking tea or coffee, and Sheila, seeing the brightness of his eye, the restlessness of his manner and the fact that he had helped himself three times to bread when once would have done, felt a cold chill at her heart.

Was it whisky?

No, it was not whisky, he was neither flushed nor garrulous, nor thick of speech. Poor Sheila knew the symptoms; old Captain Dennis had not been free of the failing, and Larry in rare moments of uplift had not been beyond reproach.

What was it, then?

"You've cut the loaf to pieces and you've scarcely eaten anything and you're not yourself—what is it that's the matter with you?" suddenly asked she, unable to hold herself in any longer. "You've something on your mind."

"I have," said he, rising from the table.

"What is it then?"

"Sheila," said he, for he had long dropped 'Miss Dennis,' "come here and sit on the couch beside me. Where's Larry?—for nobody, even Larry, must hear what I have to tell you."

"Larry's having his supper in the galley," said she, taking her seat on the couch. "There's no one to listen, and for goodness' sake go on."

He lit his pipe.

"Sheila, I don't know how to tell you it. It's the biggest news in the world, but I don't know yet whether it's good or bad, and I don't want to raise your hopes till we've got it. It's gold, maybe over a ton of gold, and it's ours if I can only buy this hooker."

"Oh, dear! Oh, dear!" said Sheila, paling with the thought that Dicky had suddenly gone clean mad. She drew slightly away, then she recovered herself. No, he was not mad; now that he had broken into the business he was quite cool and collected and instinct told her that if there was a sane man on the Mersea coast at that moment it was Dicky Sebright.

"I know," he said, "it sounds bunkum, rank craziness, but it's a fact. You know that old pig of ballast you use for an anchor for the dinghy? Well, I noticed that just where the paint is chipped at the coupling it showed yellow. I thought it was made of copper or phosphor bronze, and then the idea came to me, seeing that it looked like neither of them, that it might be gold."

"That old thing gold?"

"Yes. I chipped a bit off this morning and took it to town and had it tested. It's gold. They tested it at Ambrose's in the Strand. It's gold."

Sheila's lips parted but she said nothing.

"And there's ever so many more of them in the ballast," said he, "and they are all gold—that's why those two fellows shot each other. They were escaping with it from Russia or Germany. We're sitting on a blessed gold mine, Sheila—but it's not ours yet."

Sheila began to cry. She could not take it fully in yet, she only knew that wealth was knocking at the door. The wealth for which her father had always craved.

"Don't cry," said Dicky. "Sheila, dear, don't—it will be ours. I swear it. I'll burn the blessed hooker or dump the stuff in the Pool before anyone else gets it. Don't!"

"I'm not thinking of that," sobbed Sheila. "It's papa, poor papa, gone and always wanting money and it under his feet—and he *said* she was lucky, he *said* our fortune was in her—he knew—he knew. Well, he's gone," she dried her eyes, "he's gone where money's no use to anyone—and maybe he's happier." She sighed and gazed before her, pleating the edge of her handkerchief, a tear still on her cheek.

Regrets and tears were the first gift of the gold of the *Baltrum* that had already murdered two men.

Then like a flower recovering after rain, her face brightened, a smile came round her eyes, the gold like a sun seeming to brighten her thoughts.

"Me crying," said she, "at that grand news—sure it's ashamed of myself I ought to be. Oh, dear, to think of it, and now you'll be going off and leaving us, now you're rich." Her lips began to fall.

"But, Sheila, the stuff is yours," said Dicky. "At least it's not all mine. What on earth are you dreaming of, surely you don't think I'm such a sweep as that?"

"But you found it," said Sheila, "and you're going to buy the boat."

"Yes, and only for you I wouldn't have found it. Do you see, half's yours—and Larry's—when we get it."

Sheila began to laugh. She was not bothering about the division of the spoil, she scarcely heard him, she was quite content to take a share, but sordid considerations were far from her mind. The gold had suddenly seized her in its yellow grip and now that the first stunning effect of the revelation had passed Fortune and happy days appeared before her and she was hypnotized by the wonder and delight of the find.

The fact that she and Dicky alone in the whole world knew of the treasure cast magic around magic and the obstacles in their way brought no second thought.

Dicky might doubt, but doubt she had none that the *Baltrum* would remain in their hands. She felt that not only was fortune with them, but her father, the old man who when dying had said, "Sink her at her moorings but never let her out of your hands."

She rose from the couch.

"Not a word to Larry, at all events yet," said she. "He might get excited and go off and take whisky or something. I'll have to break it to him somehow or another—and now I want to look at it."

"The ballast?"

"Yes. I want to look at it to make sure it's there. Bring the small lamp; Larry has gone on deck, I can hear him—come on."

The ballast of a boat is stowed amidships. You can ballast with blocks of lead or iron, bags of sand, stones, or water contained in tanks. Water is an ideal ballast, for, though bulky, it is no heavier than water and will not drag a craft to the bottom if she springs a leak or capsizes. The men who owned the *Baltrum*, however, discarding all the conventional methods, had chosen to ballast her, at least partly, with gold.

A Sherlock Holmes holding the lamp while Sheila and Dicky removed the planking would have observed more perhaps than they observed, and drawn his deductions accordingly.

He would have observed—had he known anything of yacht construction—that ballast tanks had once been used and had been most carefully removed, a work of time, and that battens had been placed to prevent shifting. But more especially would he have given his attention to the oblongs of metal so carefully camouflaged and resting on a stratum of sand bags each with its rope handle attached, twenty or more of them, with sand bags here and there flung carelessly as if for a make weight.

He would have said to himself that here was the evidence of a big conspiracy carried out by men who had command of a huge quantity of gold, of a melting furnace, of sea knowledge and of time to work undisturbed.

Not only had the gold been converted into pigs and carried to some seaport or landing place, but a vessel had been prepared to receive it. Two sets of men, one versed in sea craft and the other in smelting, must have been employed under a directing brain, or directing brains, probably governmental, at all events capable of commanding secrecy in an operation shouting of itself to high heaven at every move.

Gold is more than a metal; it is a magnet drawing to itself the attention of everything high and low in the human mind. Every sort and condition of man having to do in this affair, from the smelters to the loaders, had probably either full knowledge or some inkling of the business in hand, and had remained dumb under the influence, most probably, of the only real muzzle that fits the human mouth—fear!

And then at the last, after infinite labour and precautions, assassinations, maybe, the precious cargo had turned up at a little-known English harbour with only two men in charge, and these two men had shot one another dead.

After that, silence, no inquiries, no answer to inquiries—nothing.

Our Sherlock would probably have given it as his opinion that the two dead men were the directing brains of the whole business. The men who had wielded power and commanded secrecy, and that they had put out of count any other men that might have been with them. Perhaps he would have been right.

Sheila and her companion, kneeling and holding the lamp, were troubling their heads about nothing but the sight before them—the array, vast because of their nature—of the rust-red painted blocks, tufts of rope, sand bags, all lit by the feeble light of the half-crown kerosene lamp.

Dicky, handing the lamp to his companion, took a knife from his pocket and reaching toward the nearest pig scratched the paint away for the space of half an inch, showing the royal metal, bright, yellow, hypnotizing as the eye of a magician.

* * * *

When they returned to the cabin, Dicky, relighting his pipe, constructed a whisky and soda for himself and made Sheila sit down beside him on the couch.

The fellowship that had grown up between these two was extraordinary in a way, for though both were young, good-looking and filled with the joy of life, there was nothing between them but just a bond of fellowship without any strands of sentiment in it.

They had been too busy painting, patching, overhauling sails and spars, frying bacon, fishing and digging for bait, to bother about what we call love, and of all companionships this free-and-easy companionship of two really young people of opposite sex is the pleasantest.

It is effervescent, it doesn't last, nature sees to that, and maybe she would have seen to it now only for the gold, for Dicky and Sheila, irresponsible, full of youth and almost as innocent of the ways of the world as two children, suddenly, tonight, found themselves faced with a problem that would have given pause to a syndicate of the biggest London bankers and the biggest London crooks, combined—and they knew it.

For all their innocence and worldly unwisdom they sensed the difficulties ahead.

It was not so much a question of the buying of the *Baltrum* as of the disposal of the treasure once it was theirs.

"The bother is," said Dicky, "if you go to sell gold to a chap he'll ask you where you got it; it's not like selling a horse or a yacht, it's not even like selling diamonds. You see no ordinary person buys gold—he buys everything else in the blessed world, it seems to me, but he doesn't buy gold except in jewelry. This stuff isn't jewelry. I've been thinking a lot about it coming down in the train, and the more I think of it the more difficult the whole business seems."

"Couldn't you put it in a bank?" asked Sheila.

"Well, just fancy driving up to my bank with one of those things or with a cab load of them!"

"Well, why not tell everyone?" said she. "Why hide it up and not say openly, 'Here's all this gold, we found it on the *Baltrum* and since we've bought the *Baltrum*, it's ours.'"

"Yes, and then what would the government do? They'd seize it as sure as nuts, and advertise it and hand it back to Germany or Russia or wherever it has come from, or stick to it themselves. No—I'd sooner dump it overboard."

"Well," said Sheila, "there's no use in meeting troubles halfway, there's no use in bothering about it at all till it's ours and it won't be ours till after the auction. Once it's ours, we'll manage to get rid of it—somehow."

CHAPTER 11

TUESDAY MORNING

During the five days before the auction three other prospective buyers put off to look at the *Baltrum*. They were of little account, two being small-yacht workers from Mersea and the third Selway. Not one of them, in the opinion of Larry, would bid near four hundred for the boat.

"She wants a matter of two hundred spent on her," said Larry, "and that wid four hundred would make six, and where'd their profit be? There's not a man out of the asylum that would give more than five hundred for her, new painted. Oh, be jabers, she'd want more than that—I'm forgettin' the canvas. It's good enough for us, but it's not good enough to sell her with to a gentleman that wants a yacht, and look at the price of a new set of sails nowadays. No, sir, you may make your mind aisy, she won't fetch more than three, not unless that chap Houston runs the price up on us from spite."

Larry was quite easy in his mind. He knew nothing of the gold, but as the time drew on and Sunday passed to the far-off tinkling of Hildersditch church bells, the heart of Dicky Sebright began to gnaw at his ribs and Sheila lost her appetite. On Tuesday before noon the *Baltrum* and her treasure would either be theirs, or in the possession of a stranger.

He, whosoever he might be, would take possession at once and they would have to clear out. Talking this matter over, Dicky's soul would rise in revolt. "I'll put a light to her first," said he, "or hole her and sink her at her moorings." But in his heart of hearts he knew that he would do no such thing. He knew that he was tied to the horrible position of deciding by auction whether he was to be a man of wealth or not.

You have been to an auction and perhaps you have bidden for some desired article and known the sensations peculiar to that stuffy and sordid battle.

You have seen the ormolu mirror or the Louis XV. cabinet brought in and you have heard the voices popping up from here and there in the room outbidding your bids. That was what Mr. Sebright had to face, with the object in contest not a Louis XV. cabinet but his future.

There was no way out. They had talked of carting the stuff ashore and caching it, but thrown up the idea. The sand spits always washed by the sea were impossible, the foreshore was all eyes, Hildersditch antagonistic.

Dicky had thought of taking a single pig wrapped in canvas up to town, and hiding it somewhere so that they might have something if worst came to the worst, but he did not know where to take it unless to his tailors. He had given up his rooms, even if he hadn't it was the last place he would choose for a gold cache.

"Couldn't you take it to your bank?" asked Sheila as they debated this matter for the last time.

"Of course I could take it," said Dicky, "but what on earth could I say to them? They'd know it was metal by the weight."

"What if they did?"

"Well, just think of going to your banker with a lump of iron or lead done up in a piece of sailcloth, and asking him to take care of it. No, I've thought of everything. There's nothing to be done but go the whole hog. If we can buy the old hooker there's lots of possibilities; we can take the stuff abroad or somewhere or cut it up and sell it bit by bit. We'll have time to do things in and we may get hold of someone to help. If we can't buy her we're done."

"We'll buy her," said Sheila. "I feel it. I feel that everything will turn out all right."

"I hope so," said Dicky.

* * * *

Tuesday morning dawned in a roaring cataract of rain. Dicky awoke to the sound of it on the deck and the splash of it on his face from a spot where the planking was not properly calked.

He turned on his side and put the blanket over his head and tried to go to sleep again and failed.

The rain seemed a bad omen, but it did not last. At half past seven, true to the old adage, the rain ceased, the clouds parted and a glorious day broke on the Mersea coast, a blue and bright and balmy and beautiful day turning the Pool to a sapphire, and Hildersditch to a town in Fairyland; at eight the crew of the *Baltrum* were at breakfast and before nine, rowed by Larry, they were making for the Hard.

The Hard was deserted, the road leading toward the village and station showed not a soul, the only living being in sight was Mrs. Bone hanging out washing in the yard of the inn.

Larry pulled the dinghy up high and dry. Sheila, unknown to him and with the help of Dicky, had put the "anchor" back safe among the ballast; not requiring it for fishing during the last day or two he had not noticed its absence from the boat. It was one of Larry's delightful peculiarities that a thing absent from its place gave him no trouble till he wanted it. Then instead of hunting for it he would use any old substitute. The dinghy's proper anchor was on board; he had found it again after mislaying it, but having used a substitute he continued using it without taking the bother to change.

Ashore now, he went to Bone's fence, leaned his back against it, and began to fill his pipe. Sheila took her seat on the gunnel of an old boat near by and looked about her at the Pool, blue to the sand banks, the gulls flighting above the east-centre spit, the boats at anchor, the blue sky.

On the balmy sea-scented breeze the far-off *tonk-tonk* of the bell buoy could be heard, now clear, now faint; from far away across the marshes the lowing of a cow, and above all, like starshine turned to sound, the thrilling of larks.

Innumerable larks haunt this coast, accentuating the loneliness of the sea meadows.

"Isn't it lovely?" said Sheila. "It's almost like Ireland—Larry."

"Yes, miss."

"Did you pat the paraffin stove out before we came off?"

"Faith, and I forgot," said Larry, "but I believe I did, and if I didn't it don't matter—sure it will burn itself out."

Sheila looked toward the village.

"Not a soul to be seen," said she, "and I expected there would have been a crowd. Wouldn't it be a joke if nobody came and there was only us to bid! Could you have an auction with only one person to bid?"

"I don't know," said Dicky, "but it's early yet and the London train is not in. It's due at ten-ten. Let's go up and meet it and see what it brings."

They left the Hard and came up the road through the village to the station; here they took their seats and contemplated the station master's little garden across the metals, and tried to talk, but they could find little to say.

In a couple of hours from now the lists would be set and the battle on and the whole of their future in the balance.

"Have you got that money safe?" asked she.

"Yes," he replied, putting his hand to his breast pocket, "it's safe enough." He looked at his watch. "The train's overdue."

A far-off whistle came as if in reply and away down the metals and rounding the bend came the ten-ten which was always somehow the ten-fifteen and sometimes the ten-twenty.

It drew up and discharged quite a number of passengers, nearly all men. Houston was among them. Houston carrying a yellow bag and a folded umbrella.

"That's he!" said Sheila, "the beast—and, oh, look at the others!"

They were worth looking at, this crowd suddenly disgorged on Hildersditch platform, and now making their way down the road to the village and the inn.

Men of the same type and nearly of the same age, and not one speaking to another, small dealers all of them from Shadwell or the Dock roads, some in blue serge caps, some in black suits and bowlers, some with rings in their ears, all with rings on their fingers. Not one of them able to bid above a few hundred pounds, yet all imbued with the truth of the maxim, "You don't know what may happen at an auction."

The admiralty advertisement was to these as news of a dead horse to crows.

There might be pickings or there mightn't, they hadn't inspected the *Baltrum*, they only had the specifications as set down, instinct would serve them for the rest.

"Oh, Dicky," said the girl, as they followed at the tail of this procession, "it feels like a horrible sort of funeral. If they are all going to bid, where's our chance?"

"I don't know," said Dicky. "We've got to risk it. There's no use bothering, and anyhow they look a pretty measly lot—but one never knows, the most awful-looking blighters seem stuffed with money these times. Houston is the man I'm really afraid of—wonder what he has in that bag."

Sheila was beyond trying to think.

They reached the Hard, where Bone became one of the party, Bone in a black coat put on for the occasion. Bone cheerful for once in his life at the prospect of good business and pointing out to Houston the barn where the auction was to be held.

"There's a nation of a crowd comin' from Mersea," said Bone, "not to speak of Bewick. This weather'll bring 'em like flies, but the barn'll hold 'em all, and it'll be hard biddin', I fancy."

Sheila took her seat again on the gunnel of the old boat, the crowd grew and through its murmur, from far away, she could still hear the voice of the bell buoy indifferent as the voice of Fate.

She turned her face seaward and looked at the *Baltrum*. She was not thinking of the gold, she was thinking of the days that were gone and of the old boat that had given her and her father a home.

She loved the *Baltrum* almost as though it were a living thing; it was a friend, and now—her eyes filled with tears.

CHAPTER 12

THE AUCTION

It was ten minutes past eleven when the toot of a motor horn on the breeze that had backed to west of north told every native present that Murdle, driving his Panhard, bought second-hand out of war stores and costing one hundred and seventy-five pounds, was turning from the Mersea into the Hildersditch road.

The auctioneer was twelve minutes late, but he did not apologize.

He was a round little man with an apple-red face and full of jests and good humour among people he respected at a stock or furniture sale, but mirthless as cold mutton and without a word for anyone of this shore-along crowd whom he despised—a sinister character.

He covered the bonnet of the old Panhard with the rug and led by Bone and followed by the crowd, marched off toward the barn.

Now this barn was of great antiquity. It had been built when the Hard was two miles from the sea; it was oak beamed and roomy as a small church, and it had a permanent rostrum at one end. Bone let it out for Boy Scout revels, Girl Guide festivals, dances, whist drives, and Women's Institute meetings, and maybe it was the corpse of old revelry that lent the place such an air of depression; a political meeting had not improved it by leaving old small posters stuck to the beams. There were no chairs, seats or any accommodation whatsoever, save the auctioneer's table and chair on the rostrum.

Toward this rostrum Murdle made, moving with the speed and somewhat the appearance of a dribbled football, climbed the three steps, placed his bag on the table, opened it and took out a sheaf of papers, a pocketbook and a little mallet with an ivory head. These he placed on the table. Then he sat down on the chair and looked at his watch as though reproaching the crowd for being late.

"Dicky," whispered Sheila, "I was at an auction once and it has all come back to me. Don't, whatever you do, join in the bidding at first—it only runs the price up. Wait till there's a pause, see how things are going."

"Right," said Dicky.

He was trying to hold himself steady and keep his mind clear, he felt weak, nervous, and confused, he had felt the same as a child in the anteroom of the dentist and he dared not speak more than one word lest Sheila notice his condition.

Then, all of a sudden, his sight became crystal clear and his nerves as steel.

Murdle was on his feet and the auction had begun.

The auctioneer was reading the specifications of the boat hurriedly, in a perfunctory manner, and without stops unless for breath.

He gave everything down to the ballast, iron ballast he described it as, and then started the bidding.

There was no upset price. Gentlemen were asked to bid for this capable sea boat, adaptable for alteration into a gentleman's yacht.

"Fifty pounds," said Murdle. "Thank you. Fifty-five, sixty, seventy, eighty, eighty-five, ninety."

Bids were rising like star shells from all parts of the room and from all sorts of inconsiderable people. The price rose to a hundred, to a hundred and fifty, two hundred, yet not a word from Houston. The gentleman who had bid two hundred, he had oily locks and was beginning to perspire visibly, looked slowly round him as if in triumph.

"And ten," struck in an individual with rings in his ears.

"*And* ten," said Murdle. "Two hundred and ten—twenty—thirty—thirty-five, forty—fifty—two hundred and fifty pounds."

Pause.

The oily-locked one looked round again. No one spoke, the boat was all but his. Then Houston struck in.

"And twenty."

"Two hundred and seventy pounds—two hundred and seventy pounds—any advance on two hundred and—"

"Two hundred and eighty," cried Dicky.

"Ninety," said Houston.

"Three hundred." Dicky had suddenly all but lost his voice. He recaptured it as one recaptures a hat dropped in a crowd and was himself again. All the small fry had dropped out now, it was a battle to the death between Dicky and Houston, whose voice came quite calmly right on the last bid.

"And ten."

"Three hundred and ten. Three hundred and ten pounds—twenty—thirty—forty—fifty—sixty, seventy, eighty, ninety—ninety-five—"

Sheila's heart fluttered like a bird as the bidding paused for a moment. Houston seemed done and the boat was Dicky's.

"Three hundred and ninety-five pounds—any advance on three hundred and ninety-five pounds—any—"

"Four hundred," said Houston.

In this supreme moment the memory came to Dicky of the twenty-five pounds still in the bank. He would be left without a penny—he flung that thought aside.

"And twenty-five," cried he.

"And five," said Houston, and that was the end of Dicky.

The auctioneer cleared his throat.

"Four hundred and thirty pounds, any advance on four hundred and thirty pounds—going at four hundred and thirty pounds—going—" He raised the hammer.

"Four forty," came a voice from the door.

CHAPTER 13

THE HIGHEST BIDDER

Now the night before the auction, Mr. Corder, otherwise known as James, had dined at the Ritz and danced at the "Midnight Follies."

He had clean forgotten Dicky Sebright, the story of the Dennises, Houston, and his own half promise to turn up at the sale on Tuesday, May 6th. He was awakened at seven o'clock by his valet Strutt who was holding a tea tray in one hand and turning on the electric light with the other.

James' head was aching and his tongue was heavy in his mouth. You cannot expend energy in talking, laughing, eating, dancing and drinking from seven in the afternoon till three a. m. and wake up at seven charged.

For a moment and while he drank his tea the world seemed a very black place to James, but five minutes later under a cold shower it began to clear.

Then came recollection.

Wilfred—to give him his other name—was the son of his father in some particulars. He had a kind of broken-down business sense—or, to put it more exactly, he had mixed with his joyous and generous qualities something of the low cunning that makes a business man's "sense." He had also a memory faultless when it was in working order.

The calendar on the wall of the bathroom, which Strutt attended to, pointed to the day being Tuesday, May 6th. It was also a calendar edited apparently by a madman, for each day had its text or quotation, and to-day's was "Go thou and do likewise."

James' eye fell on the calendar as he was drying himself and the date set his memory going. To-day was the day of the auction at Hildersditch, at eleven.

The last of his depression vanished. Here was something to do, something to do in the open air, away from London, and in the way of yachts.

Getting into his dressing gown, he touched the electric.

Strutt appeared.

"Strutt," said James, "breakfast at eight sharp, kidneys and bacon, a sausage and coffee."

"Yes, sir."

"Tell the car to come round at nine sharp, have a luncheon basket packed for two—one never knows whom one may pick up and I'm going into the wilderness. Also pack in three pints of Mumm." In the act of shaving now, he was speaking through lather. "Also some cherry brandy—they like it better than liqueurs. Got that down in the tabloids of your memory?"

"Yes, sir," said Strutt.

"A siphon of soda and a bottle of John Roe. I like to take my opening hours with me. Have you put out my clothes?"

"Yes, sir."

"Then that will do."

"At what time may I expect you back, sir?"

"Heaven only knows—but probably before midnight. You have the day to yourself; you had better go to the Tower or somewhere quiet. Beware of gambling, wine and women, and shut the door after you."

"Yes, sir," said Strutt.

At nine to the tick of the clock the car, a Rolls-Royce, drew in to Savoy Court and at two minutes past nine Mr. Corder appeared, stepped in and drove off.

The luncheon basket and wine had been put in at the garage. He never asked about them; so certain was he of being well served that an order once given was forgotten.

The chauffeur, Handley, drove. James did the navigating, and the route was Regent's Park, Seven Sisters' Road, Epping, Dunmow, Colchester, Hildersditch.

At Dunmow the continuous sight of shut houses of refreshment, the keen air and the vision of the bacon factory suggested in the mind of James a large whisky and soda and the John Roe was got from its hiding place.

It was got out again at a crossroads four miles beyond Colchester, where they stopped to ask the way of a country policeman who turned out to be quite a delightful person with an inside knowledge of poaching, ferrets, and the ways of wild ducks.

James would have taken this blue-bound edition of Gilbert White on board to continue the conversation only he had a bicycle with him. As it was, nearly half an hour was lost, so that when they arrived at the barn, a boy on the footboard piloting them, the auction had begun.

The bidding was at the two-hundred-and-fifty-pound mark when, standing at the doorway, he took the whole position in.

The proceedings interested him vastly, and the crowd. In that grubby and rather sordid crowd the figures of Dicky and Sheila attracted his attention; also Sheila's beautiful profile as she turned to her companion. Houston, also, stood out from that crowd.

This was the girl whose story had been told to him, and Houston was evidently the "beastly chap" who was trying to buy her boat.

The bidding went on, the knock-out blow came.

"Four hundred and thirty pounds," cried Murdle, "any advance on four hundred and thirty pounds? Going at four hundred and thirty pounds—going—" The hammer swung up.

Then, as Dempsey might wade into a street fight, Mr. Wilfred William Corder came into the business.

"Four hundred and forty."

Houston looked round. He had already gone a bit beyond his mark. He saw the newcomer and threw up the game.

"Four hundred and forty—any advance on four hundred and forty—going at four hundred and forty—going—"

The hammer fell and the *Baltrum*, ballast and all, was the property of James.

The crowd turned and pushed out of the place for drinks, and James, Dicky, Sheila, and the auctioneer suddenly found themselves alone.

James shook hands with Dicky, was introduced to Sheila and handed his card to the auctioneer.

Wilfred William Corder,

Royal Thames Yacht Club.

Murdle knew the name quite well, but he made trouble about taking a check. He wanted local references.

"And where the devil do you think I can find references in this benighted place?" said James, already writing the check from a book he had taken from his pocket. "I can refer you to Mr. Molyneux of Hatch, but that's fifteen miles from here. Don't be a fool; the Bank of England is good enough for you, ain't it?"

The sight of a check on the Bank of England—the Bank of England requires a permanent current account of two thousand pounds from its customers—was enough for Murdle. But still he grumbled.

"I take it you won't move the boat till this is cleared," said he, putting the check in his bag.

"I'll jolly well sink her if I want to," said James. "And now come out and have a drink." He put the receipt in his pocket and led the way out. Sheila and Dicky followed.

The girl was almost in tears. Boat, money, all were gone. She was not thinking of herself, but of Dicky—also of Larry.

What would Larry do now for a job? With enough money to keep them both on the *Baltrum* she had not enough to keep them both ashore, where rents were so dreadful and where one could not do one's own washing. It was only now, really, that the blessing the *Baltrum* had been to them appeared before the girl like the vision of a retreating angel. The old boat had saved them from want, given her a home, and the strange fact remained that in the mind of Sheila at this moment the gold was almost forgotten in her grief for the lost home.

Meanwhile James, the home destroyer, not looking the part in the least, was directing Handley, who was preparing and distributing drinks.

Handley was a strict teetotaler and he made the income of a puisne judge owing to this fact and strict attention to business. He was never at fault and never wanting in an emergency. In this instance he was not driven to crave glasses from Bone; tucked away in a cubby-hole of the car were five or six cut-glass Savoy Hotel tumblers, also the pints of champagne were quarts.

James, if you will remember, had ordered pints. When the man had turned up at the garage with the luncheon basket and the wine, Handley, surveying the straw-covered bottles, had asked: "What are them things? Get back with them," said Handley, "and get quarts. There's never no knowing what we want if we meet company and it's me that gets it in the neck if we run dry."

So quarts it was and fortunately, for Murdle having been satisfied and Dicky and Sheila having reluctantly enough drunk a small libation to the God of Luck, the expanding soul of James began to take in the natives in the form of two longshoremen, a crab catcher, and an old shepherd who had strayed over from Berwick Flats.

The wants of these people having been attended to, the three got into the dinghy, a tight fit, and rowed by Larry, pushed off to inspect the new purchase.

"It was jolly lucky I came just in time," said James as they left the shore. "I'd have been too late in another five minutes. I saw you were stuck; then I struck in, and now you've got her."

"*You've* got her, you mean," said Dicky.

"Me—which—oh, the boat," said James, rather confusedly. "*Me!* Why, my dear chap, you don't imagine I bought that old dredger for myself."

"Then who on earth did you buy it for?" asked Sheila.

"You," said James quite naturally, and as though he were talking of buying an orange.

"Me," said Sheila.

She had met a good many different sorts of people in her life, but she had never met anyone quite like this.

"Yes, you. I know all about the old hooker and this fellow, what's his name, who wanted to buy her; well, she's yours. Here's the receipt from that auctioneer chap, and any other papers will be made out in your name."

He took the receipt from his pocket, but Sheila would not accept it. The whole thing was like a nightmare, a pleasant nightmare; being rowed off to the *Baltrum* by a jovial and pleasant-faced stranger whom she had never seen before, a stranger moreover who had bought for her a present costing over four hundred pounds—this was a situation outside the normal, to say the least of it.

But the situation that arose on her prompt rejection of the offer and the receipt was even more curious, for James was James to begin with, secondly he was James plus far too much alcohol for that hour in the day, thirdly the philanthropist in him that had risen and had humped its back had received a snub on the nose. He had been moved by Dicky's story and in buying the boat and saving the home of the Dennises he had felt what the knight-errants used to feel when, lowering their vizors and levelling their lances, they charged.

"You won't take it?" said he.

"No, indeed, I won't—thank you more than ever so much, all the same. No, I can't."

"All right," said James, grimly. They were just alongside the *Baltrum* and as Larry hooked on James ungallantly and without a word sprang on board, and as the others followed stood looking around him.

A crab boat was passing. James hailed it.

"What are you doing that for?" said Dicky.

"You'll want to fetch your things ashore," said James. "I'm going to put a light to her."

"A light to what?"

"This hooker. She's mine, ain't she?"

"Good God!" cried Dicky. "Don't be a fool, man."

"Will you kindly get your things off," said James, "unless they're insured."

He went toward the galley, saw a can of paraffin and fetched it out. "Now we'll have some fun," said James, the snubbed philanthropist in him subsiding partly to give place to the gleeful incendiary. "I've never burned a ship before—hic; never thought of it." He turned toward the fo'c's'le hatch, having glanced at his match box to make sure it was full, and Sheila and the others saw at once that he meant work.

"Don't," said Sheila, laying her hand on his arm. "If you want me to I'll take the boat, but not before you hear what I have to tell you. Come down below. Larry, tell that crab man we don't want him and give him a shilling." She produced a starved-looking purse, handed him the coin and led the way down below.

James, who had reluctantly given up the paraffin can, followed with Mr. Sebright.

CHAPTER 14

MAC ADAM

The day had clouded over a bit as they rowed across the Pool, but now, just as they entered the cabin, the sun lit the place with beams through the skylight and water shimmers through the starboard portholes.

The place looked cozy and comfortable, and James, who had never seen a sea interior like this, stood for a moment at the doorway looking about him.

You could have got the whole of the *Baltrum* into the saloon of his yacht, the *Dulcinea*, furnished by Hollyer & Stevenson regardless of cost. But good taste backed by money has, to the appreciative eye, no chance against good taste fighting against odds, and many a humble home is to the appreciative mind a better habitation than the palace of many a millionaire who buys his taste with his tapestries, regardless of expense.

There was nothing in the cabin of the *Baltrum* to offend the eye because everything was in keeping with the sea surroundings, everything was spotlessly clean and there was only one colour to contrast with the dark oak of bulkhead and beam—blue.

James having taken the seat pointed out to him, Sheila, perching herself on the side of the table, started business right away and without preliminaries.

"I couldn't say it on deck," said she, "because Larry is there and he doesn't know yet, but you can't donate this boat. If I were to do what you ask me and accept it from you, I would be the wickedest person in the world. This isn't a boat, really, it's a gold mine."

"I beg your pardon!" said James. He had recovered almost entirely from any slight aberration due to alcohol and the auction and for a moment he thought that Sheila was joking with him, but he saw at once that she was in earnest. What on earth did she mean?

"I know it sounds mad," said she, "but I am telling you the truth. This is not an ordinary boat; she has thousands and thousands of pounds' worth of gold on board her. Oh, tell him," said she, turning to Dicky. "I can't."

Dicky got up from the seat he had taken and leaning against a bulkhead with his hands in his pockets began right at the beginning of things and went on to the end, the millionaire listening, nursing his knee, scarcely speaking a word.

He could scarcely believe, yet he believed, and the whole thing filled his mind with extraordinary sensations never experienced before. He possessed all the money he could possibly use, but the near presence of this new gold affected him almost as much as though he had been a beggar. Cupidity in a golden mantle rose gigantic in the mind of James, fronting the Spirit of Adventure and Captain Teach in all his pirate rig. Meanness, that horrid giant who is always somehow a dwarf, came from under the table and told him what a fool he had been to insist on Sheila taking the boat as a present; through the open porthole, mixed with the sea air and the clanking of the bell buoy, wafts from all the treasure stories he had ever read came spiced with the perfume of Treasure Island and the smell of rum.

"So you see," said Sheila, as Dicky finished, "why I can't take the boat. It's all yours."

The words acted like the drop of cold water that precipitates a chemical mixture and in the soul of James, grandeur, always lurking, rose like a giant reaching almost the roof.

"Nonsense," he cried. "I never go back on my word. She's yours."

Yet in the sixtieth part of a second, old Corder, who had given a hundred thousand pounds in charity yet had murdered all sorts of men financially in strictly business deals, spoke.

"The boat's yours; as to the stuff, we'll go into that later. Dicky here will want a pull out of it—by Jove, this is the biggest surprise that has ever struck me. Why, there must be near a ton of the stuff, by what you tell me. I say, those fellows must have had their heads screwed on tight to think of getting it away as ballast."

So he babbled, while all the time a voice was crying to him, the compound voice of father Corder and meanness and cupidity and Captain Teach: "Stick to it, James, stick to it, James, don't let foolish generosity get the better of you. Gold, gold, gold, tons of gold, stick to it, James."

And then, so strange a stuff is soul, the voices were shut off, and James vaguely, against his will at first and then entirely with his will, turned to the others and spoke clearly and from his heart.

"Look here, you two," said he, "we're *all* in this. It's a huge big piece of good luck and it was meant for the lot of us. The boat's not worth twopence, but she's yours, Miss Dennis; as for the stuff, we'll divide it between us."

The shade of his father, throwing up its hands at this stupidity, which seemed to read that each would take a third share, maybe chipped in, for James went on:

"I'll take half and you'll take half—how's that for fair?"

"Oh, no!" cried Sheila. "It's all yours."

"Well, see here," cut in Dicky, "I don't know that it's not fair to divide the stuff and I'll tell you why. You wouldn't have come to the auction only for me, and then again it's not only buying the stuff, but getting rid of it. It will take us all three to help in that. Sheila, I think that proposition is fair—it's more than that, it's jolly generous, but still, as I said, we have to get rid of it, turn it into money and it's a job Corder couldn't do alone."

"Well, that's fixed," said James, virtue now pouring balm on his head and saying to him, "You've done the right thing, James, you've done the right thing—you've been a damned generous fool—but all the same you've done the right thing."

"That's fixed—and now let's see the stuff. I'm aching to set eyes on it."

They led him to the ballast. He sniffed at it, touched it, tested it, gloated over it. Then they led him back to the cabin. Dicky offered drinks, but James was beyond drinks; he smoked while Sheila took up some needlework and Dicky talked, explaining the task before them. James seemed to have it in his head that the caching of the stuff was quite an easy matter.

"You see," said Dicky, "we've talked all that over for days and I don't see yet how it's to be done. If the stuff was actually our own it would be easy enough. We could take it right off to the Bank of England, but as a matter of fact, *is* it ours? We've bought the boat from the government, but taking her history into consideration, wouldn't the government barge in and claim the gold? It's treasure-trove. I believe they could and it won't do to risk it. But I tell you what we might do. There's nothing about the law my lawyer man doesn't know; we could ask him."

"Wouldn't he peach?" said James.

"Not he. I'd put it to him as a—what do you call it?—hypothetical case. If he gives it as his opinion that the government would bone the stuff, well, we must think out some other way. We've lots of time."

"Listen!" said Sheila.

A boat was coming alongside, and through the skylight came Larry's voice.

"What are you wantin'? Wantin' to see the owner—and what are you wantin' that for? Keep off till I tell the mistress." Then through the skylight, "Miss Shaila, there's a chap wantin' to come on board."

Dicky left the cabin and ran up on deck. They heard his voice and the sound of someone coming on deck. In a minute or so he reappeared at the door of the cabin, followed by a stranger.

A big glossy man attired in a frock coat and carrying a top hat in his hand.

"This gentleman was too late for the auction," said Dicky, "and he's come off to see if there's any chance to do a deal over the boat." He winked at James as he spoke, and stood aside while Mr. MacAdam—this was the name of the newcomer—advanced, placed his hat on the table and his card beside the hat.

"Haf I the pleasure of speaking to the owner of the *Baltrum*?" asked Mr. MacAdam, addressing himself to James.

"No," said James, indicating Sheila, "this lady is the owner."

"Ah, well," said the other, "it is all the same—may I take a seat?" Then turning to Sheila, "I wish to buy her. It was distinctly told me that the auction hour was two o'clock and I come too late. My partner Mr. Shelegmann and I have need of such a boat for the trade we are engaged in and as the matter is urgent to us, I haf come to make an offer. Four hundred and dirty pounds was the price named to me by the men ashore there as the price the boat changed hands at. Well, I mean good business. I would pay four sixty."

"We don't want to sell her," said Sheila.

"So. Well, maybe not, but it is urgent to us. Five hundred—what now do you say to five hundred? Seventy pounds' profit to you right away."

"No, thanks," said Sheila. "We don't want to sell her."

"Well, that is right if you do not want to sell her. I am not a man to beat pigs about the bush and seeing you are all gentle people and to be trusted, I will tell you a little trade secret. My partner and I haf some little Continental dealings and it is necessary to us to bring a cargo of what I will not say from Boulogne to the English coast. Nothing wrong, only the English government don't look with eyes of approval on such a cargo. Now I am in your hands—but it means a large fortune to me and Mr. Shelegmann and we are cornered for a boat. Saturday I went to Deal—no boat to be got such as we want; Sunday to Dover and all them ports. Yesterday came news of this boat's sale—and here I am too late. I jump the price at once in my necessity—one thousand pounds. One thousand pounds paid on this table."

"No, thanks," said Sheila. "We do not want to sell."

"Then what will you take?" said Mr. MacAdam.

"Nothing," cut in James.

"I don't say our cargo is what you call 'dope,'" said Mr. MacAdam. "I don't say it isn't, but that we should get it over by Friday night means to us a hundred thousand pounds—there, you haf me now in a bag. My name ain't MacAdam, that is my trade name. Moses Levenstein is my name, it is indeed, and the Levensteins know how to spend money to make money. One hundred thousand pounds is losing me. I could cry. Come now, good people, and if you ain't made of stone, be moved to me in my emergence—ask what you want for her. Two thousand—would that fill your pockets? Two thousand beautiful Bradburys with the King of England's head on them. Ain't that coming it? I'm bleedin' at the pores when I think of our profits being cut by two thou. Think of it! Two thou—going at two thou. Ain't you softening to it? I tell you now it's cocaine—there you've got me in a jug, that's why we want a boat like the *Baltrum*. A hundred thousand pounds' profit worth of cocaine going to leave me. Think of us sitting here and me bidding two thou. I'll go one better, three, that's my last. Three—three." He rose to his feet.

"No, nor thirty," said James.

"Then why aren't you selling her?" suddenly fired MacAdam.

"If you want to know," replied James, "it's because my name is Wilfred Corder and because I have made a present of the boat to this young lady. If you want to know who Wilfred Corder is, ask at the Savoy Hotel—or the Bank of England. And now get out and thank your stars that I don't tell the police about you."

"Oh, that's all right," said MacAdam, quite recovering himself. "We are all gentlemen here and you ain't likely to do a dirty trick on a man who has made you a good offer. Well, if you ain't selling, you ain't, and good day to you." He took up his hat and followed by Dicky strode out of the cabin.

Dicky was back in a moment.

"Well," said he, "what do you think of that?"

"If you ask me," said James, "I'd say he was one of the old firm; failing that, a gentleman in the know. We're blown on, Dicky, and it's my humble opinion we'll have every yeggman in yeggtown on top of us before the week's out."

"You think he was one of the men who got hold of the gold originally and stowed it on board here?" asked Sheila.

James was sitting with his face between his hands and his elbows on his knees; he seemed plunged miles deep in thought. Then at last he answered:

"No, I don't," said James. "I may be wrong, but it seems to me that this is some outsider who has got late news of the whole business and maybe found out by accident where the *Baltrum* is anchored and all about the sale.

"Seems to me the origin of this business was something like this: Some government doing shady work shipped the gold on the *Baltrum* to get it away to some foreign port. The two men in charge of the business did in the crew and made off with the hooker, ran her into this place, fought, and killed each other.

"Well, seems to me, we can reckon that the fellows who ran away with the stuff are all dead and accounted for, and what's after us now is the government that started the show, or some hanger-on of it who has been nosing about on his own after the *Baltrum* and only found her just now."

"You think his yarn about the cocaine was bunkum?" asked Dicky.

"Absolute," said James.

James hadn't a bad headpiece on him—it was revealed in his flashes of sanity, as now, when, seated with the tips of his fingers together, he seemed measuring the whole of this business, by and large.

"There's one thing I wish you hadn't done," said Dicky. "You gave him your address."

"I?" said James. "Never—that chap my address?—never."

"Why, you told him you were Wilfred Corder of the Savoy Hotel and the Bank of England."

"Oh, *that*," said James. "Well, it doesn't matter; what can he do?"

"I don't know," said Dicky, "but it would have been just as well to keep it dark."

Sheila laid down her needlework.

"There you are," said Sheila. "It's beginning its work already. Before we had it we were free and happy, and now we have to keep things dark; we've got that horrid man after us and what's to be the end of it all I don't know." She spoke addressing the others, yet seeming to talk to herself, with her eyes fixed a thousand miles beyond the bulkhead at which she was gazing.

James, watching her in her dark beauty gazing like that as if into the world of the Celtic twilight, suddenly received a terrible wound.

A bowman had been stalking him ever since the auction and now had fired an arrow, barbed and poisoned, at short range from the doorway against which Sheila's profile was outlined. A foul attack.

"Sure what's the good of money when it only brings trouble," finished Sheila, turning to Dicky and then sweeping her eyes round to James.

CHAPTER 15

LONDON

James did not reply. Dicky saved him the effort.

"Well, it's a lot more trouble if one's without it," said he, "and anyhow we are up to our necks in this business and can't pull out. Look into your own mind, Sheila, and you'll see that. We can't let go of the stuff."

He was right, the gold had them by a clutch tighter than any physical grip. It was physically possible to dump the stuff in the Pool, and send Larry running after MacAdam with word that they would take his offer of two thousand and so cut free of the business. It was psychically impossible—even if they had wanted to do so.

This great mass of gold clung to them like an octopus, clung to their instincts and desires by a hundred tentacles armed with ten thousand suckers, tinged their surroundings as the octopus tinges the water around it by squirting out ink—only the ink used by the golden monster was golden ink, lending a lovely laburnum tinge not only to the material world and the present, but to the future.

"No," said Sheila, with a sigh, "I suppose we can't."

"Of course we can't," said Dicky, "and we don't want to if we could. Now what I propose to do is go right up to town and see old Forsythe, my lawyer man, and put the case before him. If he thinks we're safe to trust the government, *absolutely* safe, then we'll cart the stuff right up to the Bank of England. If he doesn't, we'll have to do something else."

"That's obviously the first move," said James, who had recovered sufficiently from his wound to feel the delicious effect of the poison of the arrow. "You can come up with me in the car and see him first thing in the morning. You can both come up—I'll get you rooms at the Savoy and we'll have a jolly dinner to celebrate the event. You'll come, won't you?" said James, turning to Sheila. "*Do* come."

"I can't," said Sheila. "I can't leave Larry and the boat. You two go and, oh, *do* be careful and say nothing to anyone, because I feel," said Sheila, "I feel somehow that now we are surrounded with enemies—no, not enemies exactly, but people who would do anything to us for the sake of this money. You'll promise me, won't you, not to do anything—anything foolish?" She had gauged James' possibilities in this direction with the terrible penetrating eye of a woman, she had experience through old Captain Dennis and Larry of what men can do when in a joyful mood and she felt instinctively that the pass they were in required for safe conduct directing brains, cool, crafty, businesslike and keen in strategy.

A combination of Sherlock Holmes, Von Moltke, Rothschild and the governor of the Bank of England would have met the situation. James and Dicky, pleasant as they were, scarcely filled the bill. She felt this vaguely, but the qualities that were absent from this pair disturbed her less than the qualities they might gain through exaltation. She had seen James dispensing hospitality on the Hard.

"We have just time to catch the five-ten," said Dicky, who was consulting a time-table. "I'll fling some things in a bag and tell Larry to get the boat ready; I won't be two ticks."

Off he went, leaving them alone, and while he was gone, Sheila, face to face with the stricken one, fell to wondering what had happened to him. James had never been in love before. He had danced, flirted, carried on with girls, but this was the first time the shot had gone through his heart. The very first sight of her profile had attracted him; he who had seen so many and such lovely profiles without turning a hair! And now alone with her he felt dumb, unable to think of things to say, awkward and wishing Dicky back.

He had not to wish long. Dicky, who had packed an attaché case, appeared with it in his hand, good-byes were said on deck, and Sheila, shading her eyes against the sun, watched the little boat as it put off across the Pool.

On the way up to town James was silent, plunged in what seemed to be thought and answering only in monosyllables when spoken to.

But the atmosphere of London had a clearing effect on the mind of James, and in the Seven Sisters' Road of all places in the world he began to brighten. Regent's Park found him brighter still and by the time they reached the Savoy the full sun of his soul had unveiled itself from fog.

The joy of life had also seized Dicky, and do you wonder?

The four hundred pounds in his pocket, the precious four hundred that this morning had been his entire fortune was his to spend or do what he liked with; he need not bother about saving or scraping now, a fourth share of the *Baltrum's* golden cargo would be enough to carry him through life, and into this golden dream that had begun long before reaching the Seven Sisters' Road, Sheila had come timidly, her hands also filled with gold.

It is strange that while James had been harpooned at first sight, Dicky, who had been in contact with Miss Dennis for so long, was still scarcely scratched.

He was fonder of Sheila than of anyone else in the world, but fondness is not love, though an excellent foundation for it.

"Have Mr. Sebright's luggage taken up and a room got ready for him," said James to Handley, when they drew up at Savoy Court. "I won't want the car anymore to-day—now come on."

"What are you doing first?" asked Dicky.

"Cocktails," said James. He led the way to the American bar.

That was the beginning of things. Dicky was no believer in prohibition, but he had a very cool head and alcohol beyond a certain point had little effect on him. James was different.

He *would* dine at Romano's; a quiet dinner in his suite at Savoy Court did not seem at all the right thing on a night like this, and he *would* talk in a loud voice of the *Baltrum* and the "stuff" on board of her. It did not matter, really; there was no one in the restaurant that mattered in this respect and anyhow he soon changed the subject to Sheila.

He talked of her with tears in his eyes as one of the brightest and loveliest and best of womanhood, proposed her health, drank it in Château Larose and smashed his glass by throwing it on the floor, so that no other lips might ever drink from it.

Dicky got him back to Savoy Court quite early—about ten o'clock—and then having presented him to Strutt, the valet, went off to his own room in the hotel.

At nine o'clock next morning, Dicky, calling at the suite, found James at breakfast.

"I say," said James, "when I left you last night was there anyone else with us?"

"No," said Dicky.

"Well," said James, "it's the funniest thing—when I got up here I sat down to have a smoke and a whisky and soda for a nightcap and then I remember talking to a chap. Strutt had gone off and whether some hotel waiter brought the chap up or whether he came and knocked and I let him in myself, I don't know; to tell the truth I am rather confused about the whole thing. But I can distinctly remember hobnobbing with a fellow—he was sitting in that armchair and he wouldn't have drinks, only a cigar."

"Some friend of yours?" said Dicky.

"No, he was a stranger. Red-headed chap. Came to tell me of a big yacht he had for sale; at least that's what I think he came about."

"What did you say to him?" asked Dicky, suddenly and vaguely perturbed.

"The bother is," said James, "I can't quite remember."

"Did he say anything about the *Baltrum*?"

"I remember saying something about having bought a yacht," said James, "at least a boat—and I remember telling him about my yacht, the *Dulcinea*, you know, and where she was lying, but I tell you quite straight I wasn't in a clear state of mind."

"I wish this hadn't happened," said Dicky. "I can't help thinking this fellow, whoever he was, must have had some connection with the MacAdam man. You see, that chap had your address."

"Oh, nonsense," said James. "Where's the connection?"

"Only suspicion. There may be nothing in it, still there may. MacAdam had time to get up to town. Perhaps there's a big gang of these chaps after us now they've spotted where the gold is."

"Nonsense," said James. "Look here, my dear chap, the *Baltrum* has been lying there all winter; why didn't they turn up before? You told me Salt had told you that the government had reported her there to all the foreign port authorities."

"Yes," said Dicky, "but it seems to me that the people who are after us— if they are after us—aren't foreign port authorities, but crooks who have got in the know, yet who couldn't locate where the hooker was till that infernal government advertisement was circulated of the sale—see?"

James considered for a moment.

"Then why didn't they come and bid?"

"I don't know," said Dicky. "Perhaps they don't like publicity and public auctions, perhaps they thought it safer to wait till she was bought and then to come privately to the buyers and make a bid, perhaps MacAdam was right when he said he came too late for the sale—though I doubt it. Anyhow, James, I don't feel comfortable. I don't indeed. We've got to get a move on."

James left the table and lit a cigarette. He wasn't feeling comfortable himself. It came to him and only just now that if some gang of crooks had entered this game they must be fought without any aid from the law. He and Dicky were not exactly inside the law—unless this lawyer man whom Dicky had spoken of said otherwise. What a relief that would be; they could take the stuff openly to the bank and deposit it, and then all the crooks in London might go hang.

"How about your lawyer?" said James.

"That's where we've got to go first," said Dicky. "He won't be there till ten—he lives in Old Serjeant's Inn, and we have time to walk. It will clear your head."

It was five minutes past ten when they arrived at Isaac Forsythe's office, and when they were shown in the lawyer was in place before his desk and his morning correspondence, looking just as dry, antique and remote from human sympathy as on the day Dicky had seen him first—not a gray hair out of place or grain of dust and his glasses in just the same position on his nose.

Dicky introduced the other.

"We have come upon some awfully important business," said Dicky.

"Take a seat," said the lawyer.

Dicky took a seat, James did likewise and the conference began. Dicky had intended putting the matter as a hypothetical case, but he was no fool and when it came to the point he saw in a flash of genius that making a clean breast of the business was the only way to get any good from Forsythe. So he set to and told his story right from the beginning, the lawyer listening to the amazing tale as unconcernedly as though it were a matter of a deal in potatoes.

"I take it you have left out nothing," said Forsythe when the recital was ended, "and that what you say is, in fact, a plain statement of the affair without varnish or gilding."

"Yes," said Dicky.

"Then what do you want me to do?" asked the lawyer.

"I want to know if the stuff is ours."

"Certainly it is not," said the lawyer, leaning back in his chair and putting his hands in his pockets. "Oh, dear, no. To begin with, if you bought this vessel without knowledge or suspicion of the nature of the cargo—"

"Ballast," cut in James.

"Exactly—treasure concealed as ballast—a host of questions would arise. There is the question of treasure-trove which we will put aside—though leaving it viable—in favour of the more immediately suggested question of contraband. There is no duty on gold, but the law of contraband is elastic. Here is a cargo of great value brought secretly to an English port, possibly from one of the late enemy countries; it is a cargo that has never been declared, mark that, and it is in the province of the customs to seize this cargo for full examination and inquiry. Then the law officers of the crown would take the matter up. This concealed cargo would be held pending full examination and inquiry by the government. The stuff is evidently, or probably, stolen. You say you have bought it, but the purchase of stolen or possibly stolen goods does not make the purchaser the possessor. Oh, no. The law is quite clear on that point.

"Well, should no claimant be found for this gold, after the lapse of years, would come the question of its disposal and I may as well frankly tell you that here grows up a hedgerow of difficulties should you put in a claim. The grand old laws of England are our greatest heritage and defence against tyranny, but one has to confess that they were not framed with an eye to benefit the finders of hidden treasure; after unlimited trouble and expense you would fail, I believe, to justify your claim to any of this money. Frankly, it is in the interests of the crown to keep it and the interests of the crown are ably defended by the law officers of the crown. And so," finished Isaac Forsythe, stretching his legs out farther and rattling the coins in his pocket, "after years of waiting and ruinous law expenses you would find yourselves no longer young, worn out with litigation, depleted of money and lost to hope."

"Dicky, we're done," said James, appalled by this lugubrious picture, but Isaac Forsythe had not done, and he continued:

"That is the most favourable side of your case, and it presupposes that when you bought this vessel named the *Baltrum* you were ignorant of the treasure secreted on board of her.

"But that is not so. If I take you rightly, well knowing of this treasure secreted in the ballast chamber of this ketch, you bid for her in market overt against the government in whose possession she was, you being subjects of that government.

"That fact raises most complex questions of criminal law."

"Oh, good God!" said James.

"Questions," went on Isaac, "upon which in an ordinary case one would require counsel's opinion. Let us take one example. You might say you 'found' this gold, but the criminal law—"

"For Heaven's sake, stop," said Dicky. "The very name of the Law gives me shivers. I only just wanted to know what the beastly thing would do to us if we stick to the stuff and it seems from what you say that if we act straight and own up the law will rob us of it, and if we don't, it will put us in prison."

"You have put the thing in a nutshell," said Forsythe.

"Well, can't you give us any idea of some way out?" said Dicky. "Just a hint would do—anything."

"You forget," said Forsythe, "that I am a lawyer. The only thing I can do for you is to say nothing. My advice would be to drop this thing here and now, hand over the gold to the government and await their decision."

"Would you do that if you were us?" said James.

Forsythe laughed.

"Man never knows what he will do till he is tempted," said he. He fell into reverie for a moment, then turning to Dicky: "If you had found this gold on some desert island the whole case would be different."

"Yes?" said Dicky.

"That's all I have to say. I am going to say it again. If you had found this gold on some desert island—some island, let us say, belonging to Spain—and if you had a permit to search for it, the whole case would be different."

"I suppose it would," said Dicky, wondering what the other was driving at.

"Absolutely," said Forsythe, rising from his chair, "and now that is all I have to say. Your confidence placed in me shall be respected. I shall charge you no fee for this interview, and my advice has been to drop the business. If you had found this gold on some desert island the case would be quite different."

He opened the door and the pair went out. Halfway down the stairs they looked up. The lawyer was speaking to them over the banister rail.

"Remember what I said."

"Thanks," said Dicky, wondering what on earth he meant. But James knew. James had seized the meaning of the dusty one, this man of law who had the sharpest brain in London and yet a little bit of the boy left in his heart.

"Can't you see?" cried James, when they were in Fleet Street; "haven't you tumbled to it? He couldn't tell us to do it, but all the same he's told us what to do."

"And what's that?"

"Oh, good Lord! Can't you see? Why, take the stuff to some place and bury it same as the old pirates used to do, then discover it and claim it."

"By Jove," said Dicky, "there's something in that."

"Something! It's everything. How on earth else can we get rid of it? It's a peach of a plan. People are always going off to hunt for hidden treasure and they've never found any yet. Why, at Havana, they're always selling locations of old treasure ships to any fools that will buy. You buy a location and a permit and there you are. If you dig up the stuff it's yours. You can take it to a bank and turn it into dollars. I know the whole of the Caribbean, cruised there two winters running, and there's no end of cays and places we can dump the stuff and then run to Havana and get a permit to dig. See?"

"Yes, I see," said Dicky. "But how are we to get to the Caribbean?"

"I'll get you there and never you fear that," said James. "Can't we get the stuff on board my yacht? Why, it was built for the work. I know just the place to go to, south of Rum Cay, nothing but sea gulls and flying fish. Any more objections to make?"

"I'm not objecting," said Dicky, "it's a stunning idea, but wants getting used to—and there's Miss Dennis."

"We'll take her along," said James.

He fell into thought for a moment as if contemplating this new proposition of Sheila. Then linking arms with the other, he wheeled him into a café.

CHAPTER 16

PLANS

Leaving the café and entering the Strand, they turned into Denny's book-shop.

You can get almost any book you want at Denny's. James wanted books about buried treasure, and told his wants quite openly, and was surprised at the number and variety of the works that had been printed on this subject.

Life is a big university and every day brings some sort of examination for the scholars. Dicky and James, suddenly forced to compete for this hid-den-treasure prize, had determined to mug the subject up.

"You see," said James, as they came along toward the bookshop, "there's no end to chaps working their brains over this business and we may get tips. I'm not great on the reading business myself, but you and Miss Dennis may pick up something useful."

"Treasure Island," Knight's "Cruise of the *Alerte*" and half a dozen oth-ers having been bought and paid for, they took their way back to the Savoy, James stopping at a post office on the way to send a telegram.

"Whom are you wiring to?" asked Dicky.

"My skipper. The yacht's at Tilbury and I'm telling him to bring her right round today to Hildersditch. You don't know my skipper. Shortt's his name and long's his nature. He takes ten minutes to do a repair another man would do in five, and it wants a derrick to get him out of a port once he's taken up moorings. If I told him to come round to Hildersditch today and said noth-ing more he'd be there about this day fortnight, so I'm addressing him like this," said James, as he stood, his stick under his arm and his bowler hat on the back of his head, covering telegraph form after telegraph form with a message running like this:

Shortt. Yacht *Dulcinea*. Tilbury.

Bring *Dulcinea* round today to Hildersditch Pool, berth her at buoy two cable lengths from ketch *Baltrum*. I know *Dulcinea's* mainmast is sprung, she has opened a seam and can't possibly be moved until spars have thorough overhaul. Disregard all that, this is urgent, have her there today or you're fired.

"But is her mainmast sprung?" asked Dicky, as he read the message.

"That's sarcasm, or supposed to be. No, my dear chap, but Shortt's sprung. He's paralyzed in the hind legs of his initiative and wants hot irons to make him move."

"Fifty-eight words—four and tenpence," said the girl behind the counter, and out they went.

James' mind was now in full running order; he had taken command of things and had developed, as men develop in an emergency. Carrying the parcel under his arm, he paused after leaving the telegraph office and made his way across the Strand to a big stationer's. Here he bought an atlas, had it parceled with the books, and calling a taxi, bundled Dicky in, got in himself and told the driver to take them to the Savoy.

It was only a few hundred yards. They got out and, going up to the suite, Mr. Corder untying the parcel and casting the books on a sofa, placed the atlas on a table.

"Now I'll show you," said James, opening the atlas at the section showing the Bahamas, Florida to Tallahassee, and Cuba.

"Here's the place for us. I know every reef and shoal of it almost. I've fished it, you see; there's Great Abaco, I was nearly wrecked on it once, and there's Cat Island where they hanged Harvey—a pirate chap—and, south of Cat Island, that's Rum Cay—look, that little spot.

"South of Rum Cay there's nothing here but blue water, but the map's a fool. Give's a pen—it's all reefs along here and that keeps ships away, and here, almost in the same latitude as Acklin Island, there's a cay no bigger than your hand. That's the place for us; there's only two palm trees on it and the crabs come up there by the thousand, but they don't worry you if you have something to bat them with.

"Now you see what I mean. If we bury the stuff here it's as safe as churches. Dash it, what was I thinking of? The name of the place has come to me, Crab Cay—that's the name. It's known for the crabs that come up on it; they aren't always there. I landed and there was nothing but just the sand sizzling in the sun and the palm trees waving in the wind, but I hadn't more than walked half the length of it when I heard a rustling and behind me crabs were coming up over the coral, hoisting themselves out of the sea, hundreds of them, and hundreds of them behind me and to right and left. It was me they were after, I felt that and it wasn't a nice feeling, I can tell you."

"I should think not," said Dicky. "But why on earth bury the stuff in this beastly place? Why not hit on some spot where there are no crabs?"

"Well, you don't know the Bahamas and all round there," said James. "The place is full of small traders and fishing boats and contraband chaps always messing about. Acklin, Mariguana, Caicos; it's all the same, there's always chaps messing about that might spot what we are doing. Crab Cay is safe, no one goes there."

Dicky pondered over the map.

"There's another thing," said he. "Won't the crew see us burying the stuff? And there's another thing—we've got to transship the stuff from the *Baltrum* on to your boat; won't they smell a rat? It's not your scheme to take the *Baltrum* along, is it? Well, there you are. We have two things to do that ought to be done in secret; the transshipping of it to the *Dulcinea* and the burying it when we get there, and your crew aren't blind men, are they?"

"I'll have to have a glass of sherry and bitters to help me think over that," said James, ringing for Strutt. "As you say, those are two very important points and they haven't cropped up in my mind till now. Strutt, two sherries and Angosturas and get luncheon up at once and tell Handley to have the car here at one thirty sharp. Yes, there's no doubt about it, that the whole of this thing is not as easy a proposition as falling off a log, and there's another thing we've clean forgot—MacAdam and the possible crowd of yeggmen behind him, and the British government behind them, and the law-officers-of-the-crown chaps who may stick us in prison if one wheel goes wrong. Good gosh, Dicky, I wish we'd never gone to that lawyer chap of yours."

"Well, there's no use in meeting trouble halfway," said Dicky.

"Halfway? Why, we're in it unless we dump the stuff in the Pool and let MacAdam fish for it."

"You're not getting cold feet, are you?" asked the other, alarmed by the sudden change in James' manner.

Strutt and the sherries and bitters saved James from replying for the moment. Then when they were alone again, James, getting up, began to pace the floor.

"It's not a question of cold feet. I reckon I'm no quitter, and as for Mac-Adam and that lot, I don't care a shilling. But I've got a horrible and unholy fear of the government. I have indeed. I was in a criminal court once, and I saw an old guy in a red dressing gown with a sword hanging over his head sentencing a chap to a hundred and ten years' penal servitude for sneezing in the British Museum, I think it was—anyhow the whole business gave me the quakes."

"Luncheon is served, sir," said Strutt, opening the door.

Ten minutes later James, under the restoring influence of food and cheer-inspiring liquids, had quite recovered his balance and tone of mind. The gold had him again in its clutch, the gold and the sense of adventure and the knowledge that Sheila was in this thing with them. After all, without danger the thing would have had no spice; as it was, what could a man want better, a huge treasure, a pretty girl, danger and the land of the old buccaneers all rolled in one? What could the heart desire more?

It was five o'clock when they reached Hildersditch and by good luck they found Larry on the Hard. He had come over to fetch some parcels and he rowed them off. Sheila was waiting for them. She had spotted them through the glass and had put the kettle on to boil and when they got down to the cabin tea was made and waiting.

"I felt somehow or another you'd be back in time for tea," said Sheila. "What's in that parcel?"

"Books," said Dicky, throwing the parcel into a bunk. "We've seen Forsythe and he's not a ha'p'orth of use, only he gave us an idea. Corder will tell you."

James, who was not much of a tea drinker, took the cup presented to him, and, while he let it grow cold, plunged into the middle of affairs. His nervousness before the girl had vanished. The arrow was still there but he no longer felt it; the poisoning had entered upon its second stage and the presence of Sheila instead of sending all his wits astray pulled them together in one leash and whipped them into activity.

He explained the whole position with clearness, and not without humour, gave her a sketch of Forsythe and a brief of the plan he had formed for taking the *Dulcinea* to the Bahamas. "But it all depends on you," said James. "You are one of the partners in this business and nothing goes without your word. Will you come?"

"Of course I'll come," said she. "But there's only one question I want to ask. Won't the crew know all about it?"

"You've put your finger on the spot," said James. "You've gone right to the centre of this business. That's what we're up against. Unless we can ship a crew of blind men, they will. First of all they'll see us transshipping the stuff here, secondly they'll see us burying it."

He had placed the atlas open on the tea table while explaining matters and Sheila with her eyes fixed on the map of the Bahamas, seemed lost in reverie.

"I'm beginning to understand," said Dicky, "why the old pirate johnnies murdered people to keep things dark. They *had* to."

"Seems to me," said James, "if their position was anything like ours, they had."

Sheila raised her eyes from the map.

"I think your plan's wrong," said she quite simply. "If we do the thing at all we must take the *Baltrum*. Your yacht can come along too, and cruise in company with us. First of all, if we do that, there will be no transshipping here. Think of it, how could we? Your captain and crew would say to themselves, 'What are they bringing this ballast stuff on board for?' They might suspect nothing, but still they would think it strange. Then, when it was taken on shore to be buried, they'd be sure to suspect the whole business.

"I've just thought out the whole thing, and my suggestion is to take the *Baltrum* as she is. We three and Larry can work her. The *Dulcinea* can keep us company. At Crab Cay you can send her to Great Bahama or somewhere to wait for us. You can say we want to do some fishing. Then the three of us with Larry can easily get the stuff ashore. It will take us a few days, but that is nothing. When it is buried we can rejoin the *Dulcinea*, send the *Baltrum* home or leave her in harbour wherever it is, and sail in the *Dulcinea* for Havana, where you can get your permit to dig for buried treasure. What do you think of that?"

"Topping," said Dicky, but James for a moment said nothing.

James was fond of comfort.

"Isn't the *Baltrum* a bit small for a long cruise?" said he at length.

"Good gracious, no," said Sheila. "Father and I used to take one like her every winter to the Canaries. We took her to the Cape Verdes, once. Why, one could go round the world in her, easily."

"Maybe," said James.

"You aren't afraid of roughing it?" said Dicky.

"Me! Lord, no. I like it. Give me a simple life and I'm happy—I was only thinking of the size of her. Well, I'm not saying it's not a peach of a plan. It is, but I'll tell you what, folks, this gold is going to make us work to get it. I remember my father saying the only royal road to fortune was work. He was right, seems to me."

"What time did you say your yacht would be here?" asked Sheila.

"It's sixty miles from here to Tilbury, about," said James. "Shortt would have started about one o'clock. The wind's with him and with the auxiliary he'd do about twelve knots; that's five hours. He ought to be here at six."

Then they fell to discussing ways and means, and James, forgetting for the moment the month of hard labour and rough life before him, became as engrossed as the others in the question of stores and the time of starting.

This was no pleasure trip and there was no time for delay. Speed was a matter of urgency. While the *Baltrum* remained in harbour or within the three-mile limit many things might occur. If MacAdam and the possible men behind him were a real menace, as was highly probable, they might be boarded by night, attacked and the *Baltrum* run out to sea. It was the huge amount of gold that brought this seemingly absurd idea within the bounds of possibility, for the gold was like a magician, a spirit capable of either boundless evil or boundless good, a chemical compound that might lie forever quiescent, or handled might resolve itself into all sorts of benefits to the handlers—or explode, shattering everything around it.

That is what gold is, gold in bulk like that on board the *Baltrum*, gold unclaimed and seizable by the first comer. And they knew it.

It was theirs for the moment, but only while they could hold it. Time was of the essence of this contract; and to get to sea, clear England and give the good-bye to possible enemies, it was necessary to act with lightning swiftness. It was Sheila who took the lead. Fortunately for them she had the power to think all round a subject and an experience in ship matters and stores denied to either of them.

"We can get everything we want at MacQuoid's," said she, "and I am going to make the list. I'm provisioning her for three months; no use in getting in too much. You had better take your car and go up to town tonight with the list. Be at MacQuoid's first thing in the morning, have the things brought down by lorry. See? Then you had better arrange at your hotel, for you won't be going back there."

"Yes," said James. It was strange to hear his future being arranged for him like this by a girl, by the girl who had hypnotized him yesterday, but whose power had somehow now become merged into the power of the gold and the power of events.

She was no longer a detached being, but part of the impetus that was carrying him he knew not whither. Love under these circumstances had to wait, finger on lip and watching.

The *Baltrum* could carry to sea with her five hundred gallons of water in two water tanks; these had to be filled, and Sheila made a note of that for a start. Used to getting in stores for their winter cruises, she could tell almost exactly how much they would require per man per month. She sat adding up things on a spare bit of paper and putting down the totals on the sheet before her. No "cabin biscuits" for Sheila, except a box or two; she had seen them turn into worms too often in the heat of the sub-tropics. Hard-tack was what she ordered, hard-tack and ship's beef to supplement the tinned food, for a man sick of canned stuff will turn to junk with a relish.

While she worked, the others, having nothing to do for the moment, smoked. She made a pretty picture and as they watched, their admiration would have been increased if possible had they known what was really going on inside her head and what she was doing for them and their comfort, for it is on the little things that comfort and often safety depend.

Sheila knew, for instance, that their water supply could not be drawn upon for washing purposes, therefore they would have to wash in salt water, which is impossible without salt-water washing soap. She knew what sort of chocolate kept and what didn't, what sorts of dried fruit went mushy, the best brand of coffee and the fact that they would require four can openers.

"What tobacco do you smoke?" she asked James.

"Oh, I'll get my tobacco myself," said James. "You needn't worry to put that down."

"Well," said Sheila, "coarse navy or ship tobacco is all right, but if you smoke any fancy brands they've got to be hermetically sealed. You'd better let me put it down; MacQuoid can supply you with anything—you'd better take some extra pipes with you too. I've seen father near crazy trying to smoke a pipe he bought at Teneriffe—the Spaniards never smoke pipes and don't know how to make them. I'm ordering matches; you needn't worry about them. Wines and spirits—we don't want any wines, do we?—haven't got room for them and a dozen bottles of whisky will do, don't you think? If you want soda water we'll have to take sparklets—I'm putting them down. I suppose your clothes are all right, you'll want light things." She surveyed the list, up and down, and then went over it carefully item by item. Then she handed it to James, who put it in his pocketbook.

"How about the water tank?" asked Dicky. "It will take some filling."

"Your men can do that," said Sheila, turning to James. "If the yacht gets here tonight, they can start on it first thing in the morning, and then later in the day when the provisions come down they can help to get them on board. Has your yacht a motor boat?"

"She has," said James.

"Good! That's the provisions and water settled, and now let me see what else there is to think of. Fortunately we don't want an overhaul; everything is right, we have no sprung spars or rotten ratlines, thank goodness, and the copper is clear. Now about the navigation and instruments. The compass is all right. We can have the boat swung tomorrow to adjust it, and we have a sextant, everything we want, but no charts. You will have to get the charts tomorrow. Are you any good at navigating?" She was addressing James, for she knew Dicky's failings in this respect.

"Not a ha'p'orth," said James.

"And yet you own a yacht! Well, no matter, fortunately I'm used to it and I'll teach you as we go. And now it has come into my head that it's stupid to work her with only the four of us; we can do it but it's dreadfully hard work. We'll take two of the men from your yacht if they can be spared—can they?"

"Lord, yes," said James. "She's over-manned, she's more like a floating sailors' home than a yacht."

"Good," said Sheila. "We'll take two of your best men, and I'll choose them if I may. They can go back to the yacht when we get to the Bahamas. Well, that's all, I think, anyhow for the present."

The two men went on deck to smoke, leaving her to clear up.

"Damn!" said James. "How was I to know I'd ever want to be able to do navigating? I've always paid a man to do it just as I've paid a man to do cooking. She'll be wanting us to do the cooking next."

"I wouldn't be a bit surprised," replied the other. "I don't feel more than about one inch high. She's everything on this boat and we're nothing—not till we learn to do things."

CHAPTER 17

MORGAN

The sun had set beyond Hildersditch church when through the rose-tinted gloaming a white ghost showed up treading its way smoothly through the passage to the Pool.

It was the *Dulcinea*.

She came along in as though she knew the place by heart, past the sand spit she came, steering as though to cut into the *Baltrum*, then, the light wind shivering out of her sails, she turned, gliding, to pick up her moorings.

"Oh, what a beauty!" cried Sheila, as she watched this ghost from the sea, "and she's yours."

"Yes," said James, "and she's late. Come along."

Larry was in the dinghy, alongside, waiting, and he rowed them off. The ladder was down at the port side and as Sheila came on board it seemed to her that the heart could desire nothing better than this. There was light enough to show the sweep of the deck, the grace of the spars, the exquisiteness of the canvas, the perfection of the standing and running rigging. The *Dulcinea* wore her canvas as a duchess wears her robes. Lapthorne had dressed her, and for the first time to Sheila as she stood and looked around her the gold in the poor old *Baltrum* spoke clearly and definitely, saying: "*Now* you can see what I can do. I and I alone can create a boat like this, find her and man her and keep her, ay, and give her to you to be your own, your very own."

"Shortt," said James, addressing the foursquare person in a peaked cap and with a show of brass buttons who had received them on board, "you're late."

"Ay, I'm late, sir," said Shortt, "but it wasn't my fault. Morgan was late in coming off—overstayed his leave. But we're here now, anyhow, and there aren't no spars sprung, same as in your telegram."

James laughed, then he led the way below, Sheila following and Dicky and the captain coming after.

The electrics were on in the saloon. Cream and old gold formed the colour scheme. There were no pictured panels or fal-lals or plate, beyond a few trophies and a tarpon cup on the sideboard, but there was comfort everywhere, great cushions, ash trays where they ought to be and chairs solid and comfortable.

"Well, I won't have that," said James, who had gone down the stairs laughing and was now standing by the table with his fingers on it as he turned to the skipper.

That was a characteristic of James, which came out chiefly when brought in contact with the employés; he would suddenly strip laughter and a pleasant exterior away to show anger that he had maybe been corking up for a long time over some fault.

"I won't have that. I won't have chaps overstaying their leave, and Morgan's fired." He turned and touched an electric bell.

"Are you intending cruising right away, sir?" asked Shortt.

"Yes, right away and right down to the Bahamas."

"Then you can't fire him," said Shortt, "unless we sail without a mate. You can't get a mate in two minutes and he's my right hand."

The steward entered.

"Tell Mr. Morgan I want to see him," said James.

In less than a minute Morgan was standing in the saloon doorway; a youngish man with jet-black hair—Welsh black.

"Come in," said James.

Morgan came slowly forward. He was holding his cap in both hands and fiddling with it. He did not seem to want to come forward in the least, but he came right up to them and right into the full glare of light.

"I hear you overstayed your leave at Tilbury, Mr. Morgan," said the owner of the *Dulcinea*. "What made you do that?"

"I'm sorry, sir," said Morgan, "but I met some relatives at the last moment."

Dicky, watching Morgan, said to himself: "That chap is in the deuce of a funk about something. Either that or he's no more nerves than a kitten."

"Well, don't do it again," said James, "and hold yourself in readiness to start at once for abroad. You'll have no more shore leave."

"No, sir," said Morgan, acquiescing.

"That'll do," said James. Then he turned to Shortt.

"How much provisions and truck have you got on board?"

"There's a month's victuals for us and the crew, sir," said Shortt, "but I had to put out of Tilbury without the cabin stuff. I hadn't time to order it—your telegram was so sharp on my getting away."

"We won't want it," said James. "I'm not coming on board; I'm going to sail in that ketch over there. By the way, I haven't introduced you—this is Captain Shortt, Miss Dennis. Captain Shortt, Mr. Sebright. Yes, Shortt, I'm going to be very seasick for once in my life, I believe; sit down and have a cigar. Miss Dennis, is that chair comfortable? Yes, the three of us are going to sample the weather in that dough dish and I'm going to learn navigating from Miss Dennis, who's a better sailor even than you, Shortt. We've got to cruise in company and you've got to keep your eye on us. Have you your water on board?"

"Both tanks full," said the captain. "And when do you propose to put out?"

"Day after tomorrow early," said James.

"That's quick work," said Shortt, rolling the cigar between finger and thumb.

"Yes, it's quick work, as you say," replied James, "but you know me when I take a thing into my head, Shortt."

"Bahamas," said the captain meditatively as he stared across the cigar smoke at the old-gold plush carpet. "I was thinking it was maybe the Norway fjords you were going to make a summer trip of. Summer in the Bahamas— well, you'll find it hot, sir."

"You can't give me too much heat," said James.

"Nor me," said Dicky.

"Nor me," said Sheila.

"And it will be the hurricane season," said the captain.

"Well, we'll have to risk that," said James, "and you know a lot of that hurricane talk is bunkum. It's like the bay—give a place a bad reputation and it holds. I've been to Key West in the hurricane season and got no harm there."

"Well, sir, it's for you to choose," said Shortt. "You to order and me to obey, as the saying is. And how about your compass, may I ask?"

"We'll swing the *Baltrum* to-morrow," said Sheila.

"And your charts," said Shortt.

"Mr. Corder will get the charts to-morrow," said the girl, "also the chronometer. We have all the other navigating instruments we want."

"May I ask are you used to handling boats, miss?"

"Ever since I was a child," said Sheila.

As they were being rowed back to the *Baltrum* by Larry, Sheila, apropos of nothing and after a fashion she had, suddenly spoke up:

"I don't like that man Morgan," said Sheila.

"Why, what's wrong with him?" asked Dicky.

"I don't know," she said. "Nothing—maybe it's only a fancy."

CHAPTER 18

MAINSAIL HAUL!

Next day at dawn the business began.

They had decided last night to give themselves only one day; that is, twenty-four hours from daybreak.

Surrounded by a host of real or imaginary opponents, their nerves were on edge and the craving to get out into the wide sea beyond the three-mile limit was like the craving of the thirsty for water.

James had gone to town in the car, and he would not arrive back till afternoon. Besides the stores he had to get a log book and a chronometer, and to see to the ship's papers in conjunction with Captain Salt, on his return.

Meanwhile Sheila and Dicky had to complete their preparations on board, get ready to receive the stores, see the water brought on board and swing the compass.

The compass is the sensitive plant of the mechanical world. The chronometer comes next to it, but the compass is easily first. A compass resents the near presence of iron and goes off its balance, so to speak; or in other words suffers deviation.

To ascertain the amount of deviation due to the presence of iron on board, the ship must be swung; that is, turned right round, the pointing of the compass being noted with reference to the position of some fixed spot ashore.

Hildersditch church spire was the point fixed on by Sheila, and as soon as the light was strong enough she was at work, arrayed against the morning chill in a sou'wester and an overcoat of old Captain Dennis' that reached to her feet.

You can swing a ship by just letting her swing herself to the tide, but that takes time. The quickest way is to turn her by towing her head slowly round with a boat. This was the method adopted by Sheila and as Larry pulled the head of the ketch round with the dinghy she took careful bearings of the spire as the *Baltrum's* head came on to the different points of the compass.

She found that all the bearings did not agree as they ought, so she had to make out a table showing the deviation from each point.

This table when she had made it out could be carried with them to show the amount of error in the compass and to allow them to account for it when determining their course at sea.

At eight bells—twelve, noon—the motor pinnace of the *Dulcinea* came alongside with water breakers to fill their tanks. Morgan, the mate, was in charge of the pinnace and he came on board to direct the men.

Sheila and Dicky were away in the dinghy. They had finished their work on board, and leaving Larry in charge had gone to the Hard to see if there were any letters. When they came back they found Larry in a temper.

The tanks had been filled by the men from the *Dulcinea* and Larry had not been called upon to do a hand's turn. All the same he was in a temper and the cause was Morgan.

"Cut and carried on as if the boat was his own, and him not an honest sailorman but a damn brass-bound monkey on a shtick, bad cess to him. And then when I lift me eye off him, down he was below. 'What are you doin' below there?' says I.

"'Inspictin' the water tanks,' says he, and down I goes and there he was and him inspictin' the ballast."

"*What!*" cried Sheila.

"As sure as I'm tellin' you; him with his nose on the ballast."

"'Oh, get out,' I says to him, 'don't you know which end of a ship's which?' and he tried to soft Sawther me, but I was in a timper and told him to get on deck. I'm never houldin' with them big yachts like the *Dulcinea* over there. The afther guard's fixed up in gould lace and the crew's all white ducks and spit and polish, but I'd sooner sail in a herrin' boat full of tinkers than with a cargo of them chaps and in a scow like that beyond. Them and their exiliary ingins and 'lectric light!"

Sheila hurried down below, followed by Dicky. There was no sign of any meddling with the ballast, but Larry's word was enough.

What had Morgan been doing?

Sheila asked this question of Dicky and the only answer to it was, as Larry had put it, "inspictin' the ballast."

"It mayn't mean anything," said Dicky. "He'd be interested in a boat like this and would be poking his nose everywhere once he got below."

"Maybe," said Sheila, "but why should he go to the ballast like an arrow to a mark? He couldn't have been down here three minutes and—there he was."

"It's rum, certainly," said Dicky.

"I didn't like the look of him a bit when I first saw him last night," said she. "I took a dislike to him right off, the way he stood and fiddled with his cap and seemed as if he was cringing before Mr. Corder—but he wasn't. He'd have given impudence in a minute if he'd got the chance. Then why did he overstay his leave? What was he doing? I believe these men have got hold of him."

"You mean MacAdam and any possible men who may be working with him?"

"I do—and they are more than possible men, highly probable men, I'd call them. Mr. Corder gave his address away and you told me the night before last when he had taken too much wine he remembered talking to a stranger who called at the hotel to see him. It would be quite easy for them, once they knew his address and how rich he is to find out about his yacht, go to Tilbury and get in touch with the crew."

"Would they have had time?"

"Of course they would. It doesn't want much time to bribe people."

"Well," said Dicky, "even if it is so we've checkmated them."

"How?"

"By taking the *Baltrum*. If we had the stuff on board the *Dulcinea*, Morgan, if he *is* a scoundrel, might be able to do something. But sailing apart from them as we are, what can he do? He won't see us burying it. If it was in the old days, of course he might work the *Dulcinea* chaps up and take the ship and then go for us, but that sort of thing is not done nowadays."

"I suppose you are right," said the girl. "All the same we've got to be on the lookout. Shall you tell Mr. Corder?"

"What's the good? James is just the chap to go and make a row with Captain Shortt and give the show away, for all he'd have to say was that Morgan was looking at the ballast—which isn't a crime. Shortt would smell a rat and maybe talk some time or another. Besides, we can't fire Morgan—haven't time to get a new mate."

"All right," said Sheila.

It was four o'clock in the afternoon before James arrived and he didn't come in his car. He came in MacQuoid's lorry with the stores. He had forgotten nothing, neither the chronometer nor the charts, and ten minutes after his arrival the stores were coming off in the *Dulcinea's* boats.

The question of ship's papers was a bothersome one. James, as owner and nominal captain of the boats, had to attend to this business with Captain Salt, and it was ten o'clock and a rising moon before everything was fixed and done with.

They were short of all sorts of things but of nothing absolutely necessary except tropical clothing. They could get this at Teneriffe, where they proposed to put in before the long run across the Atlantic. Two of the *Dulcinea's* men, Hearn and Longley by name, were aboard, and Captain Shortt, having received his last orders, had gone back to his ship.

The *Dulcinea* was not to bother about keeping in sight. She was to make under all plain sail for Santa Cruz harbour, Teneriffe, touching at Plymouth on the way for oil for the auxiliary. Shortt had discovered at the last moment that the oil drums had not come aboard at Tilbury. He had only enough to run the auxiliary for five hours or so, and Mersea could not supply him, so a wire had been sent to Struthers of Plymouth to have the stuff ready.

As they watched him row off across the moonlit Pool, Sheila felt a sudden depression of spirits for which she could not account.

Every one knows that feeling of a hidden worry working beneath the mind like a mole; when hunted for it generally comes to light.

Hunting for it now, she found the cause at once. The call of the *Dulcinea* at Plymouth.

Instead of cutting their connection clean off with England on the morrow the *Dulcinea* was going to call at Plymouth.

Well, there was nothing in that. She would put in, get the stores she wanted and put out again. The whole business would take only a few hours. Still Sheila felt worried. Felt as an operating surgeon feels who finds that the tiniest loophole has not been guarded against sepsis.

Morgan would be in touch with England and he would know their destination and if he was what she vaguely suspected, well then—

What? She could formulate no definite idea of what he might do.

Being sensible, having found the worry, she put it away from her. It was not a bit of good nursing it, and there was a lot still to be done down below before turning in.

Any one who has had to get a small boat ready for sea in a hurry for a long cruise will know what I mean.

Nearly all the stores had been disposed of but there were some things that refused. A small barrel of oatmeal had taken up its place in the main cabin. Hearn and Longley, who had done most of the stowing, helped by Larry, said there was no place for it to go. Sheila found one. A bag of dried figs that had "bust itself" had to be sutured, and a drum of lamp oil deposited in a bunk—of all places—because there was nowhere it would go, had to be removed and stowed.

She knew every inch of cargo space and some of the clumsy work of these yacht sailors had to be undone before everything was shipshape. By then the west wind was bringing midnight from Hildersditch church clock across the Pool.

Then returning into the after cabin which was hers, while the two men took the bunks in the main cabin and the sailors the fo'c's'le, the crew of the *Baltrum* found oblivion, while under the moon the ketch turned slowly with the tide, as though the Fates were swinging her compass for a voyage of which no man could tell the upshot or the landfall.

CHAPTER 19

THE GIRL TAKES CHARGE

James, when he engaged in this business so blithely, had entirely left out of count the fact that he was no sailorman.

Though he could handle a sailing boat and had covered thousands of miles of sea, he had never taken charge. He paid his skipper to do that.

"Never do anything bothersome you can get another to do for you," was a motto of James', and he wasn't far wrong as long as he remained within the golden circle that Fortune had drawn round him. Yacht handling for anyone who has not an inborn passion for the business is wearisome work requiring strict attention to business, knowledge born of ignominious failures, and a clear head.

In no other trade or avocation are there so many things easy to do that surely lead to disaster of confusion, so many things that if left undone produce the same results. He had found out this fact long ago and forgotten it under the hypnotism of gold and adventure—forgotten his ignorance of the whole practice of seamanship.

The fact came to him this morning as he stood on the deck of the *Baltrum*, an inexpressibly mournful-looking dawn breaking over the sand spits, and the voice of the bell buoy coming against the wind, blowing from the west.

On board that ship there were only two people deeply learned in sea craft and capable of handling for all she was worth a craft like the *Baltrum*, and those two people were Sheila and Larry. The *Dulcinea* pair were good, capable white-painted yacht sailors but with no more initiative than a doughnut. Dicky was an amateur with all the will in the world, and you know what that means. James was hopeless till licked into shape. The only good thing about him was that he knew it and treated the fact as a joke.

"You and Larry will have to get us out and show us how to do things," said James, lighting a cigarette in the face of the dismal dawn. "It will be all right when we are once out, you know."

"Yes," said Sheila.

She was standing, in an old pea jacket with a muffler round her throat, watching while Larry and the hands came on deck. Then turning to the two others: "I'm going to pick watches with Larry," said she. "Larry, come here—I'm going to pick watches." She ran her eye over the small crowd meditatively. "I'll take Hearn," said she.

"Longley, step over to the other side," said Larry.

"I'll take Mr. Sebright," said she.

"And I'll take the gintleman," said Larry, rather grumblingly indicating James.

Sheila's was the port watch, Larry's the starboard. Sheila was the virtual captain of the *Baltrum* as she always had been, Larry mate, and the hands the rest of the crew.

James, lighting another cigarette, took in the position fully, and the comic-opera side of it. Quite naturally under the all-compelling influence of the gold, things had fallen into this shape. He, James, was serving as an A. B., of all things in the world, on an old ketch and under command of a girl, a girl, moreover, who had made him feel odd about the heart, who made him still feel rather odd about the heart when he had time to register the ordinary feelings of humanity. But that was not all; he was serving and would have to pull ropes and things with two of his own sailors. Furthermore he was sailing on a treasure expedition, not to seek for treasure but to bury it.

Mad! The thing would have been mad only for the iron chain of logical events that led up to it. Taking all the facts into consideration, nothing else could have happened; even though he and Dicky and Sheila possessed free will it had been and was of no use to them. They could not let go of the gold any more than a man can let go the poles of a powerful electric battery once they are in his hands.

It would have been an interesting question in psychology whether they were clinging to the gold or the gold to them. The result in either case would have been the same.

As he filled his lungs with cigarette smoke he recognized all this, and just like a man on a started toboggan, he recognized that he could not get out.

The sun that had been fighting the low-lying sea mists was making way, the dismal grey of the dawn had vanished and the seaward sky had taken a blue, faint, newborn and lovely, the blue of ice holding the sparkle of fire.

The captain of the *Baltrum* was looking toward it, but with no poetry in her heart. The *Dulcinea* lay in the fairway, the wind was fresh, the tide ebbing—why didn't she get out. She could see the fellows on her deck.

"What are they waiting for, Larry?" asked Sheila.

"Faith, I don't know, miss," said Larry, his contempt for fine yachts and their ways palpable to the ear. "Except maybe their exiliary ingin won't work."

"It's Shortt, damn him," said James, utterly forgetting Sheila for a moment. "Shall I row off and stir him up?"

"No," said Sheila. "There goes the winch."

The sound of the anchor chain being hove short came to them and now the sails of the *Dulcinea* began to go aloft.

"Now the winch, Larry," cried Sheila.

The winch was manned and the anchor chain hove short.

"She's a-thrip, miss," said Larry.

"Set your mainsail."

The mainsail rose slatting to the breeze, then came the orders like snow. "Your throat halyards. Gaskets off the jib. Your jib halyards—haul!"

The *Dulcinea* already was away as the orders came. "Man the windlass." She gave it as she took the wheel.

Then as the anchor came out of the mud and up to the cathead, the *Baltrum* took a new feel and found a voice, a watery gurgling voice; the main boom lifting to the breeze strained at the sheet. They were away.

The south-centre spit drew toward them as though the land were moving, the fairway broadened, and the cold North Sea, sparkling in the May morning, showed its foam gouts and its gulls and a big tanker pounding north for Hull, maybe, or the Tyne.

The sand spits passed to a shouting of gulls and the wind freshened as though the sea had given it new life, and now the bell buoy of the east-centre shoal spoke loud and clear and close to starboard and then began to fail in voice as the runways and traps of this infernal passage were left definitely behind.

"Tank-tonk—tonk-tank-tonk," said the buoy. "The *Hilda Claydon* lies here—fishing boat—lost—all hands—winter—storms—wreck—Essex boat, too—tonk."

"Lee-o!"

The wheel went over, the sails shook, the main boom listed out to port and the *Baltrum*, with the wind on her starboard beam, leaned to it, pointing due south with the sunlit coast of Essex away across the water.

Away ahead the *Dulcinea*, on the same course, showed beautiful against the blue.

Sheila handed the wheel over to Larry and dropped below to see after breakfast.

A line from the haze to the south foreland forms the arc of a great bay, a wedge-shaped bay whose conelike top diminishes till it becomes the Thames and touches London.

Larry was holding the *Baltrum* close to this line and the *Baltrum*, as though incited by the *Dulcinea*, was proving her qualities as a sea boat and for speed. Noon found them with the north foreland away on the starboard beam and the Goodwins directly ahead.

CHAPTER 20

SOUTHWARD BOUND

I have read many books on the subject, but I have never yet met an author who with his hand on his heart had told the truth, the whole truth, about the North Sea and English Channel, those sea approaches devised by the devil for the confusion of his friends the enemies of England.

Wind, currents, sand spits, fog and ships are chief among the dangers peculiar to these places and among them the most trying to the nerves of the tyro are ships.

Crossing the entrance to the port of London you meet ships. Vast ships in a hurry, high in ballast or low with freight; little ships from the Tyne, from the Humber or Channel ports, and, worst of all, Thames barges that get in the way of the traffic like dust carts in Piccadilly.

James' heart was in his throat several times that morning. Larry, on instructions from his superior officer, who was down below engaged in household duties, was l'arnin' the new hand how to steer. James had the wheel and after the first five minutes or so nothing was easier. "Keep her as she goes," said Larry, and James kept her while Larry stood off and filled a pipe.

Nothing was easier; it was even pleasant. It gave him a sense of power and of being in control and she was an easy boat to steer. Sheila came on deck, glanced at the weather and the coast and fell into talk with Larry about some trifle or another, and James, proud of his job and the way he was doing it, straightened his back and whistled. He didn't whistle long.

A ship, outward bound, and high in the water, drew his attention, a great brute of a Shireman liner with a stovepipe funnel and propellers kicking up behind like the Buffalo girls.

She was making to cut the course of the *Baltrum*. He calculated the distance and speed of the two ships and saw that if he held on collision was inevitable. But he said nothing. Sheila had glanced at the freighter, so had Larry, then they had resumed their talk as if nothing was the matter. James' lips were dry, but the palms of his hands were moist. He would have given words to express his feelings, yet pride held him. These two people who knew all about everything were content. They must have something up their sleeves to prevent collision at the last moment, and it was for them to show concern, not him.

He held on.

Sweat drops were trickling down his nose, then suddenly he recognized that collision though probable was not inevitable. They might just shave it.

A minute later he saw that he had been fooled by sea distance and want of knowledge of speeds, and that he would pass the freighter cable lengths astern.

He saw this just as Sheila turning from Larry went below.

Larry, while seeming to see nothing, had seen everything. He had been rattled the same way himself when he was a young steersman.

"Did you think she was goin' to cut into us?" asked Larry.

"I did," said James.

"Well, you'll soon know better when you've l'arned your distances. But sure, you ought to have known it was her place to do the botherin', seein' it was her place to give us the way."

"I'd forgot," said James.

"Well, then, the next time you'll remimber," said Larry.

That was James' first lesson in seamanship which is, at base, the art of self-reliance. He had to learn a lot of other lessons before he sighted Teneriffe—how to heave the log, the delights of keeping watch of a moonlit May night with lighthouses winking at you and the water populous with shipping—red and green stars to port and starboard, lights of steamers that with a shift of helm might ram you and damn you and pass on.

Down this populous street the *Baltrum* passed like a cockroach down a passage filled with tramping men, protected by the god of little ships and the sea sense of her officers and the officers of the ships around her. For a day and half a night she lay smothered in fog billows in Lyme Bay, blowing a foghorn worked by foot in the midst of a fleet all foghorns and Devonshire voices. Then the bay took her, calm as a mill pond, till in the dark of a night powdered with stars a great revolving light far to port shouted to her: "I am here—I am here—Finistère—Finistère." Far to starboard a Union Castle liner crawling home showed like a flittering insect with one bright green spot in its middle. Then came the blue sea, boundless and desolate, till one day far to the southward the sky showed a stain diaphanous yet sharp cut, cone-shaped—the Peak.

CHAPTER 21

SANTA CRUZ

They found the *Dulcinea* at anchor in Santa Cruz harbour, also an American training brig and two fruit schooners.

Dicky, standing by to help with the anchor, thought he had never seen a pleasanter place than that, so foreign to the eye, so friendly after the great sea spaces, so filled with the breath of the subtropics.

Sheila, who knew the place well, stood by Larry at the wheel; it was she who gave the word to let go and it was she who received the port officer and doctor as they came alongside, not as officials but as friends.

They knew her well, and when she gave them news of old Captain Dennis' death they flung up their hands. Then they came below, were formally introduced to James and the other, smoked cigarettes, never bothered to look at the *Baltrum's* papers, and departed leaving the cabin perfumed with Spanish tobacco.

The last time the girl had been in this place her mind had been free from care. Poor as church mice, she and her father had known nothing about care or worry and a lot about the joy of life, a life where the wind and the sea and the ever-changing sky had ringed them and roofed them, a life in which they were always altering their major environment without altering their home.

That is the charm of a seafarer's life if his boat is his own and he is free to work her as he wills. Without leaving his house he can alter his surroundings, transporting himself at will on the magic carpet of the sea. Sheila had been happy because she was free, and it was only now in Santa Cruz harbour that the fact of her lost freedom came to her fully. She had been so busy on the voyage that she had no time to think of things, but here in this place so filled with old associations she felt as a bird might feel who suddenly finds a weight attached to one wing.

It was the gold.

Of all substances in the world, gold is the most active. It cannot throw off particles like radium, but it can build cities and destroy them, build ships and sink them, cut throats, ruin men, raise them to the heights; there is nothing that it cannot do, and it is always doing. Always at work. And its work is done entirely in the world of mind, even stirring to life in that strange world forces benign or destructive, far reaching, incalculable.

Sheila, without thinking this out, felt it. The idea that the terrible cargo of the *Baltrum* had been scented by others and that men of power in the kingdom of crookery which reaches from China to Peru were out against herself and her companions, had taken hold on her mind. But it was only here, at rest in the harbour of Santa Cruz, that she felt the full weight of it as it clung.

She was no longer free, and her horizon that had always been clear and bright was hung with vague clouds.

Besides this a load of responsibility had been cast on her. On her depended the working of the ship and the safety of the crew. She was an efficient navigator, and she had seen enough of James and Dicky on the voyage to know that months of steady application would be required to make either of them efficient, and they had not months to spare—no, nor days. Then the two clockwork sailors of the *Dulcinea* were exercising her mind. They were good fellows, but obviously not satisfied with their present job and quarters. Used to big yachts and Southampton water, the *Baltrum* did not appeal to them. They were only required to stick it till Great Bahama was reached. Would they? But what troubled her most was the attitude of James and Dicky.

These gentlemen at the sight of land seemed to have cast all care to the wind, forgotten the gold, forgotten everything. They wanted to get ashore and stretch their legs.

Captain Shortt, who had come on board after the port officers, received instructions to send the pinnace along. James wanted to go ashore in style. Sheila was to go with them.

"But we can't all leave the ship," said she.

"Goodness," said James, "she's as safe as houses. She won't run away and Larry and the others will be on board."

Sheila debated with herself.

She knew that it was safe enough to leave the *Baltrum*; she would have left it joyously for a cruise ashore in the old days. But now she felt as a woman might feel who is asked to leave her jewel case in a railway cloak room—it would be perfectly safe—yet still, she would be worrying all the time about it. On the other hand, she dreaded James and Dicky going ashore alone. What might they not get up to, specially James!

James had been perfectly all right on the voyage—but ashore!

"All right," said she, "I'll come."

She went down to change and before stepping into the pinnace she gave strict injunctions to Larry to let no one on board till they came back. She took him aside to give him this order.

"No one, Larry, not even anyone off the *Dulcinea*, except Captain Shortt."

Then as she sat with her hands folded in the stern sheets of the pinnace she reviewed the whole position as only a woman could review it. Her own desperate need of money; not wealth, but just a competence; James' character—what she knew of it—and Dicky's; the gold, like a monster hidden in the *Baltrum*, the enemies or antagonists she imagined lurking out of view, ready to pounce, ready to follow them, able to trick them—she had read Gaboriau—wherever they went, ready to strike, pitiless; a dishcloth she had omitted putting to dry and the fact that she had to tell Larry to get some potatoes from one of the fruit boats that are always dodging about the shipping.

No sooner had she put foot ashore however, than being a sensible person she dismissed all this from her mind and determined to enjoy herself.

Santa Cruz was hot, it was also empty of visitors, but that did not prevent them from enjoying themselves. They sat on the Plaza under an awning in front of the Hotel Continental and had vermouths, then they found their way through the narrow callés, so-called streets, where no windows are and where the shop doors are just slits in the wall; shops like shops in the Rue de la Paix, only smaller; gorgeous shops you never would have imagined lurking in those cutthroat callés. Here they bought tooth powder and Pond's extract and other things they were short of and here they ordered tropical clothing, to be ready and delivered in two days.

Then it was lunch time and they went back to the Continental, where the waiter placed them at a table next to one occupied by the only other visitor, a French gentleman, stout, with a black beard, and a napkin tucked under his chin.

This gentleman, who was jesting with the waiter when they came in, seemed drunk but wasn't. He was Southern.

He surveyed the newcomers with a bold black stare that would have been impertinent in an English room, sang scraps of song as he broke his bread, and while waiting for his fish, and then struck up acquaintance with his neighbours.

He had arrived at Las Palmas by boat from England last night and had come over to Teneriffe that morning on business—nothing but business would take a man to a hole of a place like this out of season. Bompard was his name, born at Arles. Did they know Arles? Well, it was all the same—

By the time dessert was reached and coffee, they knew Bompard, knew all about him. He was less a man than an infection, a wonderful personality, radiating itself, and irresistible. He was in the cigar business and was going from Teneriffe to Vigo, and from Vigo to Havana; did they know Havana, *hein*? Ah, well, they had something to see yet if they never had seen Havana harbour.

Then he produced a big cigar case and gave them cigars unbuyable in the English market.

Sheila almost fell in love with him. He was different from any man she had ever met or heard of; he was the joy of life condensed and radiating itself, now quietly, now unquietly, but never offensively. Sometimes when not talking he would break into little scraps of song, songs about Provence and the sun.

He walked with them down to the landing stage and bade them a fond farewell after having accepted an invitation from James to lunch next day on board the *Dulcinea*.

Then, waving his hat to them, he turned and went off on his cigar business, and as they rowed off to the *Baltrum* he seemed to have taken some of the brightness of the day with him.

He was one of those rare persons one meets with in life who seem too good to be true.

CHAPTER 22

BOMPARD

Ship's coal from lighters in Teneriffe harbour and bits of coal falling overboard form the basis of a microscopic industry. Men come out in boats and dredge for them and half a hundredweight of coal salved by a couple of boats working half a day is considered good business.

The captain of the *Baltrum*, seated under the awning knitting a jumper, watched this work with one eye and wove it into the texture of her knitting—it and all sorts of thoughts connected with it.

She knew nothing of the economic theories of the great minds whose thoughts find expression in the British quarterlies, monthlies, and weeklies, but she knew for a fact that the world is terribly poor and that man is ready to do anything for money. The gold under her feet was talking to her as well as the picture of the poor devils scraping for a peseta's worth of coal.

This was the fourth day of their stay at Teneriffe. All their purchases had been sent on board, the water tanks were filled and they were due out tomorrow morning. The gold had been talking to her all that time, hinting, suggesting, filling her with the vague uneasiness of its presence and affecting her even against Bompard.

Bompard, James and Dicky had grown frightfully thick during the last few days, dining ashore, going excursions, consuming more cocktails than were good for them and carrying on generally like schoolboys.

This radium man had infected the two others with his own joy of life—not that James wanted much infecting, but even James had become more carefree and irresponsible under his influence, and Sheila, watching him, brooded.

She had taken James aside that morning and warned him.

"Take care of that man," said Sheila. "He seems very jolly and all that, but you can't be too cautious. You haven't told him anything about—you know what, have you?"

"Me?" said James; "not a word. But what's wrong with him?"

"Nothing, perhaps—everything, perhaps. I'm uneasy."

She told him of her suspicions about Morgan, and how Morgan had been in touch with Plymouth.

"I'm only suspecting," said Sheila. "If he is in league with any people who are after us and if he gave them word at Plymouth they would have had time to send a man by mail boat. That man might be this Monsieur Bompard. Remember, he arrived at Las Palmas the night before we arrived here."

James, whose nervousness about the whole business had been forgotten or suppressed by adventure and travel, had to take all this in.

"Confound Morgan!" cried James. "What was he doing sniffing around the ballast? I'll fire him—fire him right now."

"No," said Sheila, "we have him safe so long as he is on board the *Dulcinea* and we are on guard. If he was loose he might talk or give information or do goodness knows what—then of course we may be suspecting him wrongly. No, I'd keep him."

James brooded.

Once suspicion was roused in this ordinarily unsuspecting mind it was apt to ramp and do things.

It was roused now against Bompard. Not under the immediate spell of that fascinating presence, he began to remember things.

The way Bompard had chummed up with them at first sight, the way he had told all about himself and his affairs, the frank questions he had put as to why the party had two yachts—and such a strange-looking yacht as the *Baltrum*—Bompard was very frank; the way he had laid himself out to please—oh, lots of things rose up in the mind of James asking questions and receiving no answer.

"Look here," said he, "we promised to go with him today up to a *fonda* he knows of, and have lunch. What do you think—had we better call it off?"

"I don't know," said Sheila. "No, maybe it would be better to go—I don't believe in evading things; grasp your nettle. Besides, if he is what I almost suspect him to be you might do some good if you are clever."

"How?" asked James.

"Give him wrong information. Say we are going from here to the Cape Verde Islands."

"But he knows we are going to call at Havana."

"How does he know that?"

"I told him," said James. "How was I to suspect anything?"

"Well, tell him we have changed our plans."

"I might do that," said James.

"I *told* you," said Sheila, "to say nothing to anybody about anything—well, you have done it, but remember we may have terrible people working against us. Never forget that—people who would stick at nothing, not even killing us."

She felt easy in her mind for she felt that she had made an impression on James. She had.

It was four o'clock in the afternoon and Sheila had come on deck where Larry had put the tea things out. She had turned from speaking to him when her eye caught a boat coming toward her. It was a Spanish boat, one of the ordinary scows that ply for hire, and in the stern sheets she recognized James and Dicky.

"They are coming off," said she to Larry. "You can get the tea now." She went to the side to receive them.

They looked odd.

James flung five pesetas to the boatmen. Then he came on deck, Dicky following.

"What's wrong?" asked Sheila.

Dicky laughed a little hysterical laugh. James looked over the side to see that the boatmen were gone.

"Down below," said James. He went, the others following, Sheila with her hand on her heart, Dicky dumb.

James was hunting in a locker for whisky. "We've got to get out," said James. "Right out—quick."

"He's dead," said Dicky, with a cluck in his throat.

"*Who's* dead?"

"Bompard," said Dicky.

"He's what you thought," said James, speaking between gulps of neat John Begg. "He tried to poison us and took the stuff by mistake in wine. Luncheon—in an orange grove—miles from anywhere—we left him and ran—took wrong road. Got here at last. Get the anchor up!"

The sense of blank calamity paralyzed Sheila for a moment, then she was herself again.

"Don't drink any more whisky," cried she. "How can we get out? The wind's against us! The ship's papers are all right—the water is on board—let me think—let me think."

She stood with her hand pressed on her head. Yes, they must get out. It was not a question of escaping from the law; she knew that James and Dicky were innocent; but she knew Spanish ports, and if Bompard had any friends or accomplices here, what might not happen?

Then she formed her plan.

"Leave everything to me," said she, "and don't touch any more whisky."

She put the bottle back in the locker, came on deck and ordered the dinghy over. When she was getting into it with Larry to row her, she gave orders to Longley and the other man to get the awning down. Then she told Larry to row to the *Dulcinea*.

Captain Shortt was in his cabin at tea. She shut the door.

"Mr. Corder has sent me with orders that the *Dulcinea* is to get a tow rope over to our boat and take us out," said Sheila abruptly.

"Why, God bless my soul, we weren't due out till to-morrow," said Shortt.

"I don't know anything about that," said Sheila. "I only know those are his orders and he's in a terrible temper about something. Also he says you are to keep in sight and touch with us, steering sou'-sou'-west on a course that will give a wide berth to the Selvages. Will you kindly take all this down?"

"I've got it in my mind," said Shortt, evidently put out. "Anything more?"

"He wants to know if all the crew were on board, especially Mr. Morgan."

"The starboard watch had shore leave this morning and they're back. Yes. Morgan is on board."

"By the way, Captain Shortt, did Mr. Morgan go ashore at Plymouth?" Sheila thought that while at work she might scrape this bit of information up as well.

"Yes, he went ashore for some truck he wanted. What makes you particular to ask?"

"What I meant to ask, only I'm stupid, is did he get all the paraffin you wanted? Mr. Corder wanted to know."

"Yes," replied Shortt, struck even in his upset about starting by the idiocy of this question, yet putting the matter aside. "We got the paraffin. God bless my soul, tow you out! Does he take the *Dulcinea* for a tug? It will strain her, it'll spoil my paint and I'm doubting if I have hawser sufficient. Well, it's his boat and if you ram blam into my stern it's his lookout. I'd better run over and see him."

"You'd better not," said Sheila. "He said specially that the thing had to be done at once and that I was to tell you not to come off but get to work—those were his words."

"All right," said Shortt.

He left his tea unfinished and Sheila, getting into her boat, came back to the *Baltrum*.

James was still below, but Dicky was on deck.

"Is the whisky all right?" whispered she.

"Oh, that's all right," said Dicky, "but he's a bit upset. It's given him a nasty turn for he's awfully sensitive. He's lying down there in his bunk now, smoking cigarettes."

The awning had been stripped and now from the *Dulcinea* came signs and sounds of activity. The anchor was weighed, the auxiliary put in motion and the *Dulcinea* backed to within near distance of the ketch. Then the anchor was dropped again. Then came the boats with the line that was to lead the hawser and the hawser itself slobbering wet as it came—a messy business.

Every one was out of temper, as everyone is, as a rule, on a towing job—everyone but Sheila, who saw in imagination police boats setting out from the landing stage, James and Dicky hauled ashore, examination, delays—disaster.

But nothing came off, nothing but a fruit boat for the American training ship, the sight of which pierced everything to find the housekeeper within her.

"Larry," said she, "did you get those potatoes I told you?"

"Yes, miss," said Larry, rising from the fixing of the rope and going aft to the wheel. "Now then, stand by the winch till I give the word. Hiven mend them, what a time they are gettin' that boat aboard! Now then, stand by the winch—now then, up wid her."

The anchor was hove short, then it came out of the mud, leaving the water as the anchor of the *Dulcinea* was coming to the cathead. The *Dulcinea* was moving. Sheila gave a glance astern. No, there was no sight of police or boats or any disturbance whatever, nothing to see but the evening light on Santa Cruz town and nothing to hear but the far sound of the evening band playing in the Plaza.

Then the harbour mouth was passed, the *Dulcinea* tugging bravely and the *Baltrum* following like a mongrel dog towed by a fine lady.

The island lay astern, and then the Peak came into view. You cannot see the Peak from Santa Cruz.

The wind from the northeast breezed across the sunset-lit sea and as the towrope was cast off the sails of the *Baltrum* rose, fought the breeze, and filled.

"Thank God!" said Sheila.

Then suddenly, sprung from the depths of her mind, came the words: "James is a fool!" She was not thinking of the whisky but of Bompard. "James is a fool!" she thought.

Maybe she was right.

CHAPTER 23

LONGLEY AND HEARN

"Keep her as she goes," said Larry, handing the wheel to Longley.

Sheila looked away back where the great peak was dying in the dusk above a luminous purple sea with the islands of Heiro and Gommera vaguely sketched in the twilight beyond. They were beyond pursuit, there was nothing to follow them unless the *Tiede*, a tinpot ferryboat, the American training brig and the two fruit schooners. They were beyond pursuit and they had the gold.

Down below in the cabin a little later, James, who had quite recovered himself, gave her details of the tragedy.

"Only for you," said James, "things might have panned out a lot different. You put me wise about that chap and I was on my guard. I wasn't on my guard just at first," said James, "but directly the thing occurred I knew and was able to drag Dicky away and do a bunk.

"We started all right, went part of the way by tram then hoofed the rest, climbing all the time till we got to this *fonda* place he'd spoken of. He'd sent round the day before and they had a cold chicken ready for us and rolls and butter and salad and olives all done up in a basket and two bottles of white wine and glasses and corkscrew and all; then we hiked on, carrying the provisions with us, climbing zigzag to an orange grove that grows on a shelf a couple of miles from the *fonda*.

"Bompard said he'd spread the table while we explored round. We climbed the goat tracks to the mouth of a cave we saw, and which wasn't worth the trouble.

"When we got back there was Bompard with the feast spread. He'd opened the bottles of wine and while he was messing about hunting for something he'd dropped, I took up one of the bottles to examine the label and put it down again, but I didn't put it down in exactly the same place I'd taken it from and that must have confused him."

"How?" asked Sheila.

"Wait till I've finished and you'll see. When luncheon was over and we were lighting up, old man Bompard began to look about him uneasily. He looked at me and Dicky and then he says: 'How do you feel?'

"'I feel all right,' says I. He says nothing for a moment, lights his cigar and then drops it, clapping his hands to his—front.

"He was doubled up with pain and then he began crying out that he was poisoned—that the wine was poisoned and shouting for a doctor and a priest.

"I tumbled to the business at once. He'd poisoned one of the bottles to do us in, and owing to my shifting them he'd taken the dose instead of us. He kept shouting to us to run to the *fonda* and tell them to fetch a doctor and a priest, and we ran.

"I explained the position to Dicky as we were tumbling down cliffs and chasing along goat paths. I had enough Spanish to tell the people of the *fonda* what he'd said. I told them we'd send more help from Santa Cruz, and then we kept on running, took the wrong path and got lost, but got down at last and made for the harbour.

"We didn't know where to find priests and doctors, so I ran into that chemist man in the Callé What's-its-name, and told him a gentleman was ill and gave him the directions. That's all. Only for you putting me wise we'd have stuck to that chap and maybe have been knifed by his confederates, for I liked him and never would have believed, off my own bat, that he was up to mischief."

"Good heavens," said Sheila, "you left him!"

"Of course we left him."

"But you are sure—"

"What?"

"I don't know—" Her mind was upset. The joyous figure of Bompard arose before her. She had liked him at first sight, suspicion had cast its odious shadow upon him, but the first liking had clung, obscured by the shadow, but now peeping vaguely forth again.

The question she was asking herself was frankly this: "Could that fool of a James have—

"Are you sure it was poison? Might it only have been illness?"

"Sure," replied James. "Why, he said it himself—confessed it."

"Might it only have been his fancy?"

"Goodness, no," said Dicky. "The chap was poisoned right enough—if you'd only seen him."

Sheila brooded. Well, there was no use worrying. But to run off and leave a man like that! And, still, if Bompard was what she had fancied, what better could they have done? They had told the *fonda* people, and the chemist—

"Anyhow," said she, "you did everything for the best and there's no use bothering now. Let's have supper."

All around here between the Canary Islands, and between them and Madeira, the sea is of an extraordinary depth and a blueness almost Caribbean in its wonder and brilliancy, maybe because the bottom here has no mud or sediment. It is all coral; coral even at the depth of over a mile.

When Sheila came on deck next morning she found the sun up, the Canaries vanished and the Selvages a dun line marked with foam on the port bow.

The Selvages, or Selvagees, have a chapter of their own in the long, exasperating history of treasure hunting, the history which to my knowledge has never been marked by one find worth mentioning. Here was actually hidden a vast amount of gold and here armed with full directions as to the position of the treasure the British government sent one of their ships under Sir Hercules Robinson. He found nothing. It was like the Trinidad business, the map given by the dying sailor in all good faith to his benefactor, the chart of South West Bay, the position of the hills, the minute details as to the location of the treasure—everything—but no treasure. It was like the Voss business, it was like the innumerable businesses of which I have a list as long as my arm, which have been started to hunt for pirate gold among the islands and keys of the West India Islands—they have never found anything but mosquitoes, never will.

Sheila, her eyes fixed on the lonely rocks, sand banks and foam goats of the Selvages felt a rising of her heart. She knew these barren islands and their story, and old Captain Dennis, who was in the main a sensible man, had drilled into her mind the absolute hopelessness of the treasure gamble. So it was that now, gazing across the water at these sinister and desolate rocks where many a man has laboured like a fool, her heart rose at the thought that come what might she and her companions had at least touched *their* treasure. There was to be no hopeless digging. They had only to bury it at a well-marked spot and to unearth it again.

As she turned from the view of the islands she saw Longley and Hearn. They were in different watches, but they were both on deck at the same time, Hearn having just come up from the fo'c's'le.

Both these men were out of the picture in this expedition. They were too respectable. Dicky and James and the others harmonized with—or at least did not shout against—their surroundings, but the two yacht sailors didn't fit. They felt it, perhaps that's why they showed it. They were not used to such narrow quarters and such dingy surroundings; the fo'c's'le of the *Baltrum* "smelt fusty" and the cooking was not up to their expectations. They wanted fresh meat. They did not grumble, but they showed themselves dissatisfied and they showed their dissatisfaction without rudeness or giving offence. It was a sort of atmosphere they carried with them and Sheila, who had not much knowledge of the ways of their class, thought at first she had done something to offend them. Then she discovered she hadn't—it was only the *Baltrum*.

She had made up her mind at first to get rid of them at Great Bahama, send them back on board the *Dulcinea* and so be free of them when the time came to sail to Crab Cay and do the burying.

This morning she came to alter her mind on this subject.

She had been calculating up the man power necessary for taking the ketch to Crab Cay, keeping her off it and carrying the gold ashore, and it seemed to her that they were too short handed for safety. They wanted at least another man and Longley was the man of all men for the job.

Longley had a face unintellectual as the face of a sheep and not unlike. His people originally had belonged to the South Downs before coming to Southampton in the time of King George I., and engaging in the business of yacht sailing. Longley was a safe man, Sheila felt, safe to know nothing of their business unless it was carefully explained to him, and to say nothing even if he knew.

He was just what they wanted, a big able-bodied, stupid man, trustable to keep a secret as a steam engine. Hearn was quite different. Sheila determined to keep Longley and get rid of Hearn.

So it was that this treasure expedition with bullion at stake, greater in amount than was ever carried by any boat smaller than the *Majestic* or *Homeric*, was under sole control of a girl who put in spare moments knitting a jumper.

Longley and Hearn were ignorant of the whole business, so was Larry; James and Dicky were useless except as subordinates. They knew nothing of navigation at sea and the equally important work of navigation ashore found them wanting.

She could not trust them—at least she could not trust James; he was honour personified no doubt, but he was erratic. Dicky, when alone, was sensible, but when ashore with James he seemed to follow the leading of the other.

She dreaded what might happen at Havana if James took too many cocktails and talked too much.

Another thing was bothering her. James had exhibited to her, without knowing it, the fact that Cupid had been at work with him. The events of the voyage, the excitement, new duties and new surroundings had prevented Mr. Corder from developing on these lines, but he might begin to develop at any moment. He was a gun ready to be fired. She felt that, knew it by the sixth sense that tells a woman all about these things and the knowledge was like a grit in the eye.

Love was absolutely outside this business so fraught with terrible possibilities. Even had she cared for James the thought of philandering would have revolted her, but she did not care for him—at least in that way.

At noon that day, with the Selvages far astern, she took the sun, the first observation on a journey of three thousand miles across the Atlantic. The *Dulcinea*, which had spoken to them and received orders as to where they had to meet, was far ahead, a white wing on a sea breezed and desolate but blue as the Mediterranean.

CHAPTER 24

THE LANDFALL

The north Atlantic, like the Bay, has a bad name got mostly from winter experiences on the Liverpool-New York passage. It has a cold name, too. But the north Atlantic below 40° is as beautiful as the Pacific, as blue, and more trustable.

They had no bad weather but a favouring wind that fell to a dead calm six days out, as if resting, and then resumed work blowing across the infinite distances of the swell from a sky hung on its sea line with white summer clouds. The nights were tremendous with stars, and one dawn coming on deck they saw away on the starboard beam a fairy cloud, pearly and pink tinged, diaphanous, yet hinting of solidity—Bermuda.

The *Dulcinea* had vanished from sight days before, had outsailed them. There was nothing in all that sea but the fairy island and a freighter so far off that its hull was almost down beneath the horizon.

They had changed their meeting place with the *Dulcinea* at the last moment. Great Bahama had been chosen at haphazard, but it was too far north of Rum Cay, at least farther than necessary, it was also not a good rendezvous from the point of secrecy.

Sheila, looking over the charts on the night they left Teneriffe, had suggested this and the others had agreed. The expedition, rushed from the moment of its inception, was like a bag packed in a hurry, and this important point turned up only at the last moment and James, for once in his life, was able to give advice that helped. He knew the whole Bahama bank and he had a long memory for places and soundings.

"You're right," said James, "and Great Abaco is as bad. You get all sorts of schooners and boats from Nassau pottering round. We can't do better than meet off Turtle Island. There's good anchorage but no one's there and no one goes there, for there's nothing doing. There it is east of Eleuthera and north of Cat Island; there's no reefs to make bother and no chance of missing the *Dulcinea*, for the place isn't bigger than a dinner table. Shortt knows it—he was with me when I was there last. It's a good fishing centre."

"Might there be yachts there?" asked Sheila.

"In the winter there might," said James, "but not now."

The change of rendezvous was given to the *Dulcinea* when they spoke her that night, but on the lovely morning when all calculation ought to have shown them Turtle Island dead ahead, the sea showed nothing.

The *Baltrum* was making ten knots; there were land gulls white in the flower-blue sky, but of land there was no trace.

Sheila felt a chill at the heart as the morning wore on and the *Baltrum* sighing and sinking to the swell bravely made her way in face of the endless and unbroken azure. The ship had done her duty and the hands—only she had failed. Her navigation was at fault. But not much. Toward noon Larry who was on the lookout shouted: "Land!"

"Where away?" cried Sheila, rising from the cabin hatch and running forward.

"There isn't any land," said Larry, "but sure it's there right enough." He pointed, not ahead, but away on the starboard bow and there, thready against the sky, showed the masts of an anchored vessel.

"It's near," said Larry.

It was.

Turtle Island, too low in the water to be seen at that distance, showed as the hull of the *Dulcinea* became fully visible; Turtle Island without a tree, just a low-lying mass of rocks, foam bearded and clanged about by gulls, with the *Dulcinea* lying at anchor in fifteen fathoms a quarter of a mile from the shore.

They dropped anchor a couple of cable lengths away from the yacht and the *Baltrum*, tireless, for sails never tire, swung to her moorings, without loss of stick or rag for all her journey and just as though she were still swinging to the tide and the tune of the bell buoy in Hildersditch Pool.

CHAPTER 25

THEY TELL LARRY

"How?" asked James.

It was noon of the next day, the *Baltrum*, with the wind on her port quarter, was south of Turtle Island; and Crab Cay, if the charts and the reckoning did not lie, was due to be sighted somewhere about three o'clock. Sheila was down below with the two others giving them her opinion that the worst and most difficult part of the whole business was coming now.

"This way," said Sheila. "It's just as if we had committed a murder and were trying to dispose of the corpse—I mean the difficulty is just the same. First of all Larry will see what we are doing, and secondly, there's Longley. I took him with us because we were undermanned, and secondly because he seems so stupid. I felt sure it was safe to bring him along, but it only occurred to me last night, as I was lying awake and thinking, that stupidity doesn't stop people from talking. He may suspect nothing, but he is sure to think it's strange when he sees us bringing ballast on shore at this island and burying it."

"Naturally," said James.

"Then if Mr. Morgan is 'wrong,' as I suspect him to be, he may question Longley."

"We must keep them apart when we get to Havana, that's all."

"Well, we must try and do that," said Sheila. "Then there's Larry. I've always been afraid to tell Larry about the gold lest he'd lose his head and talk. It was a mistake. I ought to have told him and I think we ought to tell him now."

"Why now?" asked Dicky.

"Because he will be able to help to keep Longley ignorant of what we are doing. They are sure to get talking together about it."

"Will he cut up rough at not having been told before?" asked James.

"Larry! Oh, no, he's too devoted to me for that. Let's call him down right now and get it over."

A minute later the old sailor entered the cabin, shut the door at the command of Sheila and stood twiddling his cap and waiting for orders.

"Larry," said Sheila, "I've got something to tell you of the greatest importance. I couldn't tell you before because it was a secret, and the secret was not all mine."

"Yes, miss," said Larry.

"It will be the most surprising thing you ever heard; and when you've heard it, you will know how important it was to keep it a secret. You know those metal blocks among the ballast?"

"Yes, miss."

"Well, they aren't metal—they are gold."

"Yes, miss."

"Pure gold. They must have belonged to those two men who killed one another. No one has claimed them, so they are ours."

"Yes, miss. I knew that long ago."

"Knew it long ago! How on earth did you know it?"

"Sure I heard you talkin' about it, and me listenin' at the skylight," said Larry.

"Oh, good gracious!" cried Sheila. "Listening!"

"I wasn't listenin' to hear," said Larry, "but not havin' corks in me ears it come to me as I was settin' by the skylight mendin' a sail one day beyant there at Hildersditch. You and Mr. Sebright was talkin' and the ould hooker's a fiddle for carryin' sound. 'So they've got a saycret they're keepin' from Larry,' said I, and wid that I listened all the more."

"You haven't said anything?" asked James.

"Me say anythin'!—it's me that's been bottlin' it, for if I hadn't tumbled to it the hands would have heard, and you chatterin' away about it down below. Many's the time I've called Hearn or Longley for'ard so they mightn't hear anythin' comin' up from the skylight. Me talk—faith, it's you that ought to be askin' that."

"Never mind, Larry," said Sheila. "Mr. Corder didn't mean that you'd talk really—only by accident. Well, you know now, anyhow, and what we have to do is to keep Longley from suspecting anything. I don't know how much you heard when you were listening; but it's just this, Larry—there's only one way to turn this gold into money and—"

"I've tumbled to it, miss," said Larry. "Sure ould Mike Connelly did the same at Stranrac whin I was a boy. Mike, he robbed a chap of five goulden soverins and dug a hole an' buried thim and then dug them up again, pritindin' they was treasure-trove; but sure wan of thim was an Australian soverin and that give the show away on him."

"Well, we haven't robbed anyone, but that's just about what we want to do—it's our only way. Crab Cay is the place we've fixed on and we're close to it now. We have thought out everything. We have the shovels for digging and the sacks to fill with sand to take the place of the ballast we are landing, not that it will equal its weight but at all events it will be something toward it. The only bother is Longley and keeping the thing hid from him—at least keeping him from suspecting the truth."

"Faith, that's so," said Larry. "Well, Miss Shaila, if you'll give me the time to turn it over in me head I'll maybe be afther thinkin' of somethin'. Longley hasn't the sinse of a rabbit beyond steerin' and splicin'—all the same, a rabbit would be askin' questions seein' what we're afther and it's for me to put the blinkers on him."

He left the cabin, took the wheel from Longley and sent him forward on the lookout. Then the others came up.

Invisible and all to west of them lay the Bahamas and the vast flats from which they rise. These banks—and the great Bahama bank has a length of three hundred miles and width of eighty—are the tops of vast mountain ranges rising sheer from incredible depths. Could the waters of the ocean be stripped away you would see the entrance leading to the Straits of Florida like a narrow road winding past sheer cliffs rising miles high to a table-land dotted with hillocks—the Bahama Islands.

Crab Cay is the most eastwardly lying of all these hillocks, the last thing to show of land before Profundity takes charge, making the bed for the Atlantic Ocean to toss in.

Here at Crab Cay, Rum Cay, Caycos, Cat Island and Mariguana, the old blockade runners of the American Civil War used to hide and keep their depots. It was at Crab Cay that Chiselman fought Hayes, Hayes "boarding" the islet where Chiselman and his crowd were making merry, just as though he were boarding a ship. Long years before that Horne was supposed to have hidden a vast quantity of plunder in the sands of Crab Cay and in the waters to westward of it, protected from the northeast trades and southwest winter gales; some years ago the bones of a ship might have been seen, an old-time ship with the bow all smashed and gone but the poop still standing. This afternoon, however, when Larry on the lookout cried: "There she is," and the others crowded forward to look, Crab Cay far across the luminous blue of the sea showed nothing of these old-time furious happenings. Nothing but the thready tufted forms of two palm trees, wind bent by the northeast trades, lonely and lost looking.

"Keep her as she goes," cried Sheila to the helmsman. "It's all thirty-fathom water this side and to the west, and good holding ground."

Then as they drew nearer she took the wheel herself, giving the order for the anchor to be got ready. It fell in twenty-five fathom water and as the *Baltrum* swung bow on to the flood Crab Cay in its full extent and desolation lay before them.

Oval in shape, exactly like one of those cuttlefish bones you can pick up on any beach, it lay in the light of the late afternoon sun, the gulls lamenting over it as though it had been a corpse. Of all places in the world—excluding cities—Crab Cay is perhaps the most sinister. Death Valley backed by the

Funeral Mountains is horrible, but it is overdone, it shouts. Crab Cay whispers. Whispers and simpers in the sun, the wind stirring the sands and the gulls lamenting on the wind; nowhere higher than six feet above tide mark, it gives you a low horizon bounding a dark-blue desolate sea, and always when the lightest wind is blowing you hear mixed with the sound of the waves on the beach, a voice within a voice, the silky uncertain whisper of the sands.

In the sou'west storms Crab Cay shouts till its voice is heard at Cat Island. It is preferable then.

The two palm trees standing some forty feet apart and bent by the eternal trade winds leaned to the west and in all the white heat-shaken expanse to south and north not another tree showed, not a bush or blade of vegetation.

Certainly James was right; of all places in the world a better could not be imagined for the hiding of treasure. There was nothing here to attract ships or men, only the good anchorage.

The boat having been got out, Larry rowed them ashore, leaving Longley to keep ship. Then having hauled the boat above high-tide mark they walked to the palm trees, stood, and looked around them expectantly.

None of them spoke for a moment. There was something about the place that blanketed conversation, something that filled the mind with a sense of negation. It was Larry who broke silence.

"I've been thinkin', Miss Shaila," said Larry, "and turnin' it over in me head that the best way to be doin' is tell Longley that you aren't aisy about the metal ballast. Tell him it's puttin' the compass wrong, or some thrash like that—he won't know the differ. Then you can say to him you want to shove it ashore and take sand on instead—at laste, I wouldn't be sayin' it to him but to me in his hearin'. Well, then, we can get the stuff ashore and dump it, then bring the bags off for the sand and fill them and bring them on board. That ought to be all done be tomorrow night. Then at night when Longley's aslape, and he slapes like a dead policeman, row off and bury the stuff, you and me and the gintleman here and Mr. Sebright."

"I was thinking something like that myself," said Sheila.

"That's a top-hole idea," said James. "The only danger is he might wake up and find out what we are doing."

"Well, unless you murther him, there's no other way out of it," said Larry, picking up an empty crab shell, examining it, and throwing it away again.

"It's the only way," said Sheila, "and we've got to run risks—not that there's much risk about Longley, even if he did know. He's too stupid. Well, are you agreed?"

"I am," said Dicky. "Yes—we're all agreed. And now we're here, let's fix on the spot where we'll hide the stuff. Those trees seem to have been put up by Providence for a land mark; suppose we bury it midway between them. It's all soft sand, except those hillocks the trees grow from."

James, who had brought the boat hook with them, as a protection against crabs should they eventuate, prodded it in the sand till Larry told him to give over.

"That chap's watchin' us from the ship," said Larry. "I tould him to get on with the brass work and there he is hangin' his sheep's head over the side. We'd better be gettin' back. You've fixed all you want to and if you want to be doin' any more talkin' you can do it aboard."

"I don't see any crabs," said Sheila, as they turned to the boat.

"You'll see them soon enough," said James, "unless they've deserted the place."

CHAPTER 26

THE RISING OF THE CRABS

Longley stood by as they came on board and helped to stream the boat on a line.

"Larry," said Sheila, as the old man was going forward with the other after the conclusion of this business, "I've made up my mind to have the metal ballast out of her."

"Come here," said Larry to Longley, who was just about to plunge down into the fo'c's'le. "I'll be wantin' you in a minit—and what for do you want to get the ballast out her, Miss Shaila?"

"I don't want to get all the ballast out," replied Sheila in a sharp voice. "How stupid you are! I said the metal ballast. It's disturbing the compass; there's a variation that has put us miles out. I was going to have got rid of it at Teneriffe, that's why I got the sacks—then I forgot about it."

"Well, I don't see how that bit of ould iron can be disturbin' the compass," said Larry, "but sure if you're set on havin' it out—well there you are. And when do you want it shifted?"

"You'd better begin and get it on deck now," replied the other, "so's to be ready for work in the morning."

"I'll start on it wid Longley when we've had our supper, miss," said Larry.

Supper was served in the cabin a few minutes later. It was a silent meal. The gold, as long as it was quiescent among the ballast, and part of the ship, so to speak, had not troubled them. It had always been at the back of their minds and not the pull of a rope or a turn of the wheel but had been part of the business of which it was prime mover, but it had not troubled them directly.

Now it was different. It was going to leave them. It was going to take itself ashore and hide itself in the sand and they were going to sail away without it. Not till now did they know that it had become part of them.

This great treasure had become part of their spirit, almost of their flesh and blood. They would have fought for it as men fight for their homes and their ideals, intrigued for it, lied for it—as indeed they were intriguing and lying with the wretched Longley, and they would have done all these things not for the sake of gain, but of possession; not because they were sordid or little, but because the gold was great in spiritual as well as material power, a potential treasure of the mind as well as the pocket.

They had bully beef for supper because it was too much bother to cook things, but they did not notice what they ate—it was all the same. The crying of the birds from the cay came through the open skylight and they could hear the last waves of the flood beating on the sands, a low, whispering, sighing sound that loudened occasionally only to die away again.

Worries bring up worries and to James as he ate, the worry of having to leave the gold brought up other worries to help. The British government, that apparition whose judges can't be bribed, whose laws are so inelastic, whose arm is so long! Bompard—a vague dread of "consequences" arising from the death of Bompard had lately begun to disturb him! The crooks headed by MacAdam! Worry about all these things crept up from the subconscious mind of James to help the worry about leaving the gold.

Then as they were lighting their cigarettes after supper, sounds and voices came from outside—the voice of Larry admonishing Longley, the sound of some heavy object being carted on deck and dumped on the planking.

It was the gold coming up; moving like a cripple, hauled by common sailormen, dumped on the deck like old junk; the thing that could recreate or blast lives, feed multitudes, make the desert a flower garden, dumped like old iron to the tune of Larry's voice.

"Aisy, you fool, if you drop it on me toes I'll splinter you!"

They came out to help, and half an hour later the business was done and there it lay in the starlight on the narrow deck, block on block, a dusky heap with rope handles sticking out here and there.

When Dicky turned in a little later he could not sleep. The night was warm, but not stifling, for the Bahama temperature even in summer is rarely excessive; all the same, tossing under a single blanket, he could not sleep. The air felt oppressive and when he dozed off at last he was brought awake again with a start. It was as though the treasure on deck had suddenly spoken to him.

The gold was up there lying out on the deck unguarded; the fact that no one could possibly steal it was nothing, the feeling that it was there lying loose for anyone to steal was everything.

He reasoned with himself, yet the uneasiness persisted, and the desire to go up and see if it was all right grew till, throwing the blanket off, he stood on the cabin floor in his pajamas.

James was snoring.

Dicky reached the cabin door and went up the companionway on deck.

The gold was all right. Larry, as an afterthought, had flung a tarpaulin on the heap. No one but Larry would have done a thing like that, and Dicky, having lifted the corner of the covering to glance beneath, smiled as he turned to the starboard rail and leaned on it face to the tepid breeze.

What a night! The blaze of a million stars lit the sea ruffled by a breeze from the Straits of Florida; the sky was a festival; streets of light, the blaze of palaces, a city of splendour swept through by the river of the milky way.

Dicky was no poet, but the beauty and the splendour of the sky held his mind for a moment, making him forget even the gold. He watched the stars for a moment, then the sea and the streaks to southward that showed the run of the current deflected by the southern spur of the sand pit.

Then the cay drew his attention. The surface of the cay by the water's edge seemed moving and changing in tint, the white of the sand passing as though a wave of dusk were invading it. Then he knew. It was crabs.

Crabs rising like a tide.

He fetched the night glass from its sling and looked.

Through the glass it was like watching a moving carpet, a carpet broken here and parted there. Here and there, lifted against the sand background, great pincers showed only to vanish again as the host from the sea flowed up and on, breaking as they went on skirmishing parties that spread with a trickling movement north and south as though running in channels.

The sight of this horrible, sudden, silent eruption of life, like the swarming of vermin, made the glass tremble in his hand. Then, closing it, he put it back in its sling and went below.

CHAPTER 27

"HARD LABOUR"

They were up at dawn, a dawn where the sky turned from flamingo red to flaming yellow, that passed, becoming pure light as the brow of the sun broke from the sea; the sea that stretched without a break to the African coast and the Sahara Desert.

Sheila, coming on deck, forgot everything for a moment as she stood facing that heavenly morning, sea scented, filled with the warmth of summer and the breath of the tepid wind. Then she found that all her worries had vanished; the worry about leaving the gold, the worry as to how they would ever dispose of it. The warmth and splendour, the feeling of newness in the air and the breath of the wind from Florida destroyed doubt and filled her soul with the gaiety of adventure.

It was the same with Dicky and in a way with James. Even Larry seemed to move with younger limbs as he helped to get the boat over—they had brought it on board overnight—and to bring up the sacks for the sand ballast.

Then, while Longley was making coffee and preparing breakfast they set to. They had determined to bring all the stuff ashore and leave it above high water mark; then, digging midway between the palm trees, to fill the sacks with sand and cart them on board; lastly, after nightfall and when Longley was asleep, to land, carry the gold up to the sand hole and cover it over.

Larry stood in the boat below to receive the blocks while the others lowered them one by one in a rope sling. Four made a sufficient cargo, and when they were in, Larry and James rowed them off, beached the boat, lugged them out and returned for more. There were twenty-one of them—five boat journeys—and knocking off for breakfast it took them till ten in the morning before the boat was ashore and the whole heap lay on the beach, the sun lighting it and the fine sand whispering about it in the wind.

Sheila, who had come over with the last load, sat down beside them, and Dicky, tired but happy, lit a cigarette.

James was on board. Lifting and hauling these heavy weights had reduced James to a condition calling for a whisky and a sparklet soda and rest under the awning which they had rigged.

"Well," said Sheila, "that much is done. We have only now to get the sacks filled, and make the hole, and get it into it, and cover it up—oh, yes, and get the sacks on board and stow them and then the whole business will be half done—or will it? No, it won't, for we have to come and dig it up again when we've been to Havana and got our permit. Oh, dear, the whole of this thing gets sometimes like a nightmare."

"Anyhow, it's lucky for us," said Dicky, "that this bit of sand is the only bit of the Bahamas that isn't British."

"Yes, and it was clever of James to pitch on it," said the girl. "He is clever if he wasn't so stupid at times. Have you noticed anything about him lately?"

"No."

"Well, it seems to me sometimes that the whole of this business is getting on his nerves; anyhow that his mind is troubled about something. I think he'd like to be out of it if the truth was told—only he's too good a sort to let us down."

"He'd never do that."

"No, I don't think he would," Sheila laughed. "If I tell you something awfully secret you'll forget it at once?"

"Yes," said Dicky.

Sheila looked at him. Their life and intimacy had bound them together as though they were brother and sister. She would say to Dicky things she would never have said to another man.

"Well, there was a time when I thought James was going to turn sentimental—you know what I mean. At Teneriffe there were moments when it seemed to me he was going to ask me to accept his heart and his yacht. Imagine the horror of guitar business mixed up in an affair like this, and James playing the guitar! Then Bompard mercifully interposed. James has got such a fright over Bompard that he's forgotten everything else. I think he's afraid somehow that people may accuse him of having killed Bompard, or something like that."

"What nonsense," said Dicky, shrugging his shoulders.

"Of course it's nonsense—he spoke to me about it; he asked me might anything be said about our going off in such a hurry and I told him I didn't think so. We were ready for sea and going, the port authorities knew we were going, and a few hours more or less did not matter. Besides, I knew them all—they've known me and father for years. Of course," finished Sheila, "I think it was stupid rushing off like that, but when he came on board saying Bompard was dead and we must put out at once, what was I to do?"

"Well, it's done," said Dicky, "and there's no use in bothering now."

He himself had been stampeded by James' imagination. He wished now they had stuck and seen the thing through, but it was done and there was no use in bothering anymore.

"Even," said Sheila thoughtfully, as she watched the gulls flighting above the sands, "even if Bompard was one of the MacAdam people, they wouldn't have dared to do anything to us. That sort of people must work in secrecy."

"No," said Dicky, "but if he had many of them with him at Teneriffe they might have tried to rush the boat and take her out that night. There was no man-of-war or anything at Teneriffe to have chased them."

"Maybe, and maybe it's just as well James was frightened. Who knows?"

She turned, her eye had caught sight of something moving by the sea edge, close to the boat. It was a crab.

Dicky saw it too, but he said nothing. What he had seen last night might have been only an occasional phenomenon. He had told James of it, but there was no use worrying the girl beforehand. Crabs or no crabs the three of them would have to land that night with Larry and not only land but spend several hours on the spit. In his heart he cursed Longley, the cause of all this bother; only for Longley they could have worked any time and how they willed.

CHAPTER 28

UNDER THE SAND

They rested till two o'clock, then, taking Longley with them, they landed with the bags and the digging began.

"This sand by the water is no good," said the wily Larry. "It's got the say in it and iv'ry change of weather the bags will sweat. Dig your sand up be them trees, sor, it's a bit further to carry the bags, but sure what's the matter about that?"

"Right," said James, leading them up to the spot they had chosen and taking off his coat. "Give me a spade."

Larry handed him a spade. They had only two spades. They did not want more, for it was not only a question of making a pit in the sand, but of filling the bags direct with every shovelful that was taken out. Sheila held a bag mouth open for James as he dug; Dicky did the same for Longley. Larry stood by with a pipe in his mouth, directing operations and fastening the mouths of the sacks one by one, as they were filled.

One might fancy the gold, in its great heap on the beach just above tide mark, making cynical reflections to itself on the matter.

It had never made them work harder than this. Since it had come together into one corporate body of treasure it had done many and cruel things, filling everyone in cognizance of it with anxiety, desire, suspicion and the worry that wealth alone can create, but it had never worked beings harder than this—couldn't.

After the first ten minutes, James, who had never done a stroke of real work before in his life, began to wish himself further. The business was not only back breaking, but niggling. Every spadeful had to go right into the mouth of the sack that Sheila held open and there was so little in a spadeful. They were heart-shaped Spanish spades, rather larger than the English sort, but not large enough. They ought to have brought shovels.

James found himself mentally repeating this fact during the first ten minutes or so; after that he was content to work without thinking. Filling sacks with sand for ballast is the meanest form of labour, or one of the meanest, far beneath the labour of filling them with coal. Coal is a necessity. You are helping the work of the world; sand ballast is only dead weight, a substitute for old metal, shingle, lumps of rock.

The gold, having condemned them to this coolie work, kept them at it. They had to get done by dark. If they did not get the whole job done that night, it would mean waiting all the next day idling and sweltering in the sun.

They couldn't talk, either, and tell each other this, nor could they complain too much else Longley would surely say to himself, "Why are they in such a hurry?" They began to hate Longley; before they had finished that evening, with their backs to a flaming sunset, they were hating the world.

Sheila, who had been taking turns with the spade, helped Larry to tie the mouth of the last sack, then, leaving the spades by the trees, they got the bags on board and stowed them, making three journeys in all.

Then they had supper.

If that had been the whole job they would have been tired out and ready for bed. As it was the prospect before them drove tiredness away. Nature has provided for nearly all contingencies and every man has in him a reserve of strength of which he knows nothing till the moment comes and the call. All the same, though they were not tired, they were strained in temper. Sitting there at the cabin table a very little would have started a quarrel.

It was not so much the work they had been doing as the work in prospect that produced this condition of nerves. The gold seemed to hold out before them an endless prospect of labour and difficulties. When they buried it they would have to get back and join the *Dulcinea*, sail for Havana, tell lies freely as to "information they had received from an old sailor as to treasure buried on Crab Cay"—Knight's "Cruise of the *Alerte*" had suggested this dodge—get permission to dig, return, dig up the stuff, bring it back to Havana. It seemed endless, all the things they had to do, and the fact had never expressed itself so clearly as it did tonight. Especially in the case of James.

Money was a necessity to Dicky and Sheila—it wasn't to James. He had let himself in for all this hard labour and tribulation and bother urged by the craving for adventure, that lies in every healthy soul, and the fascination of the gold; it would have been much better for him to have stayed out. He had no need for more riches and as for adventure he was surfeited. So he told himself tonight. But he said nothing.

After supper when Larry had cleared the things away they sat about in the cabin, Sheila knitting, the two others smoking, Crab Cay singing to them through the open skylight. They had no newspapers or books, only "Treasure Island" and the other treasure-hunting books which James had bought at Denny's in the Strand, and the very names were noxious to them; they had nothing to talk about, the gold barred every avenue of conversation; the gold, squatting like a demon on the beach a few hundred yards away—waiting to be buried.

And they could not bury it till Longley was asleep.

* * * *

It was ten o'clock when Larry appeared at the door of the cabin.

"Snorin'" said Larry in a half whisper.

Sheila put her knitting down and James put away his pipe. They followed Larry on deck, and into a night where a new moon was setting, a night of stars and warm wind and vague voices from the wave-beaten cay.

Yes. Longley was snoring. They could hear the sound as they dropped over into the boat which the push of the tide carried toward the beach almost without stroke of oar.

Then having landed and hauled the boat up they set to work.

The rope handles helped, but it was a hard business, as anyone who has carried weight over beach sand will know.

When the blocks were all up by the sand hole between the trees, Larry took one of the spades and Dicky the other. The hole had to be deepened and broadened, and, working in double shifts, Sheila helping, this business took them nearly an hour. They had finished it and the first pig of gold had been flung in when Sheila, turning, gave a little cry and clutched Dicky by the arm.

The beach edge and all round by the boat was moving.

"Crabs," said Dicky.

He had been half expecting them.

Larry, wiping his forehead with his arm, turned to look. He seemed quite unconcerned. He knew quite well that so long as a man wears boots and is able to stand on his feet crabs can't hurt him, even in thousands. They raised no disgust in his soul, and his only fear was that they would swarm up and fill the hole.

"They'll be thravelin'," said Larry, "same as they do over the banks be Acklin Island. Come on and get the stuff in and don't be mindin' thim."

In went another pig and they were raising the third when Sheila with a little catch in her voice said: "They are coming!"

They were. Upflowing like a tide just as they had done the night before, moving like a carpet being drawn across the sands, without haste yet unceasingly, clicking and rustling, advancing toward the working party but not at them. That, to Sheila, was the heart-catching part of the business. There was something blind and elemental in this moving host; there was no convergence toward the human beings; the far line was moving forward straight ahead like the rest and all seemed under the dominion, not of hunger or enmity or any passion known to man or beast—but of clockwork.

"I'll be attindin' to thim in a minit," said Larry, and in went the third pig, then the fourth and fifth. "Wan more," said Larry, and in went the sixth.

Then, spade in hand, and calling Dicky to help, he began to attend to the unholy host that was now scarce three yards away.

"They're changin' their feedin' ground from the lift to the right of the bank," said Larry, as he began smashing into them with the flat of the spade.

"Hit 'em with the flat, sor, same's I'm doin'. That'll l'arn you, you bastes, to keep clear of your bethers, that'll tache you manners—bad cess to you!"

He kept on till a mound of dead crabs three yards long formed a barrier to the pit, then the burial of the gold resumed while the last of the host—after having devoured the remains of their dead comrades—passed over the eastern beach and into the sea.

James felt sick. His lively imagination had been stirred. He saw himself alone on this place with no spade to defend himself with, alone, and naked for choice, and surrounded by that passionless, terrible host. Sheila felt almost as bad; it seemed to her as though something evil in the gold had drawn that monstrous horde from the sea. Then, when the last of the pigs was in and the last shovelful of sand on top of the pile, she turned toward the boat with a feeling of relief.

The moon had long set and the stars ruled the night as they rowed toward the *Baltrum*, dog-tired now, yet feeling a relief at having got rid at last and for a moment of the weight they had been carrying so long.

CHAPTER 29

JAMES GOES AWAY

Next morning, and before the sun was up, they hoisted the sail, took up the anchor and started north to rejoin the *Dulcinea*.

Though refreshed by sleep and though half their work was now accomplished, they showed no exuberance of spirit.

Up to this the gold had always been in front of them, not in the form of gold but in the form of Fortune and everything that gold can buy. Now in their minds, as in reality, it lay behind them, a dead weight of metal, a burden they would have to return and pick up again.

Everything unpleasant that they had experienced since leaving Hildersditch was associated with it and the crabs had finished the business, at least in the minds of Sheila and James.

Things had come to a head with James this morning. Sincerely and earnestly he wished that he had never come along on this job. He who had everything that the world could offer had left everything—for what? For cramped quarters, barely passable food, hard work and uneasy mind; Forsythe's words about the illegality of the business; the Bompard incident; the feeling that a gang of international crooks was somewhere in the dark background of things, and dread of the British government, all conspired to make the uneasy mind. He had bought the wrong stock; he wanted to sell out and he didn't know how.

How could he leave the expedition? How could he leave the others?

He could not tell. He only knew that wild horses could not drag him back to that infernal cay to take up that appalling burden again.

Had he really loved Sheila things would have been different, but, alas, James' capacity for love was not equal to his capacity for enjoyment. Discomfort and anxiety had extracted the arrow of Cupid—or maybe mortification had produced anæsthesia. Anyhow he no longer felt it.

About seven bells—half past eleven—the wind shivered in the mainsail, died, and the *Baltrum* lay becalmed, adrift on a dark-violet sea.

James, below in the cabin smoking cigarettes and meditating on matters, had just stuffed "Treasure Island" through a porthole when the others came below.

"Dead calm," said Dicky.

"And now I suppose we'll be drifting for days," said James. "Good heavens! In this old tub."

"Well, one can't help the wind," said Dicky.

"I know," said James, "but it's not the wind so much as the boat; as a matter of fact she's too small for long-distance cruising. What I propose is that we all shift on board the *Dulcinea* when we pick her up."

"And leave the *Baltrum*!" said Sheila.

"Yes. She can follow on after us to Havana."

"Larry will never leave her," said the girl. "He doesn't like big yachts."

"Well, he can stick in her and I'll lend him two more of my crew to help work her."

"He's no real good at navigating, and besides," said Sheila, "I can't leave him."

"Why on earth not?"

"Because I don't want to be separated from him. We've always been together in thick and thin."

"But he's only a servant."

"Oh, dear, no," said Sheila. "He's much more than that. Larry's just like part of myself, more—I'd sooner lose my right arm than Larry."

"Besides," said Dicky, "it doesn't seem to be playing the game to desert the old hooker. She's carried us through till now, and done it well."

"I don't ask you to desert her," said James. "I'm simply suggesting that we go on board my boat and that she follow us on to Havana. As a matter of fact I want to stretch my legs and feel I have head-room enough to stand up in, for a while—besides, there's the cooking. I'm not grumbling, goodness knows, but it does seem insane when we can have every comfort to stick on for no reason in cramped quarters like these."

"I can't leave Larry," said Sheila, taking up her knitting, "and even if he consented to come on board your boat I would not like to leave the *Baltrum*—it would be unlucky for one thing, and, besides, there's the feeling I have for her. She has been our home for so long. No. I don't want to leave her."

"I say," said Dicky, suddenly turning to James, "you aren't getting cold feet, are you?"

It was an unfortunate question, for it touched the truth.

"I've got nothing but a wish to do the right thing," said James, "and I think I've done it all along. If you feel I haven't, then there's an end to it."

"I didn't mean anything," said Dicky. "I didn't mean you hadn't done the right thing. I only asked—"

"I know. Well, to tell the truth now that the work is mostly done, if you care to carry on without me, I shan't grumble. I came in for the fun of the thing, not for any profit, and I'm ready to stand out without asking for a cent—helping you, of course, all I can at Havana."

"No," said Sheila, "you have got to have your share. Only for you, we would never have done anything. Why, the *Baltrum* is really yours. It was your money that really started the business, to say nothing of the help the *Dulcinea* has been. It's really your expedition—we are only partners."

James said nothing for a moment. His one ambition to get out of the affair, to be free of responsibility and find himself back in his own cozy corner of life was not furthered by this generous view of the matter.

He recognized that she was speaking the truth. He had bought the *Baltrum*, bought the stores, helped with his yacht and his men, helped with his own hands. If there was any bother he would be the person held chiefly responsible—and heavens! What bother there might be! Old Forsythe's words came back to him with their hint that the whole business was possibly within the circle of the criminal law, a business romantic, appealing to the adventurous spirit, yet possibly leading to the dock.

"Look here," said Dicky, a new idea striking him. "If you're fed up with the old hooker, why don't you go yourself in the *Dulcinea*, and leave us to work her? We can do it easily with Longley and join you at Havana."

"Yes," said Sheila, "why not?"

James lit another cigarette.

"I don't like the idea of leaving you people," said he. "You'd be short-handed—unless I could leave you a couple more men."

"Longley is enough," said Sheila, "and the distance is not far; yes, do go, if you feel cramped here. We're used to small boats and you are not."

James took a lungful of smoke. "I'll think about it," said he.

He had grown visibly brighter.

By supper time that evening, when the wind had taken charge again, he had fallen in with their views. He would go on to Havana in the *Dulcinea* and they could follow at their leisure. Next morning as they lay under the loom of Turtle Island and within two cable lengths of the yacht, Larry rowed him off.

"You'll find me at the Hotel Mercedes," said he, as he stood up in the boat for a last handshake. "Sure I can't leave you anything more in the way of stores?"

"No, we've lots," said Sheila.

"Or another man?"

"No, Longley is quite enough."

"Good-by."

"Luck."

They watched him go on board, the sails rising and shivering in the wind, the anchor coming aboard. Then, as the *Dulcinea* got way on her, Sheila ran up the flag and dipped it.

CHAPTER 30

WHAT HAPPENED TO JAMES

The first thing James did when he got on board was to get into a hot sea-water bath and lie in it.

The *Dulcinea* having rounded the land was on a due-west course, the auxiliary whacked up and the sails drawing to a light and variable wind.

He felt like a man escaped from prison. In years to come memory would no doubt recall the adventure robbed of its unpleasant details, showing only the blue of tropic seas, the sunlight on white sands, nights of stars and dawns miraculous in their beauty. Just now he saw nothing but the cabin of the ketch he had left behind, the discomfort, the bad cooking, the cramped deck and the ropes he had been condemned to handle.

Then he had a Martini, served by a steward in speckless white drill, finished dressing and was himself again.

Later in the day, after luncheon, the ordinary siesta which everyone takes at sea in the warm latitudes was a failure. Lying on the sofa of the saloon with the novel that refused to put him to sleep beside him on the floor, the figures of Dicky and Sheila appeared before James, mute, unreproachful, and yet—

Had he acted right in leaving them, in cutting himself loose from them, in determining not to return with them to that detestable crab-infested cay to take up again the burden of the gold?

Absolutely. He had done more than well by them, he had started them on the way to wealth, they could have the whole treasure for themselves. What more did they want?

And still, somehow or another, James did not feel quite easy in his mind. The something that had made him ask the question was still there.

After dinner he played cribbage with Captain Shortt, Morgan looking after the ship. The possibility of Morgan being a scoundrel or at least the possibility of his having been got at over the gold business did not trouble Mr. Corder much. He had never fully shared Dicky's and Sheila's suspicions about Morgan, still, tonight over the cigars and whisky and cards he put some questions to his skipper.

"You satisfied with Morgan?" asked James.

"Oh, Morgan—I reckon he's all right," said the other, contemplating the cards. "What makes you ask?"

"I only wanted to know if you thought him a trustable chap."

"There aren't any flies on Morgan," said the captain; "a bit slack sometimes, but trustable as Jimmy. Well! No, I couldn't work with a first officer I wouldn't lay my money on as being up and aboveboard. I'd sooner sail with a bishop. Had enough of that when I was Vanderbuilder's skipper. He'd a first that was all O. K. on the outside, and him smuggling cigars. Havre it was they laid their hands on him and we were held a week bailing him out and paying fines, to say nothing of the disgrace. And I got most of the kicking and Vanderbuilder didn't wear dancing pumps when he was on that business."

"You remember Morgan held you up at Tilbury when we were leaving? What about that?"

"Oh, that. I remember, and how you carpeted him here in this saloon. Well, you wouldn't if you'd known. He ought to have told you, but he's one of the sort that won't talk up for themselves. I only found it out by chance from him—his mother was sick, that's what held him. He had to get a nurse for her and was near broke at leaving her."

"The deuce!" said James. He felt sorry as a man feels who has done another an injustice, by accident; then he forgot Morgan and his mother and everything else about him, retiring at ten o'clock to a comfortable bed to sleep the sleep of the just, untroubled by fear of being roused to take his trick at the wheel.

It was not till they were entering the great harbour of Havana that unrest came back to James attended by seven devils worse than itself.

They berthed far out, not a great distance from the old anchorage of the *Maine* and the sight of the port authorities' boat raised a little flutter in his breast. Might it not possibly be that the dead Bompard or his friends— No. The port authorities came on board smiling and bowing, had drinks and cigars in the cabin and departed in their fussy launch. No, there was nothing to fear on the score of Bompard, the cables had had plenty of time to work in and the port authorities of Santa Cruz had known the destination of the *Dulcinea*.

But that fact did not alter the determination that had arisen in the mind of James, surrounding a plan.

He had got from the port officers a valuable piece of information. The *Tennessee* of the New York, Key West, Havana line was due to leave for New York at five o'clock that afternoon; being summer time there would be plenty of accommodation on board of her.

He turned from the rail, went below and turned to his writing table, rang for a whisky and soda, lit a cigar and took a sheet of paper headed "Y. *Dulcinea*. R. T. Y. C."

Then he began to write. He wrote two long letters, tore them up one after the other, and started again:

Yes, I have got cold feet, but I have a warm heart. Honestly I wasn't made for adventuring, and London is calling me. So, look here. I'm leaving the *Dulcinea* with orders to Shortt to be at your disposal. I'm telling Shortt to be on the lookout for you, and I'm inclosing a check in this on Gundermann's Bank, where I have a deposit—they deal with our firm. The check is made out in your name, Dicky. So cut and carry on and keep the whole of the boodle. When you are rich you can pay me back the amount in the check, so don't worry about using it. My address for a few weeks will be the Hotel Plaza, New York, after that, London. I hate dropping out of the business in a way, but the thing was beginning to get on my spine.

When you've hived the stuff, let me know and we'll have a dinner at the Savoy. That reminds me, the unfortunate Strutt is still kicking his heels in London. Heaven help us!

Your unfortunate uncle,

James.

Then he wrote a check for five thousand dollars, put it in the letter, addressed the envelope "R. Sebright, Esq.," and sealed it.

"And that's that," said James, lighting a new cigar.

A weight was gone from his mind. He had done the right thing.

He rang the bell, brought the captain down and explained matters.

"I'm going to New York by the *Tennessee*," said James. "Then to London. By the way, have a boat sent off to her and engage a stateroom. Mr. Sebright and the *Baltrum* will be up here tomorrow or next day. I want you to give him this letter. You are to put the yacht at his disposal and hang on here as long as he wants, then bring her on up to New York. You can cable me how things go. You have money enough for the ship; if you are short, you can draw on Gundermann's up to five thousand dollars. I'm going ashore to see them and give directions."

He came up with the captain, who called a quartermaster to get the pinnace ready, and as they stood under the awning looking toward the distant town and the shipping, fluttering to the warm breeze the flags of all nations, the deep moist bellow of a siren made them turn to where, coming up from the half-mile channel entrance, a steamer showed ghost grey in the hot and misty blue. She was the *Seville* of the Cadiz, Teneriffe, Havana line; a four-thousand-tonner painted lavender-white like the Union Castle boats, and with two bright yellow funnels.

She came along, her wash giving the *Dulcinea* a slight roll as she drew away toward the far-distant quays across the sparkling blue of the vast harbour.

Had the *Seville* been made of glass, James, watching, might have seen in her smoke room four card players, four cigar merchants of Havana, utterly undisturbed by their entrance into port and the near proximity of their wives and families; three dried-up Spaniards and a big, black-bearded, jovial Frenchman—Bompard, or his living twin image!

CHAPTER 31

THE INDIGNATION OF CAPTAIN SHORTT

Two days later the little *Baltrum*, coming along up the Bahama passage, raised Cabo Batabano, the old Bowline Head of the pirates, while in the heat haze the shores of Cuba showed like land dissolving into sea, like sea rising into the form of land. In the summer on this coast the most astonishing effects of mirage are seen, sometimes above the land, sometimes above the sea line. It is said that Rodriguez saw Dundonald's ships in the sky, pursuing him and so escaped, making round the eastern coast to the Isla de Pinos; while, sometimes, Tampico, as if tired of its position on the mainland, rises like the flying island of Swift and floats above the Cuban shore, a phantom town in the flower-blue sky. But this morning there was nothing but coast.

James had left them a book of sailing directions, though the way in was easy enough, for the channel leading into Havana harbour has neither bar nor obstruction, is three hundred and fifty yards wide and runs from eight to ten fathoms deep on its natural bed.

At nine o'clock, or a little after, Sheila through the haze ahead saw the fortifications of the harbour mouth, beyond which lay the blue hills that seemed to float in air.

The breeze held steady and warm, a continuous breathing from the east of north, and the *Baltrum* could have steered herself as they came through the passage, the vast harbour unfolding before them and the city disclosing itself as though at the opening of a magician's hand.

Yes, there lay Havana, one of the legend cities that so few Europeans have ever seen or ever will see.

Havana of the pirate days and the plate ships, of Hawke and Morgan, Dundonald and Albemarle. Havana with its spires and streets, its *alamadas*, its wharfs, where the deep-sea ships can come right alongside, and over all the flicker of bunting and over all the lights of Cuba, luminous, consuming and, at midday, tremendous.

"There's the *Dulcinea*," cried Dicky suddenly.

"So she is," said Sheila, who was at the wheel. "Captain Shortt told me before we left Turtle Island he'd anchor not far from the opening and we could take our position two cable lengths south of his moorings and we'd be safe. Stand by, Larry."

"Keep her as she's goin'," said Larry, who was in the bow. "Mr. Sebright, will you give me a hand wid the cable. Stidy—stidy, Miss Shaila. Port a stroke—as you are now."

He stood in the bow as the *Baltrum*, the wind spilling from her sails, came crawling toward the *Dulcinea*, passed her and dropped the anchor in fifteen-fathom water, two cable lengths to southward of her moorings, and two cable lengths north of the Alacante gas buoy.

Sheila, leaving the wheel, came to the port rail and looked at the *Dulcinea*. A fellow in a bos'n's chair was doing some paint work over the stern, washing was fluttering on a line and by the rail an old quartermaster was leaning and chewing something, possibly tobacco.

Sheila could see his jaws working; there was no one else on deck and as she took in the whole ship and situation, she said to herself: "James is not on board."

The unerring instinct of the sailor told her that the *Dulcinea* was without her boss. "The owner has gone away and left me," was written in the attitude of the man at the rail, the deserted decks and the general slackness; she was a yacht out of commission for the moment, and looked it through every inch of her.

"Maybe Mr. Corder is ashore," thought Sheila, as she stood by her companion while the *Baltrum* swung to her moorings.

"Don't see James," said Dicky.

"Nor I," said the girl. "Maybe he's ashore. Ah, there's Captain Shortt."

Word had evidently gone below that the *Baltrum* was in, for the *Dulcinea's* skipper came straight to the port rail, waved his hand, and then signalled them to come on board.

Larry rowed them over and Shortt, having received them as they came up the side, invited them down below.

"Mr. Corder is not here," said he, when they were in the cabin. "He's left for N'York."

"Left for New York!" said Sheila in astonishment.

"Left for N'York," said Shortt, going to a desk and taking a letter from it. "He asked me to give you this and told me to put the yacht at your disposal."

Dicky opened the envelope and took out the letter which he read with Sheila peeping over his shoulder.

Shortt watched them. Shortt was a man with a temper; an old yacht captain, he had banked enough money to live on, and that fact gave him a sense of independence often expressed in freedom of speech, even to James.

He had never looked with much favour on the *Baltrum* crowd; it was a standing mystery to him why James had cast in his lot with them. He was frankly ashamed of the *Baltrum* as a cruising partner, and her crew did not appeal to him, neither Sheila in her old guernsey, nor Dicky nor Larry, especially Larry.

A book could be written on the subliminal disturbances set up between Larry, who looked down on yachtmen from fisherman heights, and the skipper of the *Dulcinea*, who looked down on Larry from the height of the *Dulcinea's* deck.

Dicky read the letter through without comment.

"When did he go?" asked Dicky, looking up as he finished.

"Two days ago," said Shortt. "Left the day we came in; took the *Tennessee* for N'York."

"What's the *Tennessee*?" asked Sheila, half stunned by the news in the letter, and not quite comprehending.

"Well, she was a ship when I last saw her," said the skipper, ruffled by the faces of the two people before him, and their manner.

If the *Baltrum* had been even a decent fishing yacht her small tonnage would not have mattered so much, but to think that this pair off that mud barge had established a hold on James and were evidently now disapproving of his actions was too much for Shortt.

"Well, when you next see her, or when you next see your master," blazed out Dicky, "you can tell him my opinion of him." He tore the letter in two and handed the check back to Shortt, who took it. "You can tell him with my compliments he's a quitter."

"Now then," said Shortt, folding the check carefully in three and looking at Dicky with his dark, steadfast beady eyes, honest eyes with a spark in them just then, "if you want to call him down, do it yourself. I'm not going to take any of your messages." He began to warm. "No, if you want to call him down do it yourself, there's a cable form and his address is the Hotel Plaza, N'York. Do it yourself. I don't know who you are, I only knew he took up with you and chose to cruise in your company. Seems to me he's tired of it. If he'd taken or asked for my advice, he never would—no. I call it dubious, the whole business and," finished the skipper, "if he asked for or'd listen to my advice, he'd have no more truck with you. That's straight."

"Perhaps you will remember that there is a lady listening to you," said Dicky, blazing with wrath, yet not knowing how to meet these veiled allusions.

"I wasn't saying nothing a lady couldn't listen to," said the skipper stolidly, putting the check carefully away in a drawer of the desk. "I'm only saying what I'd say to Mr. Corder and that is, keep clear of doubtful company. I'm not saying there's anything wrong with you, and I'm not saying you're right. That's the bother—I don't know. You may be highly respectable parties for all I know, but there's one question would clear it, if you have the face to answer it, and that question is—what's the grip you have on Mr. Corder? Come now, face to face and man to man, give us the facts. I get a telegram from him at Tilbury to put to sea at once and I find him at Hildersditch Pool on board of you. Out we go to sea as if someone was after us, strike Teneriffe, lay up a few days and then out we go to sea again, destination Havana, changed to Turtle Island. Drop the hook at Turtle Island and off you go, you and him, he comes back and on board, tells me to whack up for Havana. Gets here and off he goes to N'York on board the mail boat, leaving you command of the yacht—looked like as if he wanted to get shut of you. Well, what do you say? Man to man, what have you got to say on the whole of this business?"

"Nothing," said Dicky. "I can't tell you anything at all about it, except that it's a secret."

"Oh, a secret, is it?" said the captain.

"Yes."

"Well, I ain't Mr. Corder's parents and guardians, but if I was I'd be asking you these questions through Pinkertons. Pinkertons—you know Pinkertons?"

"I know this," said Dicky, "if there wasn't a lady present, I'd—Oh, come on, Sheila."

He followed her on deck, Shortt coming after in the fashion of a householder escorting dubious callers to the door.

Larry was waiting with the boat and they got in.

"You haven't sent that message to Mr. Corder," said Shortt, leaning over.

"No," replied Dicky, "you can send it yourself if you want to."

"I will," said the other, "and if you've done with Ben Longley, I'd be glad to have him back this afternoon."

"You can have him back at once."

"That's all the better," said Shortt, and the boat drew away.

"Larry," said Dicky, as they came on board the *Baltrum*, "tell Longley to get his bag and go back to the yacht." Then when he was below again with Sheila, he sat down at the table and lighting a cigarette fell into a reverie—or seemed to. Clotted anger is a better definition of his state of mind.

Yes, Shortt was right. The whole business, the command they had got over James, the way he had gone off leaving everything to them, the use of his yacht, that big check—was fishy, and yet he could not explain. The bother was that James' past evidently contained purple patches known to Shortt. That yeggmen and rogues had had dealings with James, not to the advantage of the latter, was presumable.

The *Baltrum* was a dirty old boat; he himself and Sheila and Larry did not look much in a social way, and yet they had captured the butterfly James, the haunter of clubhouses and great hotels, reduced him to their environment and held him to it for over a month. Then he had run away from them, leaving them money. That's all Shortt knew, and a little knowledge of this sort is a dangerous thing.

Dicky could not tell of the treasure. Leaving other things aside, Shortt wouldn't have believed the story, at least in his present mood.

"Don't worry," said Sheila, who knew exactly how the other was feeling. "Let him think what he likes, but I must say I'm more than disappointed in James. It was such a *weak* thing to do."

"It was worse than that. It was dishonourable to go off and leave us stuck like this."

"No, it was only weak," said Sheila. "He didn't think we'd be stuck. He thought with that money he left us and the use of his yacht and crew it would be all plain sailing for us. You see, it never entered his head that Captain Shortt might think the whole thing odd and insult us as he's done—and now," finished Sheila, "we'll be without Longley; just you and Larry and me, and we can't talk Spanish, at least only a little—so we've got our work cut out before us."

"Never mind," said Dicky. "We'll pull things through. I have nearly the whole of that four hundred pounds I drew from the bank so we aren't rushed for money." He lit another cigarette, and leaning his arms on the table went on:

"There's getting on for a ton of gold on that blessed sand bank and here we are in Havana harbour, the only people with knowledge of it—"

"Heavens!" cried Sheila.

"What?"

"Morgan—I'd forgotten him."

"Well, Morgan can't hurt us even if he's crooked, and I very much doubt if there's anything wrong with him. I don't think there was time for anyone to have got at him before the yacht left Tilbury, even though he was late in coming on board. I think it was James' imagination a good deal. I know Larry saw him poking about below and he looked at the ballast—well, he's a sailor and he'd be interested in this old hearse. No, I've got a feeling that we've all been imagining things into the situation—the wicked flee when no man pursueth, you know. You see what it has done for James, making him bolt like that. Don't let us get rattled in the same way, or we'll spoil everything."

Sheila said nothing for a moment. Her woman's mind, a measuring tape for character, had never been under any delusion about James. Then after a moment she said:

"I don't like Morgan. I may be wrong, and there it is, but I think you are right about our imagining too much. I liked Monsieur Bompard at first sight, then I began to suspect and imagine things about him and worried James. I think I was wrong. People you like at first sight generally are to be trusted. It was the wretched gold that made me suspicious of everyone. Well, what we have to do now is to forget everything but the work before us, and the first thing to do is to get a concession or permit to dig for treasure at Crab Cay. How are we to get it, and where are we to apply for it?"

"I'm blest if I know," said Dicky. "James talked of it as if he knew all about it, and now we're cut off from him and cut off from the yacht."

Sheila, sitting at the opposite side of the table, rested her brow on her hands. Yes, James had talked glibly of concessions and permits as though he knew all about them; possibly he did, probably he didn't. There was one thing certain, he knew Havana, and his position as a millionaire and owner of a fine yacht would have helped them a lot. But there was not the least use in grumbling; they were up against it with only their own wits to help them. Then at last she spoke:

"I don't know. If we go straight to the authorities here and ask for a concession to dig, we'll surely have to give them something, either a share in the business or money down—people don't give things for nothing. Then, even if we get the concession, are we sure they will keep their word? You know what foreigners are and we have no position or standing and the poor old *Baltrum* isn't a certificate of respectability. You are right. James has let us down—he didn't mean to, I'm sure; he didn't think—oh, we've made a mistake!"

"How?"

"We shouldn't have quarreled with Captain Shortt. I know you couldn't help it, he was so insulting, but he wouldn't have been if he'd known all; we should have told him."

"Well, it's done," said Dicky.

"Yes, and we can't make up with him now."

"I'd sooner cut my hand off—"

"I know—all the same if we could, I'd do it. But we can't. He had or-ders to put the yacht at our disposal and that evidently irritated him, then we definitely refused the yacht, refused James' check, refused to have anything to do with him, told him James was a quitter—and there we are. Captain Shortt dislikes us. He is an obstinate, pigheaded man and he's in a strong position—that's all."

"It's a most awful mix-up," said Dicky. "Seems as if fate or something was working against us—and still we've got on all right up to now. We've done a lot."

"Yes, we have," said the girl, her spirit suddenly lighting up, "and we'll do more. I know it—we'll come out all right yet. I *feel* it, and we'll just go ahead and trust in Providence. There's a huge fortune to be saved with all our future tied to it—where on earth would we be, you and I and Larry, if we failed?"

"We won't."

"No, we won't. The thing we have to do now is to go ashore; we can stay at that hotel James told us of—the Mercedes—and look about us and see how the ground lies. I—I—" She stopped. Something had risen in her mind. If she had been a man she would have said, "Oh, damn James!" Maybe she said it to herself in the moment when she recognized that this rotten James had let them down again.

With James everything would have been all right; staying at a hotel they would have been a "party." How could she stay alone with Dicky at a hotel, and without Larry?

Sheila was old-fashioned—but sensible.

"I'll just have to go as your sister," said she.

"Of course," said Dicky. Before he could say anything more, Larry's voice came, answering voices from overside. It was the port authorities.

CHAPTER 32

CIGAR TOWN

Sheila who was used to dealing with port officials did the business with them, and the *Baltrum* having received pratique, they departed after expressing their surprise that such a small boat should have come all the way from Teneriffe; but it was an English boat and the mad English had a reputation for doing things of this sort for fun.

"Damn' onion peddlers," said Larry, as he watched the launch go off rocking on the blue. "Them and their coffeepot. What's your orders, now, Miss Shaila?"

Sheila gave orders for the boat to be ready to take them ashore and an hour later, having packed some things, they got in and started.

Larry rowed them. Longley had gone back to the *Dulcinea*, so Larry would be alone on board. Sheila, before starting, had given him the whole position in a few words and arranged that Dicky should return on board next morning to see that everything was going on all right.

Landing them at the boat slip by the Santa Anna wharf he carried their luggage up to a taxi cab in the Callé San Pedro and received their last instructions.

"Larry," said Sheila, who had suddenly remembered James' capacity for possibilities, "you'd better row alongside the *Dulcinea* and give them an address here in case Mr. Corder should send any cable or message—there's never any knowing what he might do. Tell them the Hotel Mercedes."

"I'll tell them, miss," said Larry, and the taxi started.

Havana dies every day about half past eleven and revives about five—at least upper-class Havana; the negroes, the Chinese, and the lower-class natives don't seem to mind the heat. It was beginning to revive now, and Sheila, as they drove, was filled with wonder at the size of the place.

Even in the 'eighties Havana was a fine city. Now, modernized, Americanized and festooned at night with electrics blazing against the stars, Havana is a city to be seen.

You can smell it also.

Out of the Callé San Pedro by way of the great tobacco factory fronting the sea and passing the cathedral the cab drove into the courtyard of a palatial hotel. A man in white with a blue band on his cap and the word "Mercedes" on it was opening the door and inviting them to descend; behind him the white-marble steps led to the hotel entrance, which showed vaguely sketched against the cool interior the fronds of palms in pots and tree ferns in tubs.

It was like one of the hotels you see sometimes on the stage in those spectacular productions so dear to the heart of Mr. Cochran and the London public. It didn't seem quite real, the ladies of the chorus seemed just to have vacated those steps down which at any moment Mr. Berry might come to the delight of a full house.

Sheila got out, Dicky paid the driver in English money and a second hall porter, a pure-black negro, took their luggage.

Now this luggage, a suit case of Dicky's, and a big attaché case, very much battered, belonging to Sheila, was quite in keeping with the *Baltrum* and their expedition, up to this; but it was not in keeping with the Mercedes and it came to Sheila as she followed the luggage up the steps that their "wardrobes," to use a good old term, were not in keeping either. She was wearing a white drill coat and skirt, bought at Teneriffe, and a Panama that had cost twelve pesetas; Dicky was to match as far as material and colour went, but "ready made" was written on his garments as on Sheila's.

No, they did not match their surroundings; but the hotel did not mind; a languid woman with marcelled hair, in a plate-glass office with an electric fan above her and a great block of ice near by diffusing its coolness as a flower its scent, received them without the lift of an eyebrow, presented them with the hotel register to sign, allocated their rooms and handed them over to a chocolate-coloured boy who led them to the lift.

"I say," said Dicky, as they sat half an hour later in the lounge having tea, "what's your room like?"

"Gorgeous."

"Mine's got a marble bathroom off it and what the bill will be, Heaven only knows. Well, there's no use bothering, let's enjoy ourselves while we can."

He helped himself to cakes, and Sheila, as she sipped her tea, looked about her. This sudden change from Crab Cay and the cabin of the *Baltrum* to supercivilization was the strangest experience of her life; it was the off season in Havana, but the Mercedes is never empty. People from Matanzas and Santiago, cigar and sugar plutocrats, American business men and South Americans from Brazil and the River Plate came here in summer as in winter, bringing their wives and children with them. There were three or four family groups in the lounge; women elegantly dressed and covered with jewels, men manicured and barbered; the sons of Mary served by the sons of Martha in the form of negro attendants bearing aloft trays of coloured drinks, coffee, cigars, and cigarettes; while from the dance room beyond the inevitable band made itself heard, a gadfly voice floating above the palms and flowers, the cigarette smoke and the atmosphere of ease and wealth.

It was strange.

Sheila felt lost. Crab Cay and Turtle Island seemed homely and warm to the heart compared with this. These men and women belonged to another creation and these surroundings to another world of which she knew next to nothing. It was as though the gold were showing a new phase of itself, something quite new, something that repelled her. For the faces of these men and women, their forms and attitudes, their voices and laughter, their setting and surroundings—the whole show repelled her, she who had been always used to the fresh air and the sea and the simple things of life and the work which is the soul's salvation.

She felt lost in a world of which she knew nothing, a world that filled her with a vague dislike.

"Let's enjoy ourselves while we can," had said Dicky.

She finished her tea without showing what was in her mind, then she suddenly turned to her companion:

"Dicky," said she, "I don't like this place. I wish we hadn't come. I don't like the look of these people."

"Why, what's wrong with them?" asked Dicky, surprised by the sudden change in her manner and the conviction in her voice.

"I don't know—nothing. Only they make me feel like a lost dog without a single friend in the world. They are different from us—let's go away. Couldn't we get some quiet hotel, or rooms or something, or go back to the boat?"

"Well, we landed to poke about and see how the land lies and try and get help. I don't see the good of going back to the boat."

"We won't get any help in this place."

"Well, maybe not, but we can go out and prospect. I've just had an idea that we might try the British consul—just sound him about the prospect of getting a concession. Anyhow, there's no use going to a second-class hotel; it costs as much in the long run and as for rooms—goodness, how are we to look for them?"

"All right," said Sheila. "Now we are here, we had better stay, perhaps. Shall we go to the consul now?"

"Yes, if you're ready."

Sheila was just about to rise when a voice made her turn her head. The joyous, boisterous voice of a big, burly, black-bearded man. He was passing them toward the dance room; he was accompanied by two pretty young girls in white-muslin frocks, evidently his daughters, for he had an arm flung about each of them. The gentleman passed without seeing them. He was the dead Bompard.

"*Dicky!*" said Sheila.

"Good heavens above!" said Dicky.

"Bompard!"

"Unless it's a mistake!"

"Oh, no," said Sheila, with a little laugh. "It's not a mistake. It's impossible there could be two like him—absolutely."

"But how's he here?"

"Mail boat, I suppose. You remember he said he had business here and I remember him saying something about his wife and children—those are the children I expect—or some of them. You'd better find him and speak to him. I felt somehow or another that James was making a fool of himself."

Dicky looked uneasy.

"To tell the truth," said he, "after leaving him like that—the way we did, you know—running off—"

"Yes, it makes it difficult; all the same it's better to grasp the nettle; he's staying here and it has to be done sooner or later."

Dicky jumped to his feet.

"Wait for me," he said. He crossed the hall and disappeared at the opening leading to the dance room.

Then Sheila waited.

An attendant came and took away the tea things and placed an ash tray and matches on the table; five minutes passed and then in the archway appeared two figures, Bompard's and Dicky's; the hand of Bompard was on the shoulder of his companion and they were talking and laughing and evidently the best of friends.

"Ah, Miss Dennis," cried Bompard, advancing with hand outspread. "What a pleasure!" He meant it, and as Sheila took his hand the full measure of her stupidity in ever suspecting this man came to her as a shock.

"And the good Mr. Cordare, where is he?" asked Bompard.

Sheila explained that the good Mr. Corder had been called to New York on business, and Bompard, breaking off the conversation and rushing back to the dance room, returned with Madame Bompard, a stout, comfortable-looking Arlésienne, and the two daughters. They didn't speak English, but Bompard made up for the deficiency, and after ten minutes' talk Sheila and Dicky bade the Bompard family au revoir and left the lounge.

Outside, in the Callé Juanita, Sheila turned to the other.

"But, Dicky! Didn't he say anything to you about the poisoning and you leaving him?"

"Oh, lots," said Dicky, "and he apologized for not having come to see us off. You see, he wasn't poisoned; he thinks it was island fever or the salad that gave him the most frightful cramp in his bread basket. You know these southern French shout like anything if anything's the matter with them. Well, before a doctor could get to him the *fonda* people had cured him with brandy and they gave him so much that he slept there all night, and so missed seeing us go. He never suspects that we suspected him of being a crook out to do us in. It was all that damn' fool James—excuse me."

"Don't mention it. I quite agree with you. Well, I'm glad. He has made me feel quite different."

"How?"

"I can't tell you how—he's just so jolly and so friendly and so pleasant to meet that he has made the whole place seem different."

It was a fact, there was a warmth and radiance about Bompard, a human kindliness better than wine to her flagging soul; he was just the same as at Teneriffe, but at Teneriffe she was not feeling lonely, dispirited and lost in a strange land.

Dicky had got the British consul's address from Bompard and they called at the consulate but found the office closed for the day.

"We'll call in the morning," said Dicky. Then they dined at a café in the Plaza Bombita, went to a cinema and returned to the hotel at ten o'clock.

Dicky, sitting by his open window and smoking a pipe before going to bed, watched the great sultry southern moon as she stood casting a rosy light on the white house walls opposite.

Something new had come to him with the adventures of the day, something new and strange and heart stirring—Sheila.

Up to this she had been a jolly companion, a sister, almost a brother, but now, away from the *Baltrum*, thrown together and with her entirely depending on him, Sheila was another person.

His heart went out to her. He saw her as she was; steadfast and brave, fearless, patient as she had always been, but with an added charm, a mysterious something that turned her at a stroke from a woman to the only woman in the world.

Then he put out his pipe and went to bed and tried to put her out of his mind. He had no right to think of her, no right to think of anything till the great business in hand was through, and yet she returned in pictures that dissolved at last and faded in the darkness of sleep.

CHAPTER 33

APPLEJOHN

They rise early in Havana. At half past eight Sheila and Dicky had finished breakfast and were out looking at the shops; the fruit shops showing in their cool and dark interiors banana bunches like great candelabra, custard apples—*pommes cannelles*—christophines, monkey oranges and limes green and yellow; egg plants and pommes d'Haiti; the fish shops with their great blocks of ice and *such* fish, fresh in from the sea; perroquets black and red; sardines like mounds of silver; tunny, and pink-and-orange-tinted bourles—all colours like the jewelled fish of the "Arabian Nights," all shapes, all sizes. They inspected the cathedral and opera house, lost their way and found themselves at the railway station of the Eastern Line. Here they went in to inquire their way back to the British consulate, and, as they were coming out again, almost ran into the arms of Captain Shortt.

Shortt looked in a flurry and was carrying an attaché case hastily packed, to judge from the fact that part of a sock was exuding.

He was about to pass them when, suddenly putting himself in irons, so to speak, he came up all standing, dropped the attaché case and took a paper from his pocket.

"Here," said Shortt, "what do you make of this? Do *you* know anything of this; have you heard from him?" He handed the paper to Dicky. It was a telegram.

"Come at once to Santiago by rail. Meet you at the station. Urgent. Corder, Pinos."

"Where's Santiago?" asked Dicky, handing the thing to Sheila, who read it.

"Other end of the island, hundreds of miles. But what I want to know is what he's doing there, and what mess he's got into and why did he send the message from Pinos? Why, he left in the *Tennessee* for N'York and unless he left her at Key West and came back in some other boat, how did he get to Pinos? It's above here, first station out. He must have been through Havana. What's the sense of it?"

"I don't know," said Dicky. "I've heard nothing from him, and what's more I don't want to. You'd better go and see him. It won't take you long."

"Long!" cried the captain, "it's days, what with these island railways and the lazy scamps that run them." He put the telegram back in his pocket, furiously caught up his baggage and bolted into the station.

"Well, he's got into trouble, anyhow," said Dicky, "or else why should he be wiring for Shortt? He can't be in prison, else he wouldn't say he'd meet Shortt at the railway station. What on earth can he have been doing?"

"I don't know—but there's one thing I do know. Captain Shortt suspects that we have something to do with the business—I could tell it by his manner. He thinks maybe we are shady characters. Dicky, isn't it horrid the way this gold seems to cast suspicion around it on everyone who has anything to do with it? We suspected Morgan, who seems all right, and Monsieur Bompard. Captain Shortt suspects us—even though he knows nothing of the gold. It's just as if the thing had some wicked power—and not only that, it began by killing two men—"

"Don't," said Dicky. "Let's forget all that and keep clear of superstition about it. We have trouble enough without imagining things. It's just as if we had an elephant we had to keep hidden and to sell without anyone putting in a claim for it. Well, we'll do it or die. Here's the consulate."

They went in.

The consul was away on holiday. His substitute received them, a thin young man with sandy hair, horn spectacles; a Canadian with an American accent and his ear to a telephone.

He received them out of the corner of his eye and without removing the instrument from his ear asked them to be seated, finished his conversation and then wheeled round in his seat.

"I've come to see you—" said Dicky. Then he paused. He did not know how to begin.

"Just to ask a question," said Sheila.

"Yes, that's really it, but before I begin, I take it that anything I say will be considered as a matter of the very strictest confidence?"

"Yes," said the substitute—Applejohn was his name.

"You can confide what you want as long as it's not contraband, murder or petty larceny. Have a cigarette?"

"Thanks. No, it's just a question of buried treasure."

"Oh, my," said Applejohn. "Well, I'm listening."

"It's just this. If I knew where treasure was buried, let's say on the coast of Cuba, could I get a permit to dig for it?"

"Well, I shouldn't wonder," said Applejohn.

"You don't know for certain?"

"The only certain thing I know about buried treasure is that the chaps who go digging for it never bother about permits, for there aren't any chaps that go. It's a frost. It used to be one of the industries here, but it's bust. It's like the Spanish prisoner business—even the suckers have dropped off, and if you offered any man in Havana streets the finest treasure chart stained with blood and all for two pesetas, he'd turn you down—wouldn't look at it, not if you had black whiskers and rings in your ears. If anyone has been trying to sell you stock in this gamble, don't buy; let them keep it. There never was such a thing and never will be and the proof is the men who've been stung. Now I'll prove it to you. I'm going to ring up Bostock, the sugar man. He's the archbishop of all speculators. Yankee, knows every possibility in everything and what he refuses isn't good enough for you to touch."

He took the phone and rang up Bostock.

"Are you there? It's me, Applejohn, speaking. Yes, quite well, thanks. See here. I've just heard of a big thing and believe it's real: treasure buried right on the coast. Which coast? This coast, Cuba. Are you there—are you there?"

Applejohn hung up the receiver. "He's rung me off," said Applejohn. "Now you see how buried treasure stands in Havana."

"Well, it's this way," said Dicky. "No one has been trying to sell us a location. The fact is I got one in England from an old sailor and I believe the thing is all right, and that if we dig we'll find the stuff. What I've really come to ask you is whether, suppose I get a permit to dig and the stuff's there and I bring it to Havana, the authorities would try to nab it—or put up a lot of difficulties."

"That I can't tell you," said Applejohn, "simply because I don't know. But this I *can* tell you, that if you brought a treasure ship into Havana harbour with real Simon-pure treasure on board, in one week, or maybe two, the streets of Havana wouldn't be passable."

"How?"

"With the crowd. Every root hog from Key West to Klondike would be on the job. Your name would be in every paper in the world. No. I should think the authorities oughtn't to put up any difficulties. They'd more likely give you a medal, for it would be the making of Cuba."

"I hadn't thought of that," said Dicky.

He hadn't. It was the bother with this expedition devised so hastily, rushed through in such a hurry, that new and unthought-of things were always turning up barriers or pitfalls right in their course.

Dicky had never thought of the tremendous publicity the bringing of the gold openly to Havana would give them. James had never thought of it, nor had Sheila. It had seemed to them quite simple, once the permit was obtained, to bring the gold in, take it to a bank and deposit it. They had forgotten publicity and the fact that never yet has buried treasure been discovered except in a story book, and the use the press would make of this fact. Their photographs would be in every paper, and photographs of the *Baltrum*, and the story of her voyage. Hildersditch would read of it, so would London and Paris and Berlin, for the story would be of universal interest. Then what questions might not arise? In the blaze of this fearful limelight how would they stand before an inquiring world?

If the MacAdam crowd existed in reality as well as in their imaginations, would they take their defeat in silence? One question anonymously put to the British government—what might it not lead to?

They had never thought of all this; indeed, now, seated in the presence of the wise and wily Applejohn, it was only beginning to dawn on Dicky.

"Of course," said Applejohn, "if you've got some location you're set on exploring, I could go into the matter for you and see about the concession business, but I frankly tell you, you will be wasting your time—and money."

"Thanks," said Dicky. "I'll think over it."

Then they said good-bye and departed.

Out in the street he explained to Sheila what was in his mind. It was not difficult, for the fact had begun to dawn on her too.

"It's just this," said Dicky. "We can't make the thing public like that because, as a matter of fact, the thing is crooked. We're crooks, Sheila. I know there's not a respectable man in London who would not have gone into the business just as we did, there's not a man who would really blame us in his heart for doing what we have done. All the same, we are outside the law. We *ought* to have gone to the Board of Trade and told them, and had the stuff taken away from us, but we couldn't. No man could. Even old Forsythe— and he's the law itself—couldn't. He gave us the tip about burying it and digging it up again, and if he hadn't been tied to his rotten old business he'd have been with us. The Archbishop of Canterbury himself couldn't have resisted it. The stuff belonged to no one, it fell into our hands—no man could have thrown it away. Still, there you are—we're crooks and we'll have to go on being crooks, and what we want is someone to help us who is in our way of business; a fence, some rich man with ways and means of disposing of the stuff. I wonder would that man Bostock be any good? We'd have to tell him the whole story."

Sheila said nothing for a moment. The fact that she was called a crook did not worry her in the least. They say women have no morals in this way. Sheila had plenty of morals, but she had common sense; the gold that belonged to chance, that had been hidden and camouflaged by unknown people, that had been put into their hands by chance, was a gift impossible to throw away without rupturing every instinct that has made man an adventurous, battling and acquisitive creature. Angels might have gone to the Board of Trade and handed over to authority what luck had bestowed and what selfishness sprang to guard and keep. Men couldn't. If the law was against them, it couldn't be helped. They must risk it.

Then she spoke.

"We don't know anything about this Mr. Bostock. We only know that, considering the way he is set against treasure digging, we would have to tell him the whole story in every detail—put ourselves completely in his hands."

"That's true."

"I think what you were saying about crooks and all that is nonsense. The law mightn't approve of what we have done, but I'm sure there are plenty of quite honest men who would help us if we knew where to find them. Why not try Monsieur Bompard? He knows everyone here and I'm sure he's to be trusted—anyhow, I'd trust him, though I distrusted him once."

"Bompard?" said Dicky meditatively.

"Yes, he's good—I feel it—and he's clever too, and I think he likes us."

"Well, we might do worse. Anyhow, it would be doing something."

"You must tell him everything. It's a risk, but I don't think it's much of a risk."

"We've got to take risks," said Dicky. "The whole thing has been one long risk. I think you're right. Let's get done with the thing. What's the time? Half past eleven. Well, he'll be at the hotel most likely, déjeuner is at twelve."

They turned their steps to the hotel.

As they took their way along the Callé del Sol, Sheila, who had been silent for a moment, suddenly spoke.

"I don't know why it is," said she, "but I'm uneasy about James—I mean about that telegram. Why has James gone to Santiago? Why has he sent for Captain Shortt? Why has he not sent us a word? He said in his letter he was going to New York. I don't know, but I feel uneasy."

"Maybe there'll be a message from him at the hotel," said Dicky.

CHAPTER 34

THE REAL BOMPARD

But there was no message, no telegram on the board, or word from the attendants.

Déjeuner was served in the long room overlooking the courtyard, facing north and protected from the sun. They saw Bompard and his wife and family at the far end. They did not approach his table, but took their seats near the door so as to catch him when he went out.

"There's no use bothering him when he's eating," said Sheila. "When he's going out catch him and take him somewhere quiet. I'll wait in the lounge for you; and, oh, Dicky, be careful that no one's listening. I wouldn't give him any exact details as to the place where it is, but there's no harm in telling him everything else."

"You can trust me," said Dicky.

The meal seemed interminable, at least the meal of the Bompards, but at last it was over and the party made for the door, Madame leading. Then Dicky rose, captured the big man and passed out with him, Bompard's hand upon his shoulder.

The smoke room only contained one old gentleman, a Spaniard, yellow as ivory, seated in an easy-chair, with a red handkerchief bound round his forehead and a cigarette between his lips; some tobacco planter in from the country, a quaint survival of the old régime such as may still be met with in Havana or Matanzas.

Leading Bompard to a quiet corner and accepting a cigar, Dicky plunged right into the business on hand.

He spoke in English, slowly, arranging his facts carefully and telling practically the whole story, Bompard listening and only interrupting to ask a question or two.

Sometimes he chuckled as though at a good joke, but the strange thing was he did not express surprise. It was as though he were listening to the recital of a business deal that interested and tickled him without creating amazement.

"That's all," said Dicky. "It's a strange story—do you believe it?"

"But of course," said Bompard. "The thing is plain. That was German gold."

"German gold?"

"German money. And you have got it. *Mon dieu*, yes. German gold camouflaged like their guns, being taken to who knows where, for always under the surface, Monsieur Sebright, there is German gold, trickling, stealing, going into the foreign banks, going here, going there; paying for this or that, being secreted, and sometimes, as now, being lost through the cupidity of agents. Russian? No—Germans!"

Bompard was not a Germanophile. If there was one thing the good Bompard had on his brain, it was Germans, and Dicky, with amazing insight, saw this in a flash, saw it in the hatred disclosed by the other's voice and manner, and played up to it.

"Yes," said Dicky, "I think you are right. And now we've got it we want to keep it. But there's no use keeping it where it is. The question is what are we to do with it? How are we to turn it into money? That is why I have come to you—you know Havana, and we will offer you a share—"

"*Non!*" cried Bompard, "it is outside me. I, my friend, am a business man. I do not want any adventures. I am too old, I have a wife and family and as for money—why, it suffices!"

Dicky felt crushed. He saw at once Bompard's meaning. Though he rejoiced at the Germans being robbed of their gold, he would not help. The thing was shady and he would not risk burning his fingers.

"But—" said Bompard.

"Yes!"

"Though I do not care for outside business affairs of this sort, this nature, there is one I know of who may help, but he would want his not inconsiderable share without doubt."

"Well, he can have it, if he is any good."

"No, he is bad, but he would not play his tricks with me. I am in tobacco, I have my interests in sugar and many things here; so has he; and my interests hold him so to speak. I hold him and he would play no tricks. He is Mordiaz. You do not know the name?"

"No."

"Ah, well, you do not know Havana. Every one knows Mordiaz. He is the one man who can help you, the one man who can take what you want to dispose of—the one man who does not fear governments. If you care I will say to him: 'Mordiaz, this gentleman, my friend Mr. Sebright, knows where a large store of hidden gold is to be found.' I would not tell him your story. I would just say: 'This gentleman knows where gold is and he will give you a share if you will take it from where it is and put it on the market.'"

"Do you think he'll take it up?"

"Oh, yes," said Bompard. "Why not? It is only a question of buying what you call salvage. He will not go shares with you in this matter, he will not be a partner in what might bring trouble, but he will buy from you the—what you call location, paying you a sum to be agreed on after he has made good with it."

"I see."

"In that way he protects himself and me."

"How you?"

"I am his partner," said Bompard, with a laugh.

"His partner!"

"His what you call partner that sleeps. My name is not on his business nor his name on mine, yet often I can say to Mordiaz, 'Here is a good thing to be done. Do it and we will go shares.' Last year for instance, I was at Barcelona when I had news before anyone else that the *Pablo Poirez* was gone to the sea bottom off Andros Island; a cigar ship, with half the Vuelta Abago crop in her hold—one very special brand of cigar. Across the deep-sea cables I speak in the ear of Mordiaz. Mordiaz puts telephone to his mouth and that night he buys all the rest of those cigars for sale in the Havana market. Those cigars go up twenty cents apiece in the markets of New Orleans, Philadelphia and New York. The clubs will have them, so we make a profit of twenty cents on each cigar. Just a whisper on the deep-sea cables and a large profit. That is business. So now with you. You come to me, I believe you because I have seen you at Teneriffe in your little boat, I believe you because you are honest man—your face tells me. I go to Mordiaz and say: 'Take this matter up.' He takes it and I get my share without sharing with you in any trouble that may be. I am plain with you—my life is all business. I am business man first.

"I am two men, the man who enjoys himself and the man who makes profit. I enjoy myself with friends, but for no friend would I go in danger of trouble in business. If you choose to say to me, 'I do not care to deal,' then I will forget all you have told me; but if you say, 'Take this matter up,' I will answer, 'Yes,' and more, I will say, 'Do it at once, Mr. Sebright, and do not let grass grow on your feet, for from what you have told me you may have trouble.' Gold is like a beautiful woman—there is always someone after her."

"You think those fellows I told you about may be after us?"

"It is possible; not after you but the gold; but if Mordiaz takes the matter in his hands you have no cause to be afraid, and as to your share, it will be as safe as my own."

"I'll see Mordiaz today if you will take me to him."

"Yes. At five he is to be seen every day at his office."

"Then I will meet you here at five," said Dicky.

They parted and Dicky went to find Sheila in the lounge.

So that was Bompard, a man light-hearted as a boy, always ready for fun, irresponsible—on the other hand a man of business, swift as lightning to grasp at a deal, yet cautious as a cat in a strange larder. In this business, if it came off, he would receive his profit without the slightest danger to himself. It would be just an introduction, nothing more. If it didn't come off he would lose nothing, this Dicky saw, and also the fact that not to satisfy his hatred of the Germans, not for profit, or love of a friend, or any consideration on earth would Bompard risk entanglement in the law. It was Dicky's first encounter with a southern French business man; a perfect specimen in full flower like a blossom grown in a hothouse.

"Well!" said Sheila.

"I believe it's all right," said he. "But, Sheila, it will mean losing a lot of the stuff; we'll have only to take a share."

He explained everything and Sheila listened. She understood.

"We never could have had it all," said she, when he had finished. "It is too big for us to grasp alone. I see quite clearly that these men will want the most of it. Well, it can't be helped. I don't want a great fortune, but I do want enough to live on. If I could only get that I would be content."

A lump rose in Dicky's throat. He knew now the worst feeling that can come to a man, the feeling that the future of the being he loves is in danger. If he failed with Bompard and Mordiaz he would be left with little or no money, and Sheila with that tiny income which was a mere pittance, not enough to support herself and Larry on shore.

It was a thought paralyzing to a weak man, stimulating to a strong.

CHAPTER 35

MORDIAZ

At five o'clock to the minute Bompard appeared in the smoking room where Dicky was waiting for him.

"We will walk," said Bompard. "It is only a little way."

Out in the street he linked arms with his companion. This big man seemed unable to stand alone; his hand was always on someone's shoulder or on someone's arm, and as they walked he talked about everything but the business on hand, about the new dredging scheme in the harbour, the tobacco crop, the condition of the streets. Sometimes he broke into little snatches of song—*The girls of Avignon* or *Morbihan*. "And here we are," said he at last, leading the way through a stone entrance up a stairs and into a business office filled with the clacking of typewriters.

Bompard seemed quite at home in this place. He opened a door with ground-glass panels, showed Dicky into a little room furnished with a table, two chairs and a flaming almanac of the Union Générale's and told him to wait. He closed the door and Dicky waited.

Nearly twenty minutes passed. Then Bompard reappeared, led him through the main office and into a room where behind a desk table and writing with the aid of a pair of thick-lensed glasses, sat Mordiaz.

Mordiaz might have been fifty; a small man, stout as Sancho Panza, with a sparse grey beard and nearly bald, he looked very commonplace. You never would have imagined him to be a genius, a genius of affairs, an alchemist who extracted gold from all sorts of unlikely substances, men, conditions.

Nominally in the cigar business he moved behind everything in Havana. Hundreds of men were his shadows, bringing him information or doing his work. He had agents in Santiago and Matanzas and among other things he was the motive spirit in the Havana Los Pinos Salvage Company.

"This is the gentleman who wished to see you," said Bompard, introducing Dicky. Then as Mordiaz motioned the newcomer to a seat, Bompard went out and closed the door.

Mordiaz finished what he was writing, took off his glasses and turned in his chair toward the newcomer.

"Well, sir," said Mordiaz, speaking in English, "my friend who has just gone out has told me of this business on which you wished to see me. I never touch affairs of this sort. Let us make that clear between us once and for all."

Dicky rose from his chair.

"Sit down," said Mordiaz.

He stretched out his hand for a cigar box, opened it, presented it, struck a match and, rising, held it to Dicky's cigar.

Then he lit up himself.

You could not buy those cigars in any market. They filled the air with a fragrance heavenly beyond description, and leaning back in his chair, Mordiaz seemed for a moment to forget the newcomer and the business in hand.

"But," said Mordiaz at last, "though the question does not interest me, I may be able to tell you of a man possibly useful in the matter. He is in no way connected with me, but the business might interest him. In fact," said Mordiaz, "he puts so much trust in my sense of affairs that should I say to him, 'Take this thing up,' he would do so. There only remains the question of terms."

"Yes," said Dicky.

"In a business like this," went on Mordiaz, "there can be no contract. A contract is the child of the law, and the law—well, señor, it cannot have anything to do with this business. My friend will no doubt say to you, 'I will give you so much.' He will keep his bond because, this introduction coming from me and from Señor Bompard, it will be necessary for him to do so. You understand?"

"Yes."

"He will say to you, 'The gains from this business we will divide into three shares. I will take two and you one.'"

"He will want two thirds!"

"Yes, señor."

Dicky, for a moment, felt crushed. It seemed to him that for the first time in his life he was standing face to face with rapacity. He knew quite well that this third party, whoever he might be, was only the agent and tool of Mordiaz, that Bompard had so put the case to Mordiaz that Mordiaz would take the matter up and run it through—but at what a price!

"You will remember," said Mordiaz, "that all risk will be gone from you, all work will be done for you, and the cash placed in your hands in dollar notes. That is how this gentleman does his business."

Dicky was still thinking. Curiously enough this evidence of business rapacity, after the first shock of it, seemed to point toward reality and security. It was, in its way, an indication of honest intention. He remembered that James was out of the business and they were the richer by his share—still, one third! It seemed robbery.

"Do you mind if I don't give you a definite answer right away?" said he. "I have a partner, a lady—I would like to consult her."

"Most certainly," said Mordiaz, "but please remember that the terms I have said to you will not be altered by this gentleman, and should you decide tonight you will call and see him tomorrow. I will write you his address. He is an American. Captain Kane of the Havana Salvage Company, 30 Callé Antonio—that is it," and he handed him a slip of paper.

Dicky put it in his pocket, and saving good evening to Mordiaz, departed through the outer office where the clerks were knocking off work for the day.

One third of the gold, one third of the gold—the words kept repeating themselves in his mind as he made his way back to the hotel where Sheila was waiting for him in the lounge.

CHAPTER 36

LARRY

"Never!" cried Sheila. He had described the whole interview and given her the terms.

"Never! Never! One third! I'd sooner give the whole thing away."

Dicky remembered her words, spoken only that day—how she had said she did not want wealth, only enough to live on; he did not know that her revolt against the terms was inspired not so much by greed for money as by the fancied injustice of them. She explained this. There was perhaps another reason. What woman has ever been satisfied with the business bargain a man makes? Women have little ideas about concession.

Dicky actually and for a moment found himself almost taking sides with Mordiaz.

"I know you're right," said he. "The terms aren't good. All the same let's look at the thing fairly and squarely. All responsibility is taken from us, they run the risk and they pay us in dollar notes which is as good as payment in gold. We can't do anything alone and they are the only people I see that can help us. After all, Sheila, a third of that stuff will mean a lot of money."

"Yes, and how do you know they will pay us?"

"We've got to risk that. We can make no contract with them, but just take their word—we've got to depend entirely on Bompard, and I believe we can depend on him. Bompard is straight. He has introduced us to Mordiaz and he will not let him run crooked."

Sheila sighed. She believed Bompard to be straight and like Dicky she felt the very hardness of the bargain to be a guarantee of good faith on the part of the bargainers. All the same she felt it was dreadful to be done like this. Pure anger took the part of reason and out of some black and unexplained part of her mind came the voice that rose to her lips.

"I won't," said Sheila. "I'd just as soon bring it here and sell it in the streets for old metal. They have no right to squeeze us like this. You say they are straight. Maybe! But they are not straight to squeeze us like that. You can tell Monsieur Bompard that we won't—at least I won't—take less than half."

"Do you really mean that?" asked Dicky.

"I do."

He did not answer for a moment. This decision meant that there was no use in him seeing Captain Kane in the morning. He would have to go back and fight with Mordiaz for better terms and he felt in his soul that Mordiaz, having the whip hand, would not give in. Days would be lost. The terms were bad, but in his heart he knew it would be better to take them, perhaps because he knew that he was a bad bargainer and that Bompard and Mordiaz, having summed him up, would never lower their flag.

But he could not say this to Sheila.

However, events of which he knew nothing had taken charge of this business.

He was just about to speak when a page boy who had entered the lounge as if in search of someone, came toward them and began to speak in Spanish.

"Señor" and "hombre" were the only words Dicky could make out, but Sheila knew. "He says there's someone to see you," said Sheila. "Perhaps it's Monsieur Bompard; whatever you do, be careful."

Dicky left the lounge. He returned in a couple of minutes looking perplexed and put out.

"It's Larry."

"Larry! What on earth does he want?"

"He says he got a message from us to come to the hotel, that we wanted him."

"A message from *us*?"

"Yes—what's the meaning of it? I sent no message—did you?"

"Never. Who gave it to him?"

"They sent it over from the *Dulcinea*, said it had come there by mistake. Come outside and see him."

Sheila followed into the hall where Larry was standing twisting his cap in his hands.

"Larry, what on earth is this?" said Sheila. "Who brought you that message?"

"One of the chaps from the *Dulcinea*, miss. He rowed over and said a message had come from you and I was to put ashore wid the boat and leave her at the quay and go to the customhouse office in the street beyond and wait at the door there for you, and if you weren't there in an hour, I was to come to the hotel for you."

"What time did you get the message?" asked Dicky.

"Eight bells, sor, four o'clock."

"And it's now after seven," said Sheila.

"Some one's been fooling the *Dulcinea* people," said Dicky.

"But, Larry," cried Sheila, "you shouldn't have left the ship without anyone on board."

"I didn't, Miss Sheila. The chap said he'd stick wid her and look after her till I came back."

"Well," said Sheila, "this is the most extraordinary thing. It couldn't be James, could it, that's playing some practical joke? Anyhow, we've got to go and see."

"Where?" asked Dicky.

"We'll go to the *Dulcinea* and question them. It must be James—remember that telegram he sent Captain Shortt."

"If it is," said Dicky, "I'll break his neck—if I catch him. Come, let's go."

Sheila had not taken off her hat. Dicky fetched his from the lounge and they started, Larry following them.

Darkness had fallen when they reached the wharf and the boat was moored and under the care of the wharf keeper.

They got in and Larry took the oars. The moon had not risen and the harbour lay vast and vague under the first stars. The air was filled with sea scents and harbour perfumes and noises from the dockyard—the rattle of a cargo winch, and from somewhere at a great distance and borne on the wind, the tanging of a guitar.

Lights everywhere. Havana all aglow with electrics and out on the harbour water the lights of the shipping.

Sheila, seated beside Dicky in the stern sheets, felt lonely and depressed, perplexed. Who had sent that message, and why? James? But why? It was not the sort of thing that James would do—he might be a fool, but he was a gentleman. Who then? She could not tell, but in her mind was the old uneasiness, the sense of people antagonistic to them, people unseen, hidden, and with one objective, the gold.

"There's the *Dulcinea's* light, I think," said Dicky, who was staring ahead through the dark. "But I can't see the *Baltrum's*."

Larry turned his head.

"That's her and there's the gas bouy, musha, but them fools haven't put up our ridin' light. I'll scrag that chap—I'll put the sinse into him—"

He took to the oars.

Suddenly Sheila spoke.

"She's gone," said Sheila.

The gas buoy flung its low and intermittent light across the water at them; it seemed like an evil eye winking. The *Dulcinea* showed outlined on the night. No other ship lay near her. The *Baltrum* was gone.

"Don't stop to talk," cried Sheila, cutting short the language of the two men. "Get up quick to the *Dulcinea*. She's been stolen, that's all. I felt it—oh, dear."

"*Dulcinea* ahoy!" cried Larry.

"Ahoy!" came a voice from the yacht.

"Drop us the lather—and what have you done with the boat? Where's the *Baltrum*? Who's stole her and what were you meanin' to let her be gone? Oh, be the powers, if I get a hold of you—"

"Now then," came the voice of the old quartermaster who had been at the rail when the *Baltrum* anchored—Benson was his name. "What are you talkin' about? Nobody's stolen your boat, not to my knowledge. Mr. Morgan has took her out. Here's the ladder—mind my paint with that boat huk."

"Morgan!" cried Sheila.

"Yes, miss, Mr. Morgan took her out." He held a lantern while they came on deck, Sheila first, Dicky following, Larry remaining in the boat.

"Mr. Morgan took her out?" said Sheila.

"Yes, miss."

"Come down below," said Dicky. "We can't talk here. Put on the lights, Benson."

They went below, Benson switching on the light. Then in the saloon it was Sheila who took the wheel.

"Tell us exactly what happened," said she to Benson, "everything."

"Well, miss," said Benson, "it was gettin' on for four bells. I was in the fo'c's'le with the others when Mr. Morgan sent for me here and he says to me: 'Benson, I've been expectin' a message from Mr. Sebright which hasn't come. Send a man over to the *Baltrum* and tell that Irishman to get ashore and wait at the customhouse for an hour, and if Mr. Sebright hasn't turned up by then, tell him to go to the hotel'—he give me the name on a bit of paper— 'and meet Mr. Sebright there. You'd better tell him that Mr. Sebright has sent the order here, for that Irishman is such a thick-headed chap,' says he, 'that he'll start arguin' if he doesn't get the order explicit,' he says, 'and you can tell him we'll look after the *Baltrum* while he's gone.' And I says to him, 'I'm to send a man to the *Baltrum* and tell the chap Mr. Sebright's sent an order for him to get ashore at once and wait an hour at the customhouse and failin' Mr. Sebright's turnin' up, he's to go to the hotel,' I says.

"'That's it,' says he, 'and when you've done that, tell Longley and Hearn to get their bags ready for I'll be wantin' them on special business,' he says.

"Well, sir, I sent the order and the Irishman went ashore and Mr. Morgan he says to me, takin' me to the after rail: 'Get the dinghy down,' he says. 'I'm goin' on board the *Baltrum* to take her out and whisk her down to Matanzas, for it's a question of contraband,' he says, 'that Mr. Sebright has got himself mixed up in and there'll be hell to pay,' he says, 'for Mr. Corder and us all if the *Baltrum's* caught here with the stuff on her. I'll dump it at sea,' he says, and with that he put aboard her, takin' the dinghy, and they put out."

"Good heavens!" said Sheila.

"Yes, miss, and he'll have dumped the stuff by this and you'll find the boat at Matanzas," said Benson.

Sheila turned a chalk-white face to her companion. Dicky sat down.

He checked the outburst rising to his lips. They were done, absolutely done, at least for the moment. There was no use abusing Benson or raging or storming. Morgan was away for Crab Cay; that telegram which had fetched Shortt to Santiago was a fake; the thing was clear; there was only one chance—pursuit.

"Benson," said he at last, "we have got to get out and follow them right away."

"Yes, sir."

"Get the auxiliary going. You have the rest of the crew on board, I suppose?"

"Beg pardon, sir," said Benson, "but if you mean taking the yacht, I can't move her. Mr. Morgan gave me strict orders not to move her till the captain is back, and she's going into dry dock tomorrow sun-up."

"Rubbish!" cried Dicky. "She's got to go—it's life or death. You've got to take us. I tell you—"

"Dicky," said Sheila, restraining him. She was a sailor. She knew quite well that a man of Benson's type left in charge would die before disobeying orders.

Morgan had foreseen everything, blocked them at every point. Shortt would not be back for maybe two days, the *Dulcinea* would be in dry dock when he arrived—there was just one chance for them, something that Morgan had not foreseen and so could not guard against. Bompard and Mordiaz. If these proved rotten ropes, then everything was over.

She turned to Benson:

"You absolutely refuse to take us out?"

"I can't indeed, miss, not nohow."

"Dicky," said she, "come. There's no use in wasting time, and I have an idea."

"You'll be sorry for this," said Dicky to Benson.

"I can't move her nohow, sir," cried Benson.

"Come," said Sheila. She led the way on deck and as they were getting into the boat, Sheila turned to Benson.

"You are quite right," said she, "in not disobeying orders, but you see how we are placed. We have a boat and a man here. Will you take Larry when he has rowed us ashore and give him quarters till the *Baltrum* is back? I don't know what we can do with him at the hotel."

"Yes, miss," said Benson, "I don't mind obliging you by that. There's room enough aboard."

"Larry," said Sheila, leaning over the rail, "when you've put us ashore you're to come back here and take up your quarters. Your bag is gone in the *Baltrum*, but she'll be back soon."

"Yes, miss," said Larry. Like a dog he read the tone of his mistress and knew that he was not to ask questions in the hearing of others.

They pushed off. Then when they were out of earshot and as he bent to the creaky oars, she told him. "And all you can do, Larry," she finished, "is just to go back to the *Dulcinea* when you have put us ashore, and wait till you hear from us. We have friends ashore who may help."

Dicky heard nothing of what she was saying. The appalling fact had just occurred to him that all his money, with the exception of twenty-five pounds, was in his locker on board the *Baltrum*. He had left it there for fear of pickpockets ashore!

CHAPTER 37

IT NEVER RAINS BUT IT POURS

It was in the Callé San Pedro just beyond the wharf that he told her.

Their home was gone, their money was gone, their prospects seemed almost hopeless.

Sheila took the news of the lost money with a little shudder.

"How much have you left?" she asked.

"Twenty pounds—a little over. How could I have known? What could have been safer than leaving it on board with Larry looking after the ship?"

"It never rains but it pours," said she. "There's no use thinking of it—there's no use thinking of it. May our bad luck go with it. I know it's awful. No matter, we have a chance, our last chance."

"Bompard."

"Yes, Bompard—for one moment I fancied that Bompard might have had some hand in this, but I know he hasn't. No, that beast wanted no one to help him. Now you know why Captain Shortt got a telegram calling him away, and why it was sent from Pinos, just close here. Morgan most likely slipped ashore and sent it himself. Longley must have been spying on us at Crab Cay."

"Longley hadn't sense enough for a spy."

"Sense enough to see what we were doing. It was Morgan, of course, as first officer, who picked him and Hearn to go with us when I asked for two men, and I—I never thought of that. We were children, Dicky—we have been children in this business—but there is a Providence. Don't let us talk anymore. What time is it?"

"Twenty past ten."

"We may catch Monsieur Bompard at the hotel."

"Do you intend to tell him this?"

"Everything. He is our one and only chance. I don't mind now the bargain about the two thirds—anything—so long as he will fight Morgan. Walk quicker!"

The streets were filled with the usual Havana night crowd, negroes, yellow men, whites. Not a cab was to be had, and sometimes they had to take the roadway from the footpath.

Never even in nightmare had Dicky imagined such a walk as that. The idea of Sheila stranded in this glaring, heartless, terrible place, of himself almost helpless, of the prize just out of reach, of Morgan calmly sailing under that moon with a favorable wind—rogues always get that—of James, who could have made everything different had he been here—all these ideas projected themselves, became part of and clung to the blazing fronts of cinema palaces, the flash-light advertisements of Merilliers, Menthe, Juan Bangos tobacco, and Cacao Santa Anna.

The smells helped; Chinese and bay rum, Cuban earth, cigars and the eternal cigarettes; negroes, flowers, rotten bananas, rum.

Sheila took his arm so that they might get along quicker, and the feeling of her hand on his coat sleeve did not give him a thrill. Love has no part in ship-wreck and disaster unless in the form of heroism and devotion.

They reached the hotel and took their seats in one of the great basket couches in the outer hall to rest a moment and pull themselves together. Then Dicky went to find Bompard.

"Yes. Monsieur Bompard is in. He probably is in the dance room." Dicky went there.

The eternal band was sawing away and nearly a dozen couples were fox trotting. The chairs were filled, for residents in the town came to the Mercedes for the dancing at night.

Yes, there was Bompard, talking to a girl in pink, and Dicky, catching his eye, signalled to him.

He led him out to where Sheila was sitting and there, between them, they told him all.

"*Coquin de sort!*" cried Bompard, when the tale was finished; then for a space he fell dumb.

"Quick," he said, "you have told me all but the name of this place and the distance."

"Crab Cay," said Dicky, and gave the distance.

"Then," said Bompard, "there is yet a chance. We must go now and at once to the Captain Kane. It is late, but we may find him."

He rose up and called a boy and sent him running for a cab. Then he lit a cigar and sat down.

He was in evening dress; he remembered this and went off and fetched a light overcoat and his hat. Then he sat down again.

"The question is, can he find at a moment a boat that is quick enough to catch Mr. Morgan?" said he. "Who knows?—we will see."

CHAPTER 38

KANE

Sheila remained at the hotel. The cab took them through the blaze of streets, through squares lit as for a festival, down cutthroat byways to the waterside, past the Santa Anna wharf and the Gholem yard to a big building where it stopped. Telling the driver to wait, Bompard led Dicky through an archway, down a passage, to a big stone hall where a single electric cast its light on all sorts of junk, anchors, hawsers like coiled anacondas, oars, diving pumps, diving dresses hung on the walls—a deep-sea ship seemed to have been wrecked there as in some submarine cave and the divers to have just knocked off work.

Bompard went to a door through whose ground-glass panels light showed, knocked and entered.

It was an office and two men showed through the haze of tobacco smoke that filled the place, a big man and a small man. They were playing cards. The big man was Kane.

"Good!" said Bompard. "We have found you. No, Monsieur le Capitaine, do not rise. We will find us seats. This is my friend Monsieur Sebright. Monsieur Sebright will tell you why we have come." He opened the door and looked out to see if by any chance there might be a listener. "This is a business sent by Señor Mordiaz," finished he, "and all expenses will be chargeable to him."

"There's no one to hear," said Kane. "Hank here is all the same as myself. Bring yourself to anchor and spit it out." He moved a chair out of a corner for Dicky. Bompard took his seat on an angle of the table, and Hank, who had picked up the cards, began spreading them on the table before him as though he were telling his fortune or engaged in a game of patience.

"Everything?" asked Dicky, with a glance at Bompard.

"Yes, monsieur, everything," said Bompard. "Everything—location and all. It must be the all together or nothing."

Dicky started. As he talked he insensibly took in these two new men upon whom depended, now, his fate and Sheila's fortune. He knew that this was the hub of the whole business and he guessed Kane to be the linchpin. Kane's appearance did not justify the title of captain; he wore a guernsey under a rough coat and his hands wanted washing, but his face would have pleased an artist. It was a fine face, but rough cast. It might have been the face of an actor battered by seafaring and tanned by the tropics; he had extraordinary eyes, level gazing and far sighted, eyes that whisky or battle could fill with the fire of insanity.

This was the man who salved the bullion from the strong room of the *Paraquay*, wrecked on the black strand of Martinique and only reachable from the sheer cliffs three hundred feet high. The man who was Mordiaz's right hand in sea affairs.

On the other hand, the leathery, wizened Hank playing with the cards and seeming to hear nothing, scarcely impressed Dicky. He told everything with scarcely an interruption and Kane, when the story was over, made no comment on its strangeness.

"He'll have got seven hours' start by now," said Kane, "and it's four hundred odd miles from here to Crab. I know your boat, saw her come in and her copper wants cleanin'. With this wind he'd be making good, maybe, and there's nothing to follow him with but the steam dridger and the mail boat."

"*Coffeepot*," said Hank, without looking up from the intricate pattern of the cards.

"Oh, her—will she run?"

"Depends," said Hank. "If her fans will hold out and her propeller stick on her, she'll go. I was goin' to take her to Matanzas next week to the breakers. Her bunkers are near full."

"An old torp Mordiaz bought off the Cubans," said Kane in explanation to Dicky. "Fifty cents, I think it was he gave for her, or maybe it was a bunch of bananas. She's a holy howlin' terror, but if the string and sealin' wax will hold she may get us to Crab."

"What is a torp?" asked Bompard.

"T'pedo boat. Come out of the ark or the Spanish-American war, I forget which. Engine's a jazz band, but it plays. Hank."

"Yep."

"Off with you—we count out under three hours. Fetch Lomax, Tearle, and that chap Antonio; they'll be on the dridger. Get the men busy and the rest of the coal in her and fire up. Get all the stores out of the dridger on board of her—there's grub enough for a week. I'll bring the charts—guns—no, we want no guns."

Hank swept the cards together, put them in their cardboard box and the box in his pocket, took his hat and went out.

"That's done," said Kane. "You goin' with us, of course?" turning to Dicky.

"Yes—rather."

"Then," said Kane, "you'd better be off and make your will and get your traps. I'll want you to be at the Poirez wharf in three hours, sharp." He turned away and took charts from a locker.

"Where is it?" asked Dicky.

"I will show you it," said Bompard. "I will take you there. For the present good-bye, Monsieur le Capitaine." Taking Dicky's arm he led him out. Kane seemed to have forgotten them, up to the eyes in his charts.

The cab was still waiting for them as Bompard told the man to take them back to the hotel.

"What a night!" said he, as they started.

The good Bompard was flustered. He was used to doing business in a leisurely way, and with all sorts of precautions and screens, in a case like the present. Morgan had shattered all that.

All of a sudden it had become necessary to jump right into the arena, to take Dicky to Kane and mix himself up in this affair at firsthand. Mordiaz was still sheltered; if there was trouble over the business no man could say that he had any hand in it. He had only given an introduction, but he, Bompard, was helping to set the affair going "with his two hands" as he expressed it to himself.

However, there was no use in worrying.

"Suppose," said Dicky, as they drove, "we pull this thing off and recover the gold. Is Kane to be trusted?"

"Oh, yes," replied the other. "He will get his little commission. Again, he is one of Mordiaz's men who are all to be trusted. Again, it would be no use to him—he could not dispose of it alone, no more than you can. This Monsieur Morgan must be either a very great fool or he has men behind him who will help him to dispose of it."

"He has men behind him," said Dicky. "They got at him before we left England, of that I'm certain. Once he gets the stuff on board he has only to go home with it—he has stores enough on board for the journey and he needn't worry. He knows we can't touch him. If we cabled to stop the *Baltrum* at any port, we'd have to accuse him of running away with the ship. He knows we can't do that without giving the whole show away."

The bitterest thing to Dicky was the thought that Morgan could go in safety to England and not only go there, but, with the aid of the crooks who were backing him, cash the gold.

Another bitter thing was the almost sure fact that only for James' tomfoolery in telling MacAdam his name and position, the MacAdam crowd would never have achieved the lightning stroke of getting at Morgan and corrupting him.

However, as in Bompard's case, there was no use in worrying, and in any case there was no use in worrying about the past. The present held quite enough worries and difficulties as he found when he came to the hotel and full face with the fact that he would have to leave Sheila.

It would be impossible to take her on this business. He would have to leave her at the hotel.

She was waiting for them in the lounge when they came in and they sat down beside her and Dicky began explaining things.

"I've got to leave you, Sheila," finished Dicky, when he had told her everything. "You couldn't go on this stunt. It's too dirty and too dangerous. Bompard will look after you."

He spoke in short chopped sentences and with a catch in his throat; the idea of leaving her alone here, even with the Bompards, the idea that he might never see her again brought him as near to sniveling as a man can come without disgrace.

CHAPTER 39

THEY PUT OUT

The electrics were on at the Poirez wharf when Dicky and Bompard arrived. Dicky had forced Sheila to take the remainder of his money to pay the hotel bill at the end of the week. "There'll be some left over," said Dicky, "and Bompard will help you if—if— And there's James, should anything happen. If I don't come back or anything, he must help. You've got his address, 'Hotel Plaza. New York.' Nothing's going to happen. I'll come back all right. I was only thinking of—there, good-bye—good-bye."

Forgetting Bompard and the night porter who were standing by, he squeezed her in his arms and kissed her hair. He had never breathed a word of love to her, it all came out then, in that last moment, without a word being uttered.

Then he was in the cab, with Bompard beside him, rattling through streets now empty and only half lit, and it seemed to Dicky that he was leaving all his life behind him, all his happiness, all his hopes. It seemed to him that he would never—never—never, see Sheila again, and behind that dark obsession stood a monster calling itself the future and asking him: "What will happen to Sheila if you never see her again, Sheila alone here in Havana, without the *Baltrum*, without money?"

Through two streets and a dim-lit square this question held him and tortured him. Then with a turn of a corner and a breath from the harbour he was himself again and confidence had returned. He would come back, nothing could hold him or stop him; come back with his hands full of money, alive, to the woman he loved.

The cab drew up.

The Poirez wharf has a low freeboard; it is used for lighters discharging and the small craft that ply along the coast.

Tonight, under the moon and the sizzling arc lights, it showed forms moving here and there and echoed to an insistent drumming from the naked feet of the fellows running with the last sacks from the great coaling shed to the wharfside where the torp was moored.

Kane was standing with Hank in talk with the wharf master and a harbour official. Kane was not only captain of the salvage company; he had a hand in dredging operations and diving, and besides being Mordiaz's shadow, or one of them, knew personally all the harbour men. He could make things go, and make them go without questions asked.

"That's her," said Kane, leading the newcomers to the wharf edge and handing Dicky's attaché case to Hank for disposal on board. "That's her—she's still holdin' together."

Dicky looked down on a narrow deck along which the last of the coal sacks were being carried, a deck stripped of everything, showing nothing but its steel plates and a double-ender boat lying on it, keel up, abaft the funnel. As he looked the head and shoulders of a man black as a fiend out of Gehenna rose from a hatchway. This was Lomax, naval artisan and one of the salvage company's most priceless possessions—though he didn't look it. Close to the engine-room hatch stood two negroes, Sam and Billy, taken on to help in the stoking.

"How's it shaping below?" asked Kane, when he had introduced Dicky.

Lomax wiped his hands with a piece of cotton waste.

"Pressure's rising if the gauge isn't telling a lie. Got all your dunnage on board? Then you'd better drop down and let's get—I don't want her to blow up beside the wharf."

From the engine room a voice could be heard singing "My Coal-black Mammy"—that was Tearle. Antonio and Hank were forward of the funnel waiting to attend to the shore fasts.

Kane dropped on to the deck plates, and Dicky, having shaken Bompard by the hand, followed.

"You will bring it back here," said Bompard. "The Captain Kane has orders and will know what to do. No, you will not fail. Au revoir."

Then, as Kane took the bridge and the wheel, Lomax vanished from sight, the mooring ropes were cast off and for a moment the night hung in silence, a silence broken by the tingling of the engine-room bell and the first vibration of the engines.

The wharf began to slide away astern and now where it had been was glittering moonlit water. Dicky, glancing back, saw Bompard's figure for a moment, waving an arm, and beyond Bompard and the wharves and the cranes and great storehouses, the city sprinkled with lights.

They passed the *Dulcinea* and the gas buoy; a three-masted-schooner and a tanker waiting for the morning light to get in to the wharves; then the passage showed before them, and, beyond, the wide-rolling stretches of the open sea.

Dicky went below.

He found the once wardroom stripped clean as the deck, stores flung in corners, his baggage hove into a bunk that had neither blankets nor bedding, and a kerosene lamp, hung above a swinging table, lighting the desolation that could be smelled as well as seen.

Cockroaches, kerosene, fruit and the smell of stale tobacco took him by the throat and made his heart rejoice. Sheila was saved from all this. The more intolerable his surroundings the better; the more he had to toil and work and strive the better. The gold that had taken so many forms had resolved itself at last into a permanent shape—Sheila.

She and her future were buried in the sands of Crab Cay. They had to be rescued from Morgan, and this very real fact gave him a power and an inspiration that gold never could have bestowed, and a desire for self-sacrifice, sweat and toil that gold never could have hinted at.

He left the place and sought the engine-room, oven hot with the fires of the furnaces. Lomax, stripped to the waist, was oiling. He was greaser and chief engineer and would be stoker too when his turn came, Tearle taking his place and he relieving Tearle. He shouted this news through the music of the "jazz band" and right on his words came the ring of a bell and the swing of the indicator to full speed.

With the sound of the bell and the springing to life of the engines came a gentle roll. They had cleared the land and gained the open sea.

"Now you'll see hell," shouted Lomax through the drone of the fans and the shouting of the engines and the clash and clang from the stokehold where Tearle and Antonio were firing up. "Sixteen knots if she's doing one, and she ain't fit to be doing ten. Get into the stokehold and lend a hand. They'll show you how to shoot the coal—and you'd better be learning. We'll want you."

CHAPTER 40

DISASTER

At dawn, Dicky, coming on deck half blinded and half roasted, saw the coast of Cuba far to starboard and almost astern; day on the hills and darkness in the valleys. Kane was still at the wheel, where he had remained since leaving the wharf, and one of the negroes coming up from the fo'c's'le was pausing for a glance at the far-off coast before dropping down to the stokehold.

The chief, or one of the chief reasons of Mordiaz's power and wealth, was his knowledge of and his choice of men. Suddenly and without warning this gold proposition was put before him and almost without thinking he was able to put his finger on the men in his employ fit to work it. It had been the same with the wreck on the black strand at Martinique; she was being broken up by the sea and another tide would have done for her; Kane had salved the valuables off her because he had taken the wrecking ship out "naked," raced her against time and worked for fifty-two hours without sleep.

He hailed Dicky peremptorily now from the bridge.

"There's grub in the lockers down below," cried Kane, "biscuits and beef most, and there's a Primus. You can make some coffee—coffee cups and a pot in the basket by the doorway, can opener you'll find in the starboard after locker and knives and such. You'd better be can opener on this expedition, for we don't carry no cooks. Bring me a cup of coffee up here; I'm going to stick a while yet."

Dicky dived below to the wardroom. He found the stores and the Primus stove, and a breaker of water brought aft from the water tanks. Nothing was forgotten. That was Kane again—neither spoons nor condensed milk nor salt.

When the coffee was made he brought a cup to the bridge, then he gave word in the engine room that breakfast was ready and Tearle went aft with Hank and Antonio, leaving Lomax in charge and the negroes at the fires.

It was a strangely run ship. No watches were set, there was no lookout, no confusion, no grumbling. No man seemed to reckon on sleep except maybe a cat nap of half an hour or so. They reckoned to raise Crab Cay in twenty-four hours or under if the steam pipes held and the propeller stuck and till then they would carry on.

It was not a voyage, it was the rush of a hawk; and at eight o'clock Kane, who had given the wheel to Tearle, was figuring that they ought to be overhauling the *Baltrum* soon, and almost on his words the strong bowling breeze that had been blowing straight from the Gulf of Mexico for the last twelve or fourteen hours began to flag. Then it died. Died suddenly as if a door had been shut across the Florida and Bahama channels; a blue crystal door whose threshold was a line of deep-blue crystal sea.

"We've got the blighters!" cried Kane. "They're done." He pointed out to Dicky that the *Baltrum* with an eleven-hour start would not have made more than a hundred miles in that time. The torp that had now been running five hours at sixteen knots had laid eighty miles behind her already.

The *Baltrum* becalmed would be simply waiting for them and it was only the question of a little time. He sent Tearle forward on the lookout and Dicky with the chanting of the engines in his ears turned and stood looking at the wash they were leaving on the glassy sea.

Antonio was in temporary charge of the engine room.

In a few hours, more or less, they would raise the *Baltrum*; they would board her, they would seize Morgan. When Dicky had done with Morgan, Kane would see after the remains. They already had decided what to do with him; he would be put ashore, he and his companions, somewhere, either Turtle Island or Caicos—it didn't matter where so long as it was well out of reach of Havana and sufficiently desolate.

As he chewed the cud of these grateful and comforting thoughts, he heard the voice of Antonio through the sound of the engines, Antonio singing songs of his native land:

"Estramadura—estramadura—something—something   estramadura," came the voice high pitched and plaintive and only wanting a guitar and the moonlight of Seville to complete itself.

Then on the voice came a sudden chatter of the engines, a yell and a burst of steam from the hatch. Lomax, a biscuit in his hand, came running forward. Dicky saw him fling the biscuit away and plump on his knees beside the hatch opening, shouting down to Antonio, while through the manhole of the stokehold the two negroes were crawling on deck as the boat, losing way, turned broadside to the lift of the gentle, slobbering swell.

Estramadura—indeed!

"No, he ain't hurt!" yelled Lomax to Kane, "but the engines are gone. He's lettin' loose the steam. Come out of it, you perisher!" He clutched Antonio coming up the steel ladder and dragged him on deck through the steam clouds, Antonio, scarcely scalded, but weeping and crying aloud to his saints. Then, as the steam dispersed, they descended.

No, the engines weren't gone, and by the opening of the steam cocks the boilers had been saved, but—

The forward piston crosshead, for want of proper oiling, had heated and seized, in other words, stuck; the piston was bent and the concussion of the stoppage had dislocated Heaven knows what else.

Kane, Hank, Lomax and Tearle, four supermarine engineers, experts, magicians, and used to playing with disaster, stood contemplating the wreckage, knowing at once the cause, yet saying not a word of reproach or criticism.

Repairs to a plain mind were plainly impossible without a staff of fitters and engine-room artificers and the resources of a dockyard. They had not come unprovided for possible repairs. Kane had brought over from the dredger and the salvage company's storehouse a full outfit—still the whole business seemed impossible, and Tearle, the first to give an opinion, frankly said so.

"Get to work," replied Kane.

CHAPTER 41

SUSPENSE

To Dicky, almost more terrible than the disaster was the coolness, absence of haste and seeming indifference of these men as they set to work on their seemingly impossible task.

But they knew better. They worked as all good workmen do, without haste or fuss. Removing the cylinder cover and the piston, straightening the rod, freeing the crosshead, doing other repairs, Kane estimated all this as a two days' job—maybe three. It was all right working without pause, without sleep and almost without food when it was a matter of stoking and steering and simply chasing the *Baltrum*, but engine repairing was a different matter. It could not be rushed, and to Dicky, helpless as a woman in this matter, the leisurely sounding noises from below, the hammer blows, the voices in discussion, brought despair alleviated only by one good thing, the calm.

It still held, held all that day while he took his post as lookout or went below to prepare food for the workers; held all that night while Lomax and the negroes continued slowly with the work, and Kane and Tearle took a rest; breaking only at sunrise when the westerly wind renewed itself, blowing full and steady and giving life again to the *Baltrum* and the scoundrels who manned her. It was bitter to see it breezing up the water, coming up against the splendour of the east, and to think of the *Baltrum* taking it with all her canvas spread and Morgan at the wheel.

It lasted all day and all night, dying down at dawn only to revive again when the sun was above the horizon, and still the tinkering went on, the hollow hull sounding to the hammer blows, voices, the rasping of files, while the driven blue of the wind-swept sea showed nothing but the occasional wing of a great ocean gull sweeping above it, only to rise and vanish in the cloudless sky.

At noon on this, the third day, Dicky had almost given up hope. Wild ideas came to him of raising sail on the hulk, futile because there was not a square inch of canvas on board. Even had they been able to extemporize a mast and sail, there was no one to work her; every hand was on the engines. By night, with a still freshening breeze, hope definitely left him.

They would never be able to catch up with the *Baltrum* now, of that he felt certain. The malign something that had dogged them all along would never let them succeed; no, not even if the engines were suddenly and miraculously made whole again. Something else would happen. The prize was too great. The gold was accursed. It had begun by murdering those two men and it had finished by robbing him of all his money, leaving Sheila stranded at Havana and himself, here. And that was not the end. What would the end be?

He asked himself this as he made coffee that night for the workers. He had asked Kane at sunset how the work was going on and Kane had replied, "Bully." Nothing more. Kane seemed to have forgotten all about the *Baltrum* and the chase; his whole mind seemed concentrated on the engines. That was mainly the fact, for to Kane the work in hand was ever the all-absorbing thing.

Having made the coffee and brought it in a can to the engine-room hatch, he went back and lay down on a locker. If he only could have helped, but that was denied to him. He was useless and only got in the way of these experts, who said so quite frankly; useless, done for, drifting, with everything lost and Morgan triumphant. He closed his eyes to shut out the sight of the kerosene lamp and the steel beams and the whole of the rest of that cavelike and gloomy interior. Then he fell asleep.

He slept for hours and was awakened by a sound that made him sit straight up. A sound like the sound of trampling feet, a vibration that made the lamp chatter on its gimbals. The engines were going! Before he could get his legs onto the floor came a voice, the voice of Lomax coming down the steel ladder.

"She's whacking up," cried Lomax. "They're turning over, but Lord knows how long they'll last. Where's the biscuits?"

Dicky looked at his watch. It was four o'clock in the morning.

CHAPTER 42

A PROBLEM

He came on deck. The westering moon fronting the dawn lit the sea, and the following breeze blew strong, piling the funnel smoke and festooning it against the stars. Tearle was at the wheel.

The thud of the engines filled the night and through it came the vague sound of the bow wash from the shearing stem.

She was going, doing maybe ten knots, maybe not as much, and the *Baltrum* must by now be where? Dicky, for the first time, tried to calculate. She had eleven hours' start of them to begin with, Kane had estimated her speed with the current at ten knots. She had done perhaps a hundred and ten miles before they left the wharf in pursuit at three o'clock in the morning, close on a hundred and sixty miles before the calm took her at eight o'clock.

Then she had started again when the calm broke and had been sailing ever since. The calm had broken at sunrise the day before yesterday. She had done since then nearly forty-eight hours' sailing at ten knots, that would be nearly five hundred miles—the whole run from Havana to Crab was only four hundred. She had reached Crab by this—how long?

The wretched Dicky, trying to solve this appalling problem mentally, rested his forehead against a funnel guy. The *Baltrum* had run a hundred and sixty miles before the calm took her and, say, four hundred and eighty since the calm broke. Six hundred and forty miles. The distance of the Cay from Havana was four hundred miles. Therefore if she had passed the Cay she would now be two hundred and forty miles beyond it, that is to say, twenty-four hours' sail beyond it. But she had not passed it. She had stopped there, and she had stopped there twenty-four hours ago.

That was the way Dicky reasoned, half crazy, his thoughts all shaken up by the vibration of the funnel guy. If nothing had occurred in the way of an accident Morgan would have had nearly time by now to get the stuff on board and raise sail.

He turned to the hatch and came down the steel ladder leading into the engine room. Kane, an oil can in hand, was standing watching his work.

"Ten knots," said Kane. "They won't stand for more than that—considering they're standin' at all," said Kane, "it's not so bad—hark at them."

They weren't running sweetly, and that's the truth. There was the trace of a stutter in their speech, the ghost of a hiccup in the gasp and hiss of the pistons—yet they went. They who had been scrap iron not so many hours ago, went, and the man who had made them go, standing with a cigarette behind his ear and another in the corner of his mouth, contemplated them not without satisfaction.

"I reckon," said he in answer to Dicky, "we ought to raise Crab in thirty hours or under, say by eight o'clock tomorrow morning. Oh, Morgan, he be damned! Got the bulge on us, has he? Well, maybe he has, but being underhanded he's got a job, my son, and as sure as rogues ain't saints, he'll try to rush that job, seeing what he is and seeing what he's after, and he's not the man to do it without coming a mucker. These double-dashed yacht sailors are pretty well all tripe when you take the gold bands off them."

Dicky left him and went into the stokehold, releasing Antonio.

CHAPTER 43

THE FOOTSTEPS OF TWO MEN

At sunset that evening the wind dropped again to a dead calm that held all night and remained unbroken by the dawn.

The sun rose immense and palpitating in a haze that increased till by seven o'clock visibility was reduced to less than a mile.

"Fog maybe," said Kane, "but there's not damp enough somehow in the air for fog. See those gulls? We ain't far off now, I reckon. Oh, Lord, no. Keep her as she's going, there aren't no reefs to the west of Crab to bother about. Hark at that!"

Through the haze from far ahead came a voice, the faint chanting of gulls, a weary, creaky sound, dying off to silence and breaking out again as if in complaint.

"That's her," said Kane. He went forward with the glass. Then came his voice: "I've got the trees."

He came running aft, took the wheel from Tearle and ordered them to stand by the anchor. Dicky, standing with Tearle and one of the negroes waiting to let go, could see the trees now and vaguely through the haze the white line of beach. Sign of the *Baltrum* or any craft there was none.

The gulls were thick on the sands, held maybe from the distant fishing grounds by the haze they loathe. No sign of other living thing was there and no sign that anyone had been since the *Baltrum* had weighed anchor on the morning that seemed so long ago.

Kane rang the engines off, then astern. Then came the order, "Let's go!"

He dropped down from the bridge, helped to get the boat over and then, with Tearle and Lomax at the oars and Dicky in the bow, he took the yoke lines.

Not one of them spoke, not one of them dared to utter what the silence and desolation and the absence of any sign of sand disturbances were saying to them: "You've done Morgan—he's missed the place—he's never been here."

"He's never been here!" cried the terns, while the "Ha! ha! ha!" of the laughing gulls from the southern spit answered back through the haze as the stem of the boat grounded, and Dicky, springing out, helped the others to run her up.

"Well, what do you think?" said Kane, standing for a moment, his hand pushing back his hair and his eyes wandering round. "Seems we've done 'em—eh? Seems—" He stopped short, went forward a few paces and knelt down. "No, b'gosh!" he cried, "they've done *us*." He pointed to a footstep almost imperceptible, yet there.

"Sure," said Lomax, "and there's another."

Dicky hardly heard him. He had broken away from the others and was running toward the trees.

Here, midway between the trees, in the deep sand between the mounds of earth from which the trees grew, was a pit; in the pit, half sanded over, lay two shovels, heart-shaped Spanish shovels—the ones they had bought at Teneriffe. There were no mounds of sand beside the pit to betray its existence from a distance; the westerly wind had blown them away.

When the others came up they found Dicky on his knees by the pit like a person by a grave. It was a grave. The grave of all his hopes and ambitions, of Sheila and her future—everything.

He didn't say a word, but just pointed. He couldn't have spoken just then, for his lips were as dry as pumice stone and his throat constricted. A moment like this takes a couple of years off the life of a man; it hits the very life centres and leaves a stain on his mind never quite to be eradicated.

To the end of his life Dicky would be liable to dream of that pit in the sand, those shovels, those voices deriding him that were yet only the voices of the gulls that haunted the cay.

Lomax was just going to jump into the pit when Kane stopped him.

"This is where you dug the stuff in?" said he to Dicky.

Dicky nodded.

"Your shovels?"

"Yes," said Dicky, regaining his voice, "ours. There's no use us bothering. We're done."

Kane said nothing for a moment. He seemed turning something over in his mind.

"Sure it's just here?" asked he.

"Yes."

"Well," said Kane. "I'm used to sand. This hole's been dug a couple of days maybe, maybe not so much, but what gets me is that those footsteps down there on the beach were left some time last night. They're new, and there's only the tracks of two men. There's not a trace of a step round here because this is all powder sand; the beach stuff is harder. But it's not hard enough to hold a man's traces for any time if there's a wind blowing.

"Those tracks were made after the calm fell at sundown last night, that I'd swear. There's more'n that. You noticed the rum look of the beach sand, same as if it'd been swept. That's crabs. Crab swarms come up here same as they do on the spit south of Caicos. Night's their time, and last night they were here—those indications aren't more'n a few hours old. Well, those man tracks were made after the crabs had been, else the crabs would have wiped them out. I tell you folk there were men here, two men, not more'n a few hours ago. Well, that being so, where's their boat? Unless they went in a power boat or a rowboat, which isn't likely, how'd they get away? It's been dead calm since sundown."

"There's no show of a boat having been beached or pushed off," said Lomax.

"No," said Kane, "because it's high tide. If she'd beached or put off at low water or half flood, her traces would be covered. You can get into the pit, Lomax, if you want to, but you're wastin' your time."

He stood with arms folded and brow contracted while Lomax, dropping into the hole, grubbed about, finding nothing. Then he turned back to the water's edge, the others following, and took his stand by the boat.

Kane had twenty years' experience of the cays and islands, of the ports and harbours, of the tricks of men and sand. He knew for a certainty that two men had been on the beach quite recently; the crabs he had never seen had told him that; but Kane had also a sixth sense, half psychic, half common, born, perhaps, from his long trafficking with events. He felt almost certain in his mind that these two men he had never seen were from the *Baltrum*, and that the *Baltrum* had been here only a few hours ago. He smelled her. How then had she put out without any wind to fill her sails?

She was gone—how?

Standing considering this matter, he suddenly struck himself on the side of his head with the flat of his hand.

"Say," cried he, turning to Dicky, "has this chap Morgan been used to the waters round about here?"

"I think so," said Dicky. "He was with Mr. Corder, first officer on his yacht, and they used to be often round here."

"Get aboard," cried Kane.

He seized the starboard gunnel of the boat and helped to run her out.

"What's up?" asked Lomax, as he took an oar.

"Get aboard," said Kane. "Put your backs into it. The blighters have let her drift, that's what they've done; finished getting the stuff aboard her, couldn't get away for want of wind and funked staying—pulled the hook up and let her go on the current. That's what they've done. It runs hard from here and strikes right northeast—three knots maybe it would be, with no wind to break it."

They scrambled on board, the boat was had in and Hank, who had been playing a game of patience with the old greasy pack that never left him, came forward. He had been playing with one eye on the cards and one on the exploring party.

"I reckon those chaps have got us," said Hank.

"I reckon they haven't," said Kane. "Get down to the stokehold and swing a shovel. Where are the men? Raise steam on her."

He called to Lomax and Tearle to stand by the winch. It was a steam winch fed from the boilers. Then he went up to the bridge and stood by the wheel, looking across the cay to the sea beyond.

The visibility had become a bit better with the climbing sun, but it was true heat-haze weather. Supersummer. Weather so gorgeous that one forgot the heat, weather that suggested less the tropics than an English July of the old-fashioned type—magnificent.

"We've just got to steer nor'east with the current," said Kane to Dicky, who had come up and was standing beside him. "If what I'm thinking is true we'll hit them unless this durned haze turns to fog. If what I'm thinkin's bunkum, we won't." He called down the speaking tube to the engine room, then he shouted to Tearle to start the winch, and the rattle of the winch pawls sounding across the cay made the gulls rise in flocks, rise and scream and pass in a cloud like a spiral nebula beyond the southern spit, only to return and circle far above as the ringing of the engine-room bell started the engines and Kane at the wheel turned the spokes to starboard.

They sheered away from the beach and then, Kane altering the course, they rounded the north spur of the cay and headed nor'east, the heat haze holding them in a gauzy blue circle, a magic haze of mist giving visibility now for less than a mile.

"Oh, cuss the thing!" said Kane. "If we had clear weather we'd spot them. They're dough dishin' round somewhere on the current line, I'd swear to that, but whether we'll hit them, or miss them by a foot there's no saying— by a foot. I tell you in this sort of thickness if you can just see a thing a mile off, and shove it a foot farther, it's gone."

With his eye on the binnacle card he relapsed into speechlessness.

One thing was certain: if his suppositions were right and if the message that the footsteps and the crabs had given him was not a lying message, and the theory built on it not a house on sand, the *Baltrum* and her crew would not be far off.

Very likely Morgan was within earshot, for the trumping of the engines would carry across long distances of this calm dead-silent water.

And what a row they were making just now.

Antonio on the deck below looked up at Kane.

"De engines are knocking," said Antonio.

"Yes, damn them!" said Kane. He knew it was the packing of the piston that was at fault, that and a lot of other things. The engines were not suffering alone from the carelessness of Antonio; age had its grip on them. Age and neglect.

The rest at Crab Cay had broken them down. You often find that in men and machinery; it is a dangerous thing sometimes to rest. If they could have gone on driving they might have made those engines keep going till the bunkers were swept. It was easier for them to go than stop, but the fatal rest had given them time to think; things had contracted with cooling, packings had found themselves insufficient to hold the steam.

There was nothing dangerous, but they were working in a steam bath that nearly choked Hank, who had come down as a consulting physician.

"They're deader'n doughnuts," said Hank. "Goin' because they've forgot to stop—now they're remembering. Gosh, it's like a sheep coughing. It's not us; it's the packin', and we hadn't any other. And them nuts in the cylinder head—they weren't much more than solid rust. There she goes."

With a vast shudder the engines died and ceased to move. There was no need to open steam cocks to save the boilers, steam was exuding from all sorts of places where it shouldn't.

Still he opened taps and things and they came on deck in a cloud to find Kane leaving the bridge.

The firemen came up. They would not be bothered anymore with rake and shovel and that was a comfort. All the same, the situation was unpleasant.

It was no longer a question of the gold; it was a question of the current taking them out to sea, sweeping them into the Atlantic on a helpless hulk.

The *Baltrum* would be in quite a different position. She had masts and sails. There was nothing at all on the torpedo boat that could be used for locomotion. They had the boat, it is true, but they had no mast and sail for her. They might row, but had they all crowded into it the boat would have been dangerously overloaded. They were at least eighteen or twenty miles northeast of the cay. To row back they would have to row against the current. They had no boat compass.

It was not a cheerful prospect. As Kane stood considering it, the glassy circle of sea within the haze ring dulled to the northeast and the rag of bunting on the jackstaff gave a lift.

Wind was coming, heralded by the phantom of a breeze that died off and then revived and strengthened.

"It's going to clear," said Kane.

"It's clearin'," said Hank.

They held silent for a moment gazing to windward.

Then as they looked a picture showed revealed by the thinning haze, the vaguest outline of a boat with sails set, ghostly, vague, a phantom that seemed to have materialized from the mist.

Then as the flag on the jackstaff lifted again, and the wind came stronger, the picture strengthened in outline and the sun laid a finger on hull and canvas.

It was the *Baltrum*.

CHAPTER 44

THE "BALTRUM"

"Over with the boat," cried Kane.

The boat was got over; Dicky, Hank, Tearle and Lomax crowded in, and Kane took the yoke lines. The distance was perhaps a mile and a half. The movement of the air had strengthened to a steady breeze and the sails of the *Baltrum*, clear to the sight and with the sun full upon them, filled now to the wind and now, as though the helm had been shifted, shook the wind from them.

Kane, staring straight ahead, suddenly spoke.

"She's derelict. Put your back into it, boys. Derelict she is and driftin'. Here's luck—make her go—make her go!"

He had no need to urge the rowers.

Yes, the *Baltrum* was derelict. Clawing and snatching at the wind, now filling, now falling off, she shouted the fact across the sea. As they came up with her no sign of life showed above the rail and as they fastened on, no man stood to receive or prevent them.

Kane was the first on deck. After him came Dicky, then Tearle, Lomax and Hank.

On the deck now shadowed by the mainsail, now sunlit as the main boom swung to the wind, lay two forms, Morgan and Hearn, stretched on their backs dead—with sleep. Dead with exhaustion.

Kane, kneeling by Morgan, shook him.

"Wake up, you blighter," cried Kane.

Morgan's eyes half opened, closed, opened again. Then he moved, lifted himself on his elbow and stared at the men before him. He saw Kane and Lomax and he saw Hank and Tearle, who were getting Hearn on to his feet, but he did not see Dicky.

Dicky had dived below. There was no sign of the gold on deck nor in the saloon. He made for the ballast.

Yes, there it was, laid just as when they had left Hildersditch. The extra sand ballast they had taken up at Crab was gone. How these men must have laboured, how they must have worked and strove, discharging the sand ballast, digging up the gold, casting it block by block on board, stowing it—always in dread of pursuit or the coming of some fishing boat. No wonder that sleep had fallen on them like that. Well, it was over, and everything was right at last—or seemed so.

He rose up and came on deck and gave the news to Kane, who was standing over Morgan, sitting now propped against the port bulwarks. Hearn was on his feet, leaning against the rail.

"Good," said Kane, when he got the news. Then turning to Morgan, he took up again something that he had been saying while Dicky was below.

"So you hadn't no other man with you," said Kane. "Well, just tell that to Mr. Sebright."

"Morgan," said Dicky, "what have you done with Longley?"

The sight of Dicky coming on deck had brought the colour to Morgan's cheeks. The others had been quite unknown to him. Where they had come from he could not tell, or why they had asked him the questions they did.

Now he knew everything at once. He struggled to his feet and stood holding on to the rail, then he hooked his arm round it.

"Longley," said he. "Don't be asking me about Longley. Ask Hearn. He knows."

"You lie," said Hearn.

Kane, who had been watching both men, suddenly put up his hand before Dicky, who was about to speak. Then he turned like a tiger on Morgan and Hearn.

"One word more out of either of you two," said Kane, "and I'll clap you in the fo'c's'le and take you back to Havana, see? I want to hear nothing more about the chap Longley. I guess you're both liars. Now get forward. Tearle, take the wheel and run us down to the torp. Come below."

He took Dicky by the arm and they went below to the saloon.

"They've murdered him," said Dicky.

"Looks like it," said Kane. "That's why I stopped their jaw. Another moment and they'd have been accusing each other and then we'd have had to take them back to Havana to have them tried and hanged."

"Aren't you going to take them back?"

"Oh, gosh, no—where's the good? That chap Longley was either done in for his share of the money, or maybe in a quarrel, but there's no witnesses. Those chaps would never get hanged, but the whole of this story would come out—gold and all—and where would you be?"

"Then what are you going to do with them?" asked Dicky.

"Make them a present of the torp. Of course they'll get took off by some ship—bound to be—but they're muzzled. They never dare go back on us, or peach, or say a word; seems like Providence, don't it?"

They came on deck.

The *Baltrum* was hove to a couple of cable lengths away from the torpedo boat. Kane ordered Tearle and Lomax to bring the two negroes on board;

when that was done he ordered Morgan and Hearn into the boat and rowed them off.

Dicky watched them crawling up the side of the hulk followed by Kane. Kane, when he led them on deck, seemed lecturing them. He didn't take long over it and they did not seem to be making any reply to him.

Hank, who was standing beside Dicky chewing tobacco and spitting into the water, chuckled.

"Them chaps have done a lot of work," said Hank, "an' they'll do a lot more if they want to get thim ingins to go. I reckon they'll get through most of the grub on board her before they get picked up by some ship, and the worrying will do them good."

It was the first time Hank had held any conversation with Dicky since coming on board. Then he turned and went below to continue the interminable game of patience, which the events of life were always interrupting.

Dicky saw Kane drop into the boat which turned back to the *Baltrum*. In all the wheel of sea stripped now of haze to the horizon there was sign neither of wing of bird or sail of ship, nothing indicative of life but the *Baltrum*, and the hulk and the boat moving toward the *Baltrum*. They got the boat on board and, Lomax going to the wheel, they put the *Baltrum* before the wind.

The two men on the hulk, watching, stood motionless as two figures carved from wood. Then as the ketch drew far away, one of them, Morgan, Dicky thought, ran along the deck and up to the bridge and then down again to the deck; ran forward and then aft and then forward again; the tiny figure moved like quicksilver and Dicky shuddered as he watched it reappear on the bridge, only to vanish and resume the race along the deck.

He went below and straight to the ballast. He did not go to reassure himself of its safety, he went urged by the instinct that draws men to the dramatic, the curious and the terrible. There before him lay the sinister rust-coloured painted pigs, the sheer mass of dead metal that was yet a machine infinitely more powerful and intricate than any engine conceived by man, a machine that took men on to act as its working parts, destroyed their bodies with labour and their souls with lust and flung them away, only to renew itself with the bodies and souls of other men.

So it seemed to Dicky, and again, as he looked at those metal oblongs, it seemed to him that he was looking at something more wonderful than radium; at energy, condensed, trapped, always active, always ready to strike, yet never diminishing in volume and power; not though it worked till the end of time.

He would have been afraid of this thing but for the fact that fear was taken from him by the thought of Sheila.

The thought of Sheila, actually like a good fairy, had been with him all the way from Havana. He had worked for her, not for the gold, and so was not its slave.

He rose up and came to the saloon; the thought had just come to him, and only now, of the money he had left in his locker.

He found the locker. It had been ransacked, everything in it was turned upside down, but the precious bundle of bank notes was there, safe in a corner. Morgan had found them, of course, and left them there, thinking them safe enough as long as he was on the ship. It seemed a good omen.

When he reached the deck again the hulk had all but vanished from sight astern and the gulls of Crab Cay were showing in flight far away on the port bow. The *Baltrum*, going free before the increasing wind, was on her course for Havana, and Kane, standing by Tearle at the wheel, had the air of a workman well satisfied with a completed job.

"There's two things I like about this hooker," said Kane, as Dicky drew up to him. "First and foremost she don't want stoking and oiling, and second, the damned engines can't break down."

CHAPTER 45

THE END OF THE CRUISE

And was that the end of the labours and intrigues, the worries and dark works that seemed inseparably connected with the gold of the *Baltrum*? Oh, dear me, no.

From the moment when the *Baltrum* touched sides with the Poirez wharf and Dicky departed for the hotel, leaving his fortune and Sheila's in the hands of Kane, there began a series of intrigues and dark works in the subfinancial world of Cuba that Mordiaz alone could cast light on and that were guessed by Dicky owing to the odd manner and absences of Bompard, the disappearance of Madame Bompard, who had gone to Santiago on a mission, the vanishing of Kane, who went to Matanzas, and the fact that Mordiaz, when Dicky called one day to make inquiries, repudiated any knowledge of any business that Kane might have been engaged in.

The conversion of nearly a million in bullion into fluid money, and with secrecy, takes time. But a day came when Bompard entered the lounge of the Mercedes, his hat on the back of his head, a big cigar in his mouth and all anxiety gone from his face. Finding Dicky and Sheila, he linked arms with them, whirled them into the street along the Callé Antonio, across the Plaza del Sol into a building and up a stone staircase to a door marked "Saumarez."

Through an office where typewriters were busy into a private room filled with cigar smoke and where at a desk table sat a yellow little man to whom Bompard said: "This is the gentleman, Saumarez."

"Oh, this is the gentleman," said Saumarez. He made a little bow to Sheila and bade them be seated. Then opening a drawer he took out a filled-in check.

"A gentleman," said Saumarez, "who wishes not to be named, has left with me a benefaction to be delivered to you, sare—for services of great value rendered to him in past times. He wishes not to be named, nor do I know his name. With me he left this amount in notes of the Bank of Brazil, in dollar notes of Amérique and in a draft on Gundermann's payable to bearer, which I have deposited in amount in the treasury of the Bank of Cuba and of which this is the chaique."

He handed the check to Dicky.

Bompard had asked Dicky's Christian name yesterday, and Dicky now knew why.

It was a large pale yellow check made out to R. Sebright, and Dicky read after the dollar mark these figures: 1,200,000. Twelve hundred thousand dollars—two hundred and forty thousand pounds sterling!

* * * *

Out in the street, holding Sheila by the arm and making for the Bank of Cuba, Dicky felt neither pleasure nor excitement. He was stunned. After all the labour and difficulties, the sweat and toil, the suspense, the heart burnings, this great success, this enormous fortune had knocked him out of time. The thing was so complete.

These experts of Havana into whose hands he had drifted by chance had—it was like a beautiful surgical operation—separated the gold from its past, cut all avenues connecting it with them and him, converted it into currency—and played fair with him. It was the full knowledge that these men were so great in their strength, so subtle in their dealings, so widespread in their connections, that gave him the sense of security which made the punch of success so powerful. There was no dread attached to this money, no anxiety.

"Oh, Dicky—Dicky—Dicky!" Sheila kept saying; she could not find any more words. She was white, on the verge of tears, leading him, for during Dicky's absence she had explored Havana thoroughly and knew every building. Looking at them as they went you would have said they were the victims of some tragedy.

As they drew near the great bank building with its flight of marble steps and as Sheila pointed it out, he began to come to.

Halfway up the steps he stopped, placed his hand on Sheila's shoulder and laughed. It was all coming to him now with a rush, the pleasure, the joy and the excitement of the new life made possible for Sheila and himself by the piece of yellow paper in his pocket, that note of introduction to Midas signed in an impossible scrawl:

Alphonse Saumarez

That is the end of the story of the *Baltrum's* gold and the beginning of the life story of two people who were married a fortnight later at the British consulate in the presence of Bompard and Larry, who was no longer a guest on board of the *Dulcinea*.

Shortt, who had got back from his insane journey to Santiago to find Morgan and two of his best sailors gone, and Larry in their place, was about to fire the unwelcome guest off his ship when the latter, taking him aside, unveiled the story of the stolen *Baltrum* in such a way that the unhappy captain, fogged, bewildered and amazed, almost began to believe himself an accomplice of the thief.

A cable from James calling the yacht to New York gave him an excuse for departing before the return of the *Baltrum*; but no cable ever came from James to Dicky and Sheila; no letter, no word; for James could excuse a man for calling him a good many names, but never for calling him a quitter.